By the sa

FICTION

The Shaitan of Calcutta
(Parthian April 2010)

The Lucknow Ransom
(Parthian June 2013)

To Rik

good luck

The Day I Died

The Day I Died

Published by The Conrad Press Ltd. in the United Kingdom 2021

Tel: +44(0)1227 472 874
www.theconradpress.com
info@theconradpress.com

ISBN 978-1-914913-18-1

Printed and bound in Great Britain by Clays Ltd, Elcograf S.p.A

Typesetting and Cover Design by The Book Typesetters,
www.thebooktypesetters.com

The Conrad Press logo was designed by Maria Priestley.

The Day I Died

Glen Peters

Part One

Prologue

An open and shut case

A fisherman found me at sunrise, floating on the waves some five hundred yards from the beach.

I was stone cold dead.

My name was Ceridwen. They spotted my red bra top, the only piece of clothing still on me. I was dragged onto the shore like some beached sea creature and my body was covered with a filthy gunnysack until the police arrived.

The early morning sun was already warming up the air around my body and a few seabirds circled, expecting me to be their next meal. I'd have preferred to be of some use to this planet after death rather than being cremated many months after, while they argued about the evidence. It should have been an open and shut case from the start.

The papers back home in Wales said I was 'just a little tart waiting for an accident to happen.' The binge drinking, the drugs and the casual sex to get my own way were all part of me carving out a life for myself. What they didn't print was that no one had ever taught me about survival. Well... nobody I trusted. Not my mam or any of her rotten blokes, who would have tried to shag me given half the chance.

I really didn't expect to die so young, certainly not on my birthday. The evening had been a blur. I remembered hammering a whole bottle of local hooch, but then the rest of the night had been wiped from my memory. How did I end up as a corpse on the beach I'd come to love so much? I could have done with having Mam around that day. Shit, I was only just sixteen.

I'd remembered reading somewhere that, when the time came to die, most people were quite prepared to pass away, and for most of my time growing up in Fishguard at that dead-end school of mine, living or dying wouldn't have mattered much. The place was a shithole, but coming here to Goa had changed everything. It was as if I'd been carried off on a magic carpet to a land of limitless possibilities, even for a no-hoper like me.

That land was Anjuna. A beach like many others in Goa, where I spent most of my time, mooching, smooching, making good money, growing up faster than I could have ever imagined. Literally, every day seemed like a year of my life just going whoosh in twenty-four hours. The world was here, with all its excitement and opportunities and yes... snags, too.

Goa's easy-going boozy ways were thanks to the Portuguese, who ruled the place three hundred years ago. Their Indian descendants just carried on celebrating the culture and Catholic religion, well after the Portuguese were kicked out.

If it hadn't been for my unofficial husband-to-be and spiritual guide Harpo back in Wales, I'd have never become aware of my Gypsy roots in India. When my mam mentioned Goa as a place for me to go and chill with her, I felt that part of me was going home, giving me a chance to get out of dead-end Fishguard and start another life.

My world centred around Anjuna's hottest beach bar, the Sunset Lounge. It could be a place of total fun, but there was also the hassle of dealing with some absolute pricks, who came to show off their fake Rolexes and try and pull for the night. It was also HQ for the Beachboys, the local gang that had adopted me for all the wrong reasons, but hey! I was just taking it one day at a time and right then their protection mattered. It gave me almost limitless freedom to grow into a woman, an adult, all in the space of a few weeks.

What wasn't there to live for?

The Beachboys weren't saints. If you double-crossed them you were history... a flick of a blade, a guitar string wound around your neck. The only other gang on the beach were the Ukes, probably the most evil gang on earth. These guys were hardened criminals from Kiev, who had fled to Goa to escape their country that was going down the toilet. They could be all smiles one moment and breaking your neck the next, and, if you wanted to work and live on the beach, you had to choose between these two psycho gangs.

Of course, the other official gang were the men in khaki... the pathetic Goan Police Force, trying to keep law and order. They just filled their pockets with payouts and their head honcho Inspector Braganza, topped the payouts up with regular BJs from his favourite female pimp, conniving Karina, who was the real brains behind the Beachboys.

Don't get me wrong, on the surface this was one of the prettiest places on the planet with its mile of sandy beach lined with coconut trees and the beautiful people from all over the world who'd come to enjoy the sun, the dirt cheap sundowners, the readily available drugs, plus the seemingly simple Goan principle that life is just one big party... but just scratch that surface and you'd see a different world beneath.

So here I am, lying stiff as a board on the beach. All my hopes of starting a great life, becoming Young Beach Entrepreneur of the Year and giving the gypsies someone to be proud of, all dashed to the ground.

But then again, who'd have wanted to stay in Fishguard forever?

Chapter 1

Harpo

I was an unwanted baby and my mam tried to zap my foetus with every trick in the book of old Welsh termination remedies.

'There's no way I wanted another brat in my life!' she told me many times. 'So just be careful with those plonkers at school, or else it'll ruin your life. Just like it ruined mine.'

'Thanks, Mam,' I'd reply. 'It's nice to feel wanted.'

'If it wasn't for the thirty pounds Social I get for you, Cariad, you'd be a real liability.' Mam calling me *Cariad*, which means 'Love' in Welsh, is as close as she ever got to showing affection for me.

The prefab concrete council house we lived in hadn't been touched by the building department for many years. It stood out like a turd in the snow amongst the others that had been bought by the tenants and sold off to incomers from England, who had painted them yucky pastel colours to disguise their essentially ugly looks.

Maybe it was because I had tough genes that shrugged off rejection, or maybe I was born smart, but I sailed through my early years. I was jabbering away at one year old, walking soon after, and by the age of three I could read. Christ knows how, because I got no encouragement at home. All my knowledge came through the telly, which was on all day long.

Tad-cu had a little fishing boat, which he took me out in every week. It was Grandfather who taught me how to fish for mackerel and dog fish and catch spider crabs. My next door neighbour was a retired lady, who took me under her wing. She allowed me to play in her garden and gave me children's books she picked up from the charity shops. Fishguard, the old harbour town, was full of them.

Mam always had a smelly incense stick smouldering away in the house. I hated the sickly smell. She'd been to India many times, where she had affairs, I'm sure, with all sorts of weird blokes, healers, fakirs, gurus, or whatever she called them. She told me she'd take me there one day when I was older, so that I'd appreciate my life at home a little more. I never knew my father, but I knew from the only photograph of him that he was a gypsy. My mam had screwed around with him in the hot summer of 1994. I couldn't quite see it, but Mam told me that I was the image of him, but with blonde hair and tits.

At Fishguard Secondary, that was always in 'Special Measures' according to the school's inspectors, the name-calling started around my ninth birthday. I was never part of any one gang, nor did any kid invite me back to their place to play. Sleepovers were only for the few posh kids. Us council house kids strolled around the deserted pavements every evening in gangs. I'd try to join in by buying favours, like going into the chippie to buy a bag of chips with the occasional change that the kind lady at Number Ten gave me to get a lozenge.

A small bag with salt and vinegar liberally sprinkled over its contents went a long way towards buying me permission to hang around with the other kids for a few hours. I once took on a bet to shag the trumpeter of the school brass band to lose my virginity. I was unimpressed by the experience and the boy was shamefaced forever as he came in his pants well before the act. Yuk! *Ych a fi* as we say in Welsh. I kept his secret and the lanky buck-toothed girl, who was in the *Stryd Mair* gang, kept her end of the bet that she would get me into any pub I wanted.

Harpo was the only other pupil at Fishguard High who had gypsy blood and no one picked on him because they'd have been pulverised. Most of the older girls had been his moll at some stage or another. He could have had his pick of anyone. He was dark, mysterious, and never much in school, as he spent a lot of time in juvenile detention.

'Watch out! Harpo's about!' the word went out whenever he was back from detention. In pubs they'd be saying 'Lock up your chain saws and your daughters.'

In the periods when he was free, the crime wave in Fishguard went sky high as every potential thief took the opportunity to pinch something, in the hope that Harpo would get the blame.

The Deputy Head, Mrs Jones, referred to him as a nice bad boy due to his popularity with the pupils, especially the girls. When he was at school, he was always volunteering for duties which earned him a soft spot with the head, who tolerated him despite the trouble he kept getting into.

Alwyn Hughes, the PE teacher, who considered himself Mister Tough Guy, was the biggest sleazebag of all the teachers. His greasy ponytail, did nothing to disguise his baldness, making him look repulsive. Like a cross between a human and a seal. He kept baiting Harpo at every opportunity, almost forcing him to react, and so he absolutely deserved the regular damage which Harpo inflicted on his car, whenever it was parked out of sight. The deflated tyres, the etched lines on the paintwork, and the Vaseline smears on the windscreen, all helped to inflame the rage that Hughes felt towards us.

The Bell was the only pub in town, run by a freakish hippie couple, who were lax about serving underage drinkers like me. Their folk singing nights were the perfect occasion to go in with your mates and pretend you'd come to hear the awful finger-in-the-ear droning that passed for singing. The red-eyed landlady, who had a face like a guinea pig, would sell us a bottle of cider provided it was served in half pint glasses. This gave us the giggles as we sat in a far corner of the bar, killing ourselves at the awfulness of the sounds.

'Shit! Unbelievable!' said my classmate Alison. 'Pervy Hughesy just came in with a guitar.' I looked around and saw him. He looked at me and nodded as if to acknowledge my presence. 'Right, girl, you're nominated to go to the bar and try and order for us.'

'No way!'

'You wanted to come drinking with us, didn't you?'

'You scared or something of that perv?' asked Alison's friend, who was a year younger than me. 'Two quid says you're a scaredy-cat.'

I was on my way to the bar. The singing continued and I hoped that I could achieve my mission under the cover of the chorus that had now begun to take hold. *Heave away, haul*

16

away, they shouted out to a sea shanty. The guinea pig hadn't acknowledged me yet, when I felt a presence behind me.

'Hello, *shwmae,* didn't know you liked this sort of music.' It was Hughes. Yuk! 'It's okay.' I stammered.

'Look, let me get you one,' he offered, standing uncomfortably close to me. 'I'm with my friends. There's three of us.'

'*Swr, swr, dim problem.* No problem. Suz!' he called to the landlady, 'a bottle of your weak cider for my friend Ceri, with three glasses.' The woman obliged without comment. 'Come and join us. You probably know some of the songs.' I didn't answer and tried to smile away the request as I picked up the drinks.

That was when he put his right arm around my waist and I swear he tried to give my right breast a squeeze. I froze, stunned by his brazen approach, but then recovered quickly and scurried away.

'*Thank you* would be nice!' he shouted as the chorus of 'Heave away' concluded. The others thought it was hilarious, when I told them.

'Go get another fondle and we'll be drinking free all night!' chortled Alison.

I collected my two quid but continued to feel sick and left the Bell soon afterwards. I stayed awake for most of the night, thinking of how I might get my revenge against Alwyn Frigging Hughes.

The local *Enquirer* routinely ran stories about Harpo's court appearances. They could almost have had a special column devoted to him. He was represented by a solicitor named Mr Charles Owen, who must have made a killing out of the Legal Aid fees, defending his client.

Boy stole to save his dog, ran one headline. *Mr. Owen, speaking for the defendant known as Harpo, told the magistrates that his client was in a state of inebriation after his pet collie had fallen ill. He thought that the shoulder of lamb from Tesco would provide the necessary remedy.*

Boy who hospitalised farmer says he was acting in self-defence, ran another headline, after Harpo said that he was attacked by a farmer for going out with his teenage daughter. And so, the stories ran on and on, which made Harpo a legend in Fishguard.

Whenever he was around at school, he would nod at me and smile. One break time he said loudly for all to hear, 'Hey, come by 'ere, girl. Anyone calling you a gypo just let me know, huh?' I nodded and smiled in thanks.

I wished I wasn't so young. I wanted so much to be Harpo's girl, for not only did we both have gypsy blood, but we were joined in our hate of Alwyn Hughes.

Then one Friday, I bunked off school and caught the bus to Whitesands, the surfing paradise for people like me. Mam said that, as a Pisces, I was a Water sign, strong and intuitive. I loved the sea and could stay out on the surf for hours without feeling the cold or tiring. The beach, a mile and a half of glorious sand, was empty that day. Life couldn't be any better.

I'd left my kit bag with clothes and towel on the beach, but when I returned they weren't there. I scanned the sands around me, but there was nothing. Just nothing. They were worth fuck-all, but I couldn't get home in my wets.

I walked to the car park in the hope that someone might

have seen my bag. The only vehicle there was a van with *Clean me I'm dirty* scrawled on the back. I walked towards it in the hope that I might see someone in the driver's seat. As I approached, a guy got out. It was Harpo.

'Harpo!' I shouted.

'Hi, you look wet,' he responded.

'Someone's taken my kit.'

'Get in. I've got it in the back of the van. It's safer there.'

'Ugh, you have?' I said, almost relieved.

'Yes, now get in the back of the van and change into your dry clothes, while I drive you back.'

'I don't understand. What are you doing here? How come you have a van?'

'Brother's. I always come here on Fridays to worship the sea. It's an old neopagan purification ritual.'

I got in the back of the windowless van. He got into the driver's seat and drove out of the car park, while I fumbled around for my towel to dry my hair.

'No school today, huh?' he asked.

'It's my birthday tomorrow, so I'm celebrating a day early. Might go out to the Bell tonight for a drink.' I said, trying to sound very grown up.

'Ah, good. How old are you tomorrow?'

There was no use lying as he probably already knew. 'Fifteen.'

'Oh, cracking on, huh?' He laughed at his own humour. 'It'll be a good year for Pisces you know. Water signs are big this year and you'll get up to fantastic stuff. Might even get to travel to far distant lands.'

'Yes, Mam spends a lot of time in India. She wants to take

me there. I don't know what I'd do in India.'

'You know it's where our lot came from initially, many moons ago, down the old silk roads and all that.'

'My dad was a Romany, you know. So, I'm half gypo. Can't say I fancy India.

Heard it stinks and you catch terrible diseases.'

'I'd really like to go and discover my gypsy roots. Can't say I feel part of this place, until I fully understand where I came from. Do you feel a full Welshie?' asked Harpo.

'No, I guess not, with all that name calling and people always picking on me.'

I was still rolling about in the van, trying to get changed as it rocked from left to right down the winding country lanes. Harpo kept up the stories about the gypsies and their customs until I noticed that we were stopping in the middle of nowhere, with cliffs all around us. This was nowhere near Fishguard.

'Where are we?' I asked.

'Oh, I thought I'd give you a treat and we'd celebrate your birthday eve at St Non's Holy Well. This is a really sweet place that goes way back... hey it matches your water sign. After all, we're both part gypsy and part Celt. So here we are. Is that cool or what?'

I'd never been to St Non's Holy Well before, but it did send a shiver down my spine as I got out of the van. 'Here, can I hold your hand as we walk down to the well? These stones can be slippery at this time of year,' asked Harpo.

He held my hand. It sent an electric shock down my arm. Why was he being so nice to me? He was one of the most desired blokes at school and here he was holding my hand.

Why, why, why? I was only just fifteen and he was nearly a man at sixteen.

This must have been one of the most stunning places I'd ever seen or can remember. We were in the middle of a small green field with cliffs and crashing sea below us. Amidst the sound of the waves roaring in from the Atlantic, I could hear the haunting sounds of a seal colony down below. When we reached the Well, we sat down together.

'Close your eyes.'

I did as he said. In a few seconds, between the sound of the crashing waves, I heard the crying of baby seals.

'Can you hear the sounds of our past ancestors?'

'They're baby seals.' I replied.

'No, think beyond those seals and breathe in deeply.'

'Hmmm, I see what you mean.'

'Ancient Celts worshipped here amongst these rocks for thousands of years. Just think thousands of years ago, well before Christianity arrived. Amazing! Look, you must wonder why I've brought you here.'

'Yes, but I'm not complaining.' He put his arms around me and looked into my eyes. I got goose pimples. 'I want you to be my woman,' he murmured softly.

'But,' I stammered, 'I'm…'

He put his forefinger to my lips. 'Don't say anything, just hold me.'

I was shivering. Was it fear or excitement? Everything had happened so quickly and I couldn't think straight.

'My ancestors have spoken to me,' he pronounced. 'They say I've gotta find the girl I'm gonna marry before she's fifteen and she's gotta be a virgin. God, I've been watching you for

21

ages... and you've got the same blood as me – we're perfect, like as if you're my gift from *Kali Mai* the Hindu goddess. '

'I'm just in a daze. I don't know what to say.' I burbled.

'Have you fucked anyone? I mean are you still a virgin? It's quite important for me to know.'

'No, I mean yes,' I said lying.

'Perfect!' he exclaimed with a flourish and a thumbs up gesture. 'This is just so cool. It's our custom for a man to kidnap a bride of his choosing, who must be a virgin not yet turned fifteen. Can you see what I'm doing?'

'I'd have to tell my mam first,' I hesitated. 'She'll be a bit surprised, but she's quite open minded. She's been telling me to go to the docs and get on the pill just in case, you know, if I take a fancy to one of the douche-bags in school.'

'No, no this can be our secret until it's time to start a family.'

'Hey, that's way off for me, Man.'

'No, it's not that long. With you in my life I know I can settle down and get a job and become a responsible guy and begin looking after you. We can go off to India together and discover the real gypsies, back to our ancestral homelands. Now kiss me.'

We kissed. Not one of those deep-throated French jobs, but a gentle meeting of each other's lips. The dream was now clearing, and I could see reality emerging from the fog. I'd just been proposed to and it looked like I'd accepted.

'I've got a bottle of cider here in my bag. Let's celebrate our betrothal.' He reached into his leather shoulder bag and took a large gulp, handing it to me to do the same. I gulped, too. We continued to drink from the large plastic bottle until I began to feel warm and light-headed. This was my engagement celebration. My feelings were a mixture of joy, fear, shock and anticipation of what might happen next in this bizarre ritual.

'Feeling good, toots?' asked Harpo as he rolled over from the stones on to a patch of grass, dragging me down with him.

'Yes.' I said. 'Still a bit in shock.'

'Let's stay here and watch the sun go down. Would you fancy a tab, perhaps?'

'A tab?'

'Yep, some E. Nice way to celebrate in an altered state.'

'I've never tried it.'

'Okay, just a half then,' he said, biting a little blue tablet and handing me the other half. We were both now gazing up at the blue sky and I watched a jet trail crawling across, out toward the west.

'Harpo, have you done this before?' I asked. 'Am I really your first woman?'

'To be honest, I've had a few other girls, quite a few actually, but none I'd have liked to be my bride. I can hear my ancestral voices talking to me loudly in my brain.'

'If you want to fuck me, it's okay. I wouldn't mind losing my virginity to you.' I heard myself say. Was it the cider talking, or perhaps the early effects of the tablet?

'This is not about sex, you know. Hell, I fancy you rotten.'

'And I think you're hot, too.'

'I'd like us to practice that tantric thing.'

'Tantric?'

'Yeh, like holding off and building up a real yearning.'

23

'Like those seventies rock stars?'

'Yeh, I read about them. They're into that. It'll make our big moment seem monumental,' he said earnestly, and I relaxed, although I was beginning to feel randy as hell.

Harpo told me more about his Neopaganism, which he learned about whilst in detention. It seemed a strange place to learn about world religion. The sun began to set, the sea lit up in yellow and in minutes the air turned cold and it was dark. Harpo pulled out a bulbous object from his satchel and began to blow into it. It sounded weird, like a cross between a bagpipe and the wailing cry of a young baby seal. It reverberated around the cliffs and back again.

'This is a *poongi*. The instrument of the *Banjara* gypsies, thousands of years old.

They still play it today.'

He puffed up his cheeks with air, blew into the mouthpiece, and a loud reedy noise wafted out, sending a shiver down my spine.

'Doesn't it put you in a trance?'

'I'm getting cold now, Harpo, do you have a blanket or something warmer in your van?'

'Sure, toots, let's go to the van and play some music. I've got some rags you can put on.'

He threw me an old sweatshirt. 'Bit smelly, I'm afraid, but it'll do the job.' He put on some gypsy fiddle music in the van and we swayed outside in our own private, open-air club, whilst the effects of the E began to take control and the music became more bizarre.

Harpo began to take off his clothes whilst he swayed and I followed, garment by garment, until we were both starkers in the freezing cold.

'Race you to the beach!' he challenged, and we both skipped along the footpath down to the rocks and swam in the freezing water, yelling our heads off with a mixture of madness and pain.

It didn't take long for the temperature to become unbearable and he was helping me back up the rocks to the van, where the music continued to play as we got dressed.

'Hey, toots, I love you with the kit off. Looking forward to our first night together.'

'Me, too,' I responded.

'But now we've got some other things to do. We've got to sacrifice a living being.'

'What, kill someone?'

'No, not a person. Some unfortunate animals, to free them from their suffering or pain, so they can move on to another life.'

I'd no idea what he was saying, but my mind was in such a confused state that all I could do was hop into the van with him. Off he drove erratically back through the dark lanes and hedgerows, to God knows where and I didn't care. I could have been the sacrifice, but it didn't matter to me. I was with Harpo, my pagan lover-to-be, and that's all that seemed to matter in that moment.

'Oh toots, I'm *soooo* fucking happy! This is it. This is it.'

We slowed down and all I could see in the headlights was a farm gate, which he opened, then drove through into a rutted field. We drove up the farm track with the lights off. There was no sign of any houses or buildings anywhere and then we stopped by a long line of fencing. He took out a flashlight and a pair of pliers.

'Come on, toots,' he whispered. 'Look there beyond that shrub.' He shone his light and I saw a pair of gleaming eyes in the pitch black, then another and another.

'What are they, Harpo?'

'Wolves. I was a wolf in my previous life and I absolutely love these guys. I worked here, for this bastard landowner who keeps them. I had to feed them once a day and all he gave me was a few scraps of lamb from his kitchen. The animals are skin and bone, see.'

I couldn't see anything, but the eyes began to converge towards us slowly, accompanied by the sound of whimpering.

'Come on, my lovelies,' called Harpo, as he began to use his pliers to cut open the wire fence.

'What are you doing?' I asked.

'I'm freeing them, it's my act of sacrifice.'

'But they are dangerous animals. They'll kill the sheep and cause total chaos.

They'll be hunted down and shot.'

'Exactly, and that's our sacrifice. These guys will die happy, going to their next world. Trust me, toots. I know what I'm doing.'

I think there were about six wolves that hovered around the gap cut in the fence. We got back in the van, waiting for the animals to feel confident about crawling out to their new freedom. One hopped out, followed by the others in quick succession, and they were gone into the dark of the night.

'Way hey!' shouted Harpo and I found myself shouting too, but then I began to feel sick. I opened the door of the van and sicked up a whole lot of stuff I had no idea I'd eaten.

'It's the tabs, toots, doesn't agree with everyone. I'd better get you home now. You need to drink a lot of water and lie down,' he advised, starting up the van. I wound down the window and retched all the way home.

Mam was mad when I got back way after ten o'clock. I looked terrible and told her I'd eaten a dodgy kebab after school. I didn't sleep all night. By morning I felt worse than ever. Thank God it was a Saturday and I could stay in bed for as long as I liked.

That evening I heard someone talking to my mam about wolves being on the loose and farmers armed with guns patrolling their properties. Police cars were driving past with sirens blaring and it sounded as if the world had gone crazy, like in those American disaster movies. All this in sleepy old Fishguard, where the only action to be seen were drunken lads on the piss at the weekend.

On Monday I went to school looking out for my secret lover Harpo, but the hot news in the playground was that he'd been arrested and was back in detention again. On Tuesday the *Enquirer* carried the following report:

Youth held as prime suspect

A juvenile and pupil of Fishguard High has been arrested in connection with the release of wolves into the estate of Maesgwyn Mansion. Two dozen sheep were mauled to death before local farmers were able to track down the wolves and shoot them, but not before a local youth known as Harpo frustrated their efforts by banging a drum to ward off the hunters. The defendant's solicitor, Mr Charles

Owen, told the magistrate that his client was in a distressed state after finding the animals were about to die from malnutrition. The magistrate reserved his judgment, until he had taken advice from local social workers.

I wouldn't see Harpo, my husband-to-be, ever again.

Chapter 2

Yule bash

My favourite teacher was Miss Jacobs who took us for English. She'd ask the class to write a page about their thoughts every week, on some random idea. I loved doing those notes on life and she believed I might be a creative writer one day. I'd write in my black textbook and hand it in for her to read. She asked me to read out one of my scribbles to the class once, as an example of what she described as 'creative expression'.

I never want to have babies, it began. *After all, why does the world need more children? There are enough people around in the world and we certainly do not want more babies here in Wales, where our town is dying on its feet. There are no jobs unless you work for the Council doing dustbins or pushing some geriatric around a nursing home.*

My friend got preggers and we all knew the guy whose plonker stuffed her up.

She'd decided to have the baby and end her schooling or whatever was left of it. She'd gone up the duff and is being so cool about it. Me, I'd be taking a knife to cut off that bastard's dick, if I had the chance.

With Harpo locked away in a remand centre somewhere far out of sight of Fishguard, I was left to fend for myself at school. The wolf incident had earned me a bit of respect and the usual bullies seemed to have been silenced. However, there was one exception, Alwyn Hughes. He seemed to have taken a particular dislike to me now and our relationship was about to sink to a further low point during a lesson on Citizenship, which was about 'Mixing sex with alcohol'.

Our usual teacher who took us for Citizenship had gone sick and Arsehole Hughes came to take our class.

We'd first seen a video of a pupil called Veronica in some Californian school, droning on about how she'd dorked some ugly fat boy in her school, after downing a bottle of wine. *Been there done that* was the general opinion in the classroom and now, she was describing how she always made sure she had a condom when she went out on the razzle, and had cut down on the pop to keep her head.

But when Hughes began to single me out to answer some of the questions he had on his crib sheet, I could have kicked him. 'Now, Ceri, what do you think Veronica can do to protect herself, if she continues to want to mix drinking and sex?'

'Why are you picking on me?' I replied. 'You trying to tell me something, sir?'

'I'm asking you; I'm not picking on you. Do you know the difference?'

'Yes, I do, and I think you're picking on me. Most of this class looks to get laid on a Friday night after a few cans of cider from the offie and that's because there's sod all to do, in this piss hole town of ours.'

'There's no reason for that sort of language!' rapped Hughes.

'Okay, the best thing that Veronica can do, if she wants to continue to mix drinking and sex, is to fuck off and find a place where there's some future.'

'Consider yourselves lucky to live in a place like this. There are many millions of young people out there in the world, who'd happily trade places with you.'

'They're welcome to it!' I sneered, and Hughes decided that he was wasting his time on me and moved on to complete his lesson on the importance of protection, condoms and moderation when getting rat-arsed with the opposite sex.

Oh, how I hated this man! When Harpo was out of detention, we were going to concoct a horrible fate for him that will have him branded a paedo and driven out of our lives forever. I began to think of all sorts of ways that we could trap this disgusting fellow and expose him for the nasty piece of shit that he was.

I was soon going to be able to test out my theories at our school annual ball, where the Year Ten and Elevens would go to the Bay Hotel for our annual bash, for some serious downing of alcohol and, if we were lucky, a good bit of shagging behind the kitchen waste bins.

This was a free-for-all where even the teachers let it all hang out and morals sunk to an all-time low. The year before, the art teacher, a hippy dippy woman with Rasta hair, had fallen off a parapet, taking one of the teaching assistants down with her and had broken her leg. At eleven, when parents came to pick up their darling children, they'd been horrified at the carnage of vomiting and pissing teenagers in the bushes. I was totally looking forward to it. It was the highlight of the school year.

Girls had been talking about what they were going to wear for ages. Copies of *Heat* and *Pony* had been circulated and they were always looking on eBay for ideas. Of course, I couldn't afford any of those red-carpet glitzy gowns, but Mam said I could have a tenner to see what they had in the Factory Seconds shop.

Now a tenner wouldn't normally even get you a decent pair of knickers, but in the Factory Seconds shop there were always surprises if you were happy to put up with a bit of faulty stitching here or a button missing there. Mam never shopped anywhere else.

So, on Saturday morning I went off to the High Street to look for a £10 dress for the ball. There was tons of crap piled high here and there. Lots of outsized things that were good for elephants and some hideous colours. Then I saw this black satin off-the-shoulder number, which was one size smaller than mine. I tried it on.

'Fuckin' el, Gel!' cried out one of the weekend shop assistants from my school, 'That looks amazing on yer. Go for it, I say.' An elderly woman browsing the rails shook her head. I knew I was wearing a shape shifter.

So, decked out in my little black dress, in the middle of winter, I arrived at the ball. All the other girls were strutting their stuff too, in far more expensive rags, whilst the boys hung around looking their usual scruffy selves... barely cleaned jeans, trainers and shirts half hanging out of their pants. Most of us had one thing in common. We'd smuggled in booze, in handbags, pockets, and some had even come earlier in the day and hidden cans around the gardens, like squirrels concealing nuts for later consumption. I had taken a few swigs of vodka at home from mam's drinks cabinet.

Oh, if only Harpo could have been here, that would have made my day. I hadn't missed him much, because I knew he'd return for me one day, but tonight would have been special. He'd have been so proud of me, his woman.

None of the other girls had dared bring an overcoat, so we were all pleased to be out of the cold in the hotel, where the noise of the playground reverberated off the walls of the main banqueting hall.

'Ello, 'ello, 'ello,' asked one of the girls in my street. 'Who're you gonna pull tonight then?'

'Oh my God... I know,' giggled another

'Arsehole Alwyn PE Hughes.'

'Don't bloody start that sluttish stuff now you lot!' I snapped.

And then the evening completely went down the toilet when Hughes himself turned up and said he was the designated teacher on our table. 'Okay you lot, don't enjoy yourselves too much,' he warned. 'I'm joining you for the evening.' The silence on the table said it all.

I would have walked if he came and sat by me. Thankfully he chose to sit exactly opposite me and continued to try to make eye contact.

'Don't mind if I have this beer, do you, guys and gals? Sorry I can't share. School rules,' he joked. Everyone continued to remain stone faced. This was looking like it would be the worst Christmas ball we'd ever had.

As soon as we'd got through the rubbery chicken and soggy chips, posing as food, we got on the dance floor, girls only of course. The boys were all huddled in a corner trying to look cool, some were outside finding their cans of lager and sharing roll-ups. Hughes sat at the table on his own sipping his beer. What a saddo!

But the music was good and we swung around to the tunes, taking breaks for a quick swig from someone's half bottle of vodka hidden in a handbag. I was feeling good again. Some creep from Year 11 came up to me, shouted in my ear that he liked my moves and asked would I come outside for a drink and a smoke. I shook my head and gave him two fingers.

I finally got desperate for a pee and joined the girls queuing for the toilet. I was beginning to get frantic, so I decided to nip out into the cold and do it in the bushes, just like the boys. It was freezing outside after the warmth of the hotel, so I found the nearest, darkest bit of greenery, pulled my knickers down and relieved myself.

As I was finishing, I felt a man standing behind me. He then spoke. 'Hey, I think we should kiss and make up, don't you?'

It was Arsehole Alwyn Fucking Hughes. I pulled my knickers up and tried to stand up. But he was now holding me from behind with his right arm gripped around my waist and his left hand holding my mouth, stopping me from screaming. I tried to wriggle free, but he was strong and I was caught in a vice-like grip. My left arm was free, however, and for one brief moment I felt his ponytail brush against my wrist. I grabbed it and pulled with all my might. His head yanked back and in a true Harpo-inspired move, I head-butted him right on the nose with the back of my head. He reeled and I ran into the hotel. Then all hell broke loose, with Hughes coming after me with a broken nose and blood

34

flowing freely from his face, down his white shirt. Two of the teachers had to hold him back, or he would have hurt me too. The girls thought it was hilarious. Just another Friday night in Fishguard, except this time I thought I'd got off lightly. Or had I?

On Monday morning my mam and I were summoned into the head's office for a second time in the same term. I was expecting the worst and that's exactly what I got.

'Now then,' said the head, looking at us as if I'd robbed the town bank, 'you know what I've called you in for?'

'Yes, I have an idea. It's about that paedo Hughes, isn't it?' said Mam.

'Now, now, there is no need for that sort of language here. Your daughter has needlessly and viciously attacked Mr Hughes our PE teacher for no rhyme or reason.'

'He was trying to make a move on me, Miss, in the dark, when I had my kickers down.' I sneered, 'He didn't tell you that?'

'I'm sure that was all in your mind, Ceri. You're jolly lucky you're not being sent away with that Harpo fellow you were embroiled with.' She turned to my mam. 'I'm afraid we're going to have to exclude your daughter from our school for the next term. Right now, I can't guarantee a place for the rest of next year. That will be down to the governors.'

'But what am I going to do with her around the house all day. You're asking her to get into more trouble, aren't yer?'

'That's my decision now and it's final,' Mrs Jones snapped, standing up to indicate that it was time to leave.

'You can't friggin' do that!' yelled Mam.

'I'm going to have to ask you to leave. Now!'

Chapter 3

Goan night

'This is a fine mess you've got us into, Ceri,' my mam complained as we walked home.

'Mam, it was he who attacked me. How fair is that?'

'He's a fucking man, *Cariad,* they all believe him. You're just a girl from a council estate with a reputation for bad behaviour. You know who wins in that game?'

'But we could appeal! My mate Alison said.'

'Useless bloody waste of time. They're all in this together, these bloody teachers.

Now, you do realise that you're almost certainly never going back to that school?'

'But what about my exams and all that?'

'It's not going to happen, not in Fishguard. Next term would have been your last one to get you ready, but now you're excluded you're going to have to educate yourself.'

'What right here in dead-end Fishguard?'

'Look, why don't you come with me to Goa? At least there you'll learn about real world things, like survival, and maybe my *Bhagwan* will show you a bit of meditation and yoga to help sort you out.'

I was used to Mam going on about her *Bhagwan*, who I gather was some kind of spiritual guide. To me he sounded phony.

'Goa, is that in India, where you go?'

'Yes, you'll love it, *Cariad*. Paradise on earth.'

Mam had a cleaning job for a few families, who lived by the posh Lower Harbour end of town. Every Christmas they gave her a little bonus, which this year was just enough with her social payments to pay for two cheapo flights to Goa, departing shortly after the New Year. Harpo had made me curious about going to India to find the first gypsies, who had travelled across the world to Europe. He said I would understand myself better, if I met my ancestors from way back.

'What am I going to wear?' I asked in the hope that Mam would give me a few quid to visit the Factory Seconds shop.

'Remember it's boiling there, so you won't need much in the way of clothes. No bikinis. You'll get leered at a lot, as they don't see much female nudity. A few T-shirts and shorts should do it.'

I ignored Mam and bought a bikini in shocking pink, which had been marked down to three quid in the sales, and a cut-off pair of jeans which I tore holes in. I thought I was ready for Goa.

The Thomas Cook flight to Goa arrived at ten minutes past midnight, packed with passengers who had come for a cheapie couple of weeks in the sun. Most of them would decamp in coaches to iffy hotels with all-in deals, so they could lie in the sun for the duration and stuff themselves as much as they liked with poppadoms and curries.

But Mam and I were different, a cut below the others. We couldn't afford any deals. Mam had only just scraped the money for cut-price tickets to Goa that had cost her a month's wages and her bonuses. That had cleaned her out completely. She told me that she knew a guy in a shack on the beach in Anjuna, where we could sleep on the floor for a few days. I'd no idea what she'd planned after that, but Goa was to be my refuge from Fishguard High, while things cooled off for a few months and Mr Hughes's smashed up nose and reputation recovered from the injury I'd caused.

How we were going to live or eat for the next few months, I did not know. Little did I know, mam didn't either.

She got plastered on the plane by convincing a steward to give her unlimited plastic bottles of wine because he came from Carmarthen and she made out she'd spent most of her youth in the pubs on Castle Street. As a result, when we got off the plane, she could hardly walk in a straight line and I had to carry her weight for most of the way through Immigration and Customs.

The officials were glad to wave her through to save embarrassment and most of the passengers seemed glad to have nothing to do with a fellow Brit, who had sadly started the holiday a little too early. Once we were out of the terminal building into the open air, the hard reality of getting a bed for the night began to sink in.

There was a swarm of taxi drivers offering us a ride, but Mam said that we couldn't afford it on the few rupees she had left. We'd have to bum a ride or sleep in the airport till morning, when we might be able to catch a bus in the direction of Anjuna.

Then Mam threw up, narrowly missing one of the taxi drivers, which could have probably got us killed. After I'd taken her to the ladies room and had her cleaned up, we came back out to find that the meet-and-greet crowds had dispersed and nearly all the coaches had departed.

We looked a sorry sight. Two penniless women backpackers from Britain, stuck in an airport in the early hours of the morning. None of the taxi drivers wanted to have anything to do with us. It looked like we'd have to spend the night outside the airport, being hassled by people trying to sell us stuff. Perhaps in the morning someone might get us to Anjuna, where Mam was sure we could find refuge with her friends.

I never worked out why at the time, but one of the taxi drivers with a scar across his face asked us if we wanted to go somewhere and I just said 'Yes,' not caring that we didn't have the fare to even get down the road.

And so, we dumped our rucksacks into the cab and climbed in. The taxi was surprisingly new and smelled like it had just been delivered. Mam still smelled of puke.

'Hello, good morning, ladies, welcome to our beloved state of Goa. My name is Tony, and I'm able to help you with anything you want here in Goa. Please sit back and relax for the journey, which will take us about an hour. I know it's still evening for you back home, so I'll let you sleep for the rest of the journey.'

I dropped off to sleep immediately. The uncertainty of where we were going to end up didn't matter. Tiredness had taken over. I dreamed of Mr Hughes, with a broken nose pinning me down on the ground trying to rape me, Harpo pulling him off and the two of us kicking the hell out of him. I awoke with a jolt as the taxi stopped and Tony announced, 'Okay, Madams, we're arrived.'

Mam was still confused and her distress showed in a weird mumbling. I wasn't much help. 'Mam, what are we going to do, here in the middle of nowhere?'

Tony punched a number on his mobile. Someone answered. He spoke in some language I had no idea of. Tony listened then hung up.

'Look, I know of a place for you to stay, you will be safer there,' he reassured us.

'Oh Tony, that's brilliant!' I replied, oozing all the thankfulness I could manage at three in the morning. Mam was still dazed.

We arrived at an enclosure surrounded by walls. The place was in darkness, so I couldn't make out exactly where we were. There was a large veranda, in which I could make out a number of other sleepers on the floor, who could have been homeless people like us. 'You can sleep here,' Tony said, 'there are others like you here.'

'Tony, I have no money at the moment. Can I pay you later maybe?' I asked in my best pleading voice.

'I know,' he replied. 'Come to the Sunset Lounge on the beach and ask for Scorpion. You pay him.'

'How much will it be?'

'He will tell you,' and with that our Goan Knight drove off into the darkness.

We both had sleeping bags tucked in our backpacks, which I rolled out onto the veranda floor. My mam was still useless, so I had to put her down for the rest of the night. None of the half-a-dozen lying bodies stirred, while we made our bed. I was completely drained by now, my eyelids were leaden, in seconds, I fell asleep.

This was not the way I'd expected the first night of my foreign holiday to end.

Who was Tony really? Was he our Goan Knight or was he luring us into something we'd forever regret? Right now, I was thankful to be horizontal and I had many dreams, none of which I could remember.

We were woken with bright sunshine streaming down on our faces and the sound of church bells. In my half-asleep state, I thought I was still back in Fishguard. Do they have churches in India? Apparently, they do.

The morning air was fresh with an unfamiliar, strong scent of cooking and sea air. The noise of screeching birds in the trees, mixed with beeps from traffic on the road outside, also added to a sense of unfamiliarity.

I stripped off my heavy clothing, which we'd worn to reduce our baggage, down to a vest and my cut-off shorts and I could feel my skin breathe again.

A priest, all decked out in an ornate white dress with a big green cross, addressed the half slumbering dossers like us on the floor 'Good morning, my dear friends, I'm Father Michael. I hope you had a restful night. We're celebrating Mass in a few minutes and you're very welcome to join our congregation, after which there will be coffee and refreshments in the hall next door.'

Mam was still comatose, but the thought of coffee and refreshments was enough of an inducement to get me up. I noticed a fellow sleeper also rising and rubbing her eyes. We looked at each other. She looked around my age. She smiled a little at me. I smiled back a little, too, and asked, 'Hi, where does one have a piss around here?'

41

'Come, I'm going there too. I'm Melita,' she replied.

She looked Goan but spoke with a Brummie accent. She showed me a door marked *Ladies*, through an arch, next to the church, and let me go first. I was bursting! Melita had tried to tell me about herself, but a combination of an aching bladder and being half asleep meant I had not registered all the details. I looked in the mirror and didn't like what I saw, so I gave my face a splash of water and dried myself on my sleeve. I still looked a mess though. I'd been bitten by something on my neck during the night. It had left a large red mark.

A crowd had already gathered outside, waiting for the nine o'clock morning Mass to begin. They were mostly men, all dressed in suits or jackets, having their final drag before the service began. The church, St Anthony's, had seen better days. The crumbling, whitewashed Portuguese façade had twin towers, from which bells tolled loudly. The smokers began to put out their fags and drift inside.

Melita joined me after her visit to the toilet, suggesting, 'Let's go in. I was brought up a Catholic. It's worth a cup of coffee and some mince patties afterwards.' She led me into the church, and I felt a hundred eyes following me, the only white face, to the only empty pew, which had probably been reserved for us dossers. Melita was confident about her surroundings and acknowledged the people who looked at us with a smile.

I'd only ever been to a chapel once, when *Tad-cu* died. This was nothing like a Welsh chapel. There were ornate statues of white men and a woman in blue all around me. They were dusty, chipped and in need of a good cleaning. Melita handed me a hymnbook. A guitarist started strumming to the accompaniment of a tambourine and Melita opened the hymnbook for me on No 348, 'As I Kneel Before You'.

The singing was surprisingly good, with many harmonies given in full throated passion, by the mixed talents of men and women, and delivered in a style somewhere between Willy Nelson and Dolly Parton. Women occupied most of the left-hand side of the church and men sat on the right, separating the sexes.

Father Michael, accompanied by half a dozen youths in cassocks, processed to the altar. One was swinging a bowl, from which emanated the smell of pungent smoke. I coughed a little, as it caught my throat. Father Michael, a tall man with a dark crop of jet-black hair, looking like he was still in his forties, spoke when the hymn finished.

'Dear parishioners and friends who have joined us for Mass,' he greeted us, holding out his hands in a welcoming gesture. There were a lot of prayers which everybody, including Melita, knew and I just followed along, longing for my cup of coffee and mince patties. The longer it went on, the hungrier and more fidgety I became. Then there was the sermon, during which Father Michael got quite theatrical.

'You know, in the time of Jesus, they used to stone women who committed adultery, and when Jesus came upon such a stoning, he said, 'He that is without sin, let him cast the first stone.' So let us stop judging other people and start by looking at ourselves. Let's welcome people of different faiths and nationalities into our hearts. I see two people here today who were sleeping outside last night and walked into our church here to be with us. I hope you will welcome them and many others afterwards.'

At the end of the Mass, the congregation drifted out of the church and the smoking young men resumed their ritual and their stories, probably about bikes and girls, accompanied by much laughter. The girls kept to their own company, appearing to tease each other in light-hearted exchanges with passing glances at the boys, each one followed by fits of giggles in a post-Mass dating game.

The priest made a point of coming up to talk to us, 'Good that you could come to Mass. I hope you can stay for coffee and Mrs Castellino's delicious pasties.'

'Thank you.' I said, as I had already consumed several of these pasties in my head to satisfy my hunger pangs and I lost no time heading inside, where the smell of minced beef filled the room. I helped myself to three, thinking I'd save one for Mam, who was probably still nursing her hangover. We sat down at a table, watched suspiciously by some of the parishioners, who'd probably seen dossers like us come and eat their lovely pasties and live off their generosity.

'How long are you staying here for?' asked Melita.

'I don't know really, depends on my mam and how we can support ourselves. We're a little like exiles here. I was thrown out of school, so this is sort of my punishment for my bad behaviour.'

'Why don't you come and help me here with this orphan charity. I'm running away from home in a way, too. My Goan parents in Worcester want me to become a doctor or something like that and I just want to see the world a little, discover more of my roots.'

'I've never even worked in a charity shop before.'

'They give you this rubbish tat called jewellery, that you

have to sell, and you get to keep a quarter of the sales. The more you can push the stuff the more you make. Give it a go. You and I could make a team. The Fab Floozies.'

'I'm not sure I'm a very convincing salesgirl. I've never done this before.'

'The earrings are in a fake silver, with bracelets and necklaces to match. The foreigners love this sort of stuff. Try it out tomorrow on Anjuna beach. A couple of days a week and you and I could afford to rent one of those shacks on the beach, right on the water's edge.'

'Really?'

'Go on, it's for charity. A good cause.'

'Tidy.'

'Is that yes or no?'

'We'll give it a go.' I took a couple of patties for Mam, who had finally woken up. She was sitting talking to a man who had greased back hair and a black Armani T-shirt, not a kindly sort of dude.

'This is Scorpion, *Cariad*, he's come to say hello. We've him to thank for the taxi ride.'

He shook my hand with a surprisingly weak handshake for a tough-looking guy and I thanked him.

'Come by the Sunset Lounge on the beach, girls. I may have some work for you'

'He seemed a nice sort of fellow,' remarked Mam when Scorpion had left.

'Oh? I thought he was a bit sleazy.'

'Not at all, he asked me if I wanted anything while I was here in Goa. I said I needed to get to Pune to see my *Bhagwan* and he lent me the train fare.'

'So, I assume he thinks that I'm going to be paying him back, through whatever work he has in store for me.'

'Don't look a gift horse in the mouth,' said Mam.

I'd been in Goa for a day and hadn't been in the sea, me a Pisces of the water sign. I went into the ladies toilets to change into my swimmers, my head felt groggy as I looked at my face in the pockmarked mirror. I wish it had been less round. I had great hair, which was blonde. Real blonde, which went even lighter from the sunshine, and set against my golden skin. I knew I could turn heads all day on the beach and, yes of course, a fantastic figure that seemed to come naturally. 'I don't know how you do it, darling, or where you put it. Me I just have to look at food!' my mam would say, as she eyed me up and down when I'd been for a swim. Jealousy or what? I slipped on my Factory Seconds bikini top and stepped into a pair of cotton paisley pyjama pants. Mam had told me that knicker bottoms were far too provocative on the beach and these were about the only words of advice I had followed.

The early evening sun was turning the sky a bright golden colour. I watched a flock of sea birds hover around a fishing boat out at sea, through my cheap pair of imitation Gucci glasses, whilst walking barefoot on the hot amber sand.

At the water's edge, the waves formed a long line of froth at least a metre high and crashed down on the shore from their journey across the Arabian Sea. A few hundred metres ahead, the grounded hulk of an abandoned oil tanker obscured the sharp blue line of the horizon.

I plunged into the waves and the magical sea began to work wonders in soothing my throbbing head. Lush. I swam to the next wave and then floated for a while on my back to allow the sea to carry me gently ashore. The throbbing deep in the back of my head began to subside and I wished I could bob around in the moving water motionless, for the whole day.

A semi-naked man on the shore in sawn-off jeans waved to me. 'Hey, watch out for the turds, hah!'

'I can only see one, and he's ashore!' I shouted back.

'Hah, hah, very funny. English humour.'

'Not bloody English. Welsh, I'm bloody Welsh, man.'

'Welsh, English, Scottish, you're all the same, from the White world.'

'If you think that, then you're an ignorant turd as well,' I yelled, now standing up knee deep in the water and walking back to the waterline.

'Hey, I'm Jaz. You need anything today?'

'If you mean drugs, no. I'm going to be a good girl on my holiday.'

'Holy shit, no? But you should be bad on your holiday, *yar*. Yes? Let your hair down, hah?'

'But if I did, I'd be bad all the time, eh?'

I walked out of the water; a comforting glow returned to me as I ran my hands through my hair to squeeze out the heavily salted water. The wet pyjama bottoms now clung and I noticed Jaz looking at me in a way that gave me the creeps. I returned his gaze with my silent, defiant look and hoped that he would go back to where he'd come from.

'Come and see me, hah, and we'll have a nice party for you. I'm the bar guy at the Sunset, over there.'

'I'm Ceri. I might be seeing you soon.'

'Hey great, Ceri!'

I didn't reply and walked away, turning my back on the barman. I would soon realise that there was something wrong with these Goan boys that I couldn't work out. They went to church every Sunday, loved partying just like the best of the boys back home, but when it came to any white foreign woman, they thought we were slags. They'd never dare chat up a Goan girl on the beach, probably because they wore such hideous clothes, which weren't Western or Eastern. They looked like some sort of satin hybrid out of the seventies. The boys joked that they wore tin knickers, which their parents had welded on to them until their wedding day.

That made girls like me and Melita, my Brummie Goan friend, open game and we both had to learn to play it skilfully, to get our own way.

This first morning I kept to the wet sand, hard and flat from the receding tide. A woman fully clothed in her sari, half sat in the water ahead of me, holding on to her young son, who shouted with joy every time a rush of water came up and splashed them. They exchanged smiles in a silent greeting. Where was my mam?

I just couldn't rely on her to be with me on Anjuna. That evening she caught the night train to Pune to see the man they called the *Bhagwan*, who seemed to have put a spell on her. There were pictures of him in her bedroom back home and she read books by him and listened to his lengthy speeches in his sing-song Indian accent. I just didn't get it. Now after only one day in Goa, she was happy to leave me with people I'd only just met and didn't appear to have the best reputations, to go and seek her inner peace with this strange man. And you know what, I didn't care. There was never a great bond of love between us and I'd always felt that my existence was only tolerated. That's why I became jealous of Melita and the fact that she had parents who cared, although in the wrong sort of way.

It would be the last I'd see of Mam.

Chapter 4

Beach entrepreneur

That night Melita and I went to the Sunset Lounge to meet Scorpion and see what he had in store for us. We'd been for our first swim in the sea and I felt totally refreshed, ready for the evening. I still wore my cut-off jeans and Melita wore a cotton sarong, which made quite an impact when we entered the empty beach bar.

The bearded bartender Jaz, who I'd met earlier on the beach, seemed to be in charge and he stared at us both as if we'd arrived from Mars. 'Hey, you're the Welsh girl. The boss said you'd be coming here tonight.'

'I'm Ceri and this is Melita,' I answered. 'Scorpion said something about work?'

'Ah yes.' he looked over our heads, as if to acknowledge someone else. A tall, blonde, heavily made up woman in black mascara and a red blouse, came up to us and introduced herself in a thick Russian accent.

'I am Karina.' She didn't offer her hand. 'Give these girls a drink. Jaz does the bar and I look after the guests,' she explained.

'What's it to be then?' asked Jaz. 'I'll fix you my very special *Sex on the Beach*,' he giggled through his teeth. We didn't respond, but he proceeded to mix up something that looked green with ice.

'Now then, we want you to occasionally help Jaz out behind the bar, but mainly it's talking to our guests who come here and you pretend, well…' Karina hesitated, 'to be here on holiday.'

'What, like to make conversation…?' asked Melita.

'Yes, to make them comfortable, you know, give them hope they may be lucky with girls like you. But no fucking, okay? Understand? My girls do that for money and you are just preparing the punters for the time of their lives. Scorpion will pay you at the end of every night, depending how successful you are of being clearly understood?'

That was all fairly clear to me, but Melita looked unsure. 'I'll try it out for a couple of nights. You see, we already have a job selling jewellery for a youth charity.'

'Okay, your choice, but you will make more money here, than selling that crap and by the way, Scorpion controls all the vendors on the beach. Just so you know.'

Our job interview was over, and Karina disappeared behind a screen. We sipped the sickly green cocktail. The evening was quiet with mostly couples out for the evening. We chatted for most of the time with Jaz, who led us to understand this was the best bar in the world and that we had landed on our feet, with Scorpion as our employer.

On my third day in Goa, I found myself on Anjuna under a shady coconut tree with a tray of rubbish jewellery and a sign on my hat which said, *Help Orphan Children*. I had a badge, which I pinned to my top, just above my right boob, which said *I Love Cymru*.

A whole half day passed by and I still hadn't sold a single item. I was about to give it all up when Melita came over to see how I was doing.

'Oh, please don't jack this in. Maybe the two of us would work better. We're the Fab Floozies after all. The income we get from these sales means a lot to those kids.'

Melita was bubbly, quite the opposite of me. I was the sultry one, who looked suggestively at the punters from the corner of my eye. So far, I'd failed as one of the two Fab Floozies. Things had just got worse for me, as Mam had left me to fend for myself. I only had a mobile telephone and few rupees to tide me over till she got back from the Pune *Bhagwan*.

'It's no good staying here away from the main punters. We've got to take the loot to them, further down there by the shore!' decided Melita the optimist.

We giggled like schoolgirls on an outing, as we carried our tat the few hundred yards or so to the beach, where we set up our new hot spot, just near the hotel. The beach was empty. There was a *bhangi* woman, selling wooden spoons and bowls that had been turned from a dark wood. She looked at us with disgust. Most of the Indian women vendors regarded us not only as unwelcome competition, but also as low-life hookers. I'd later discover that they came from the very bottom of the caste ladder and were treated like muck by higher caste Indians.

We didn't care. This was for a charity that would eventually help those orphaned kids. Probably for the first time in my life, I felt I was doing some good. *Tad-cu* would have been proud of me. I could have sold just about anything by the time we'd finished rehearsing our chat-up lines.

And then… we had our first sale!

A woman in very classy silk beach pants came along,

walking hand in hand with a local Goan man. She looked twice at my badge, stopped and asked, '*Siarad y Cymraeg?*' *Do you speak Welsh?* I replied that I did, and she got quite excited, explaining to her muscly squeeze, that I came from her land. In fact, she came from Cardiff, but I didn't mind, even though I hated Cardiff. She bought hundreds of rupees of stuff. I think because she was quite excited to find a fellow countrywoman on a beach in Goa.

Out at sea, there were a few people in the water trying to battle with the might of the ocean waves, which made swimming only possible for those who were strong and capable. An Indian woman, fully clad in her sari, stood half in the water saying prayers to her god. So, we had someone's god looking over us and it felt good.

The Cardiff woman's purchases seemed to help our sales for the rest of the day. I later learned of the superstition of *bohni,* the first purchase of the morning. If made generously, would lead to good sales for the rest of the day. Oddly this proved true for the rest of the week. The dirty old men were especially easy game, as we strung them along and Melita scored particularly well, because they probably thought she looked exotic and came from Brummie land. My English worked for the Americans, Brits and Germans, and Melita's Spanish, French and Italian just about covered the rest of the rich world.

The Japanese just passed us by, completely preoccupied by their ambition to walk the length of the beach unmolested, in their funny sun hats. We saw Russians here and there, but none of them spoke English. They were grumpy, too, and not interested in our tat.

Melita and I became the best of friends and I moved into her beach shack, which was cheap and brilliant for jumping into the sea twice a day. After our first full week of work, we counted our money and Melita squealed with delight at the princely sum of two thousand rupees, clear of all our costs.

'This is just too much fun, Ceri, you and me.'

'Definitely. How long do you think we could do this without having to stop being teenagers?'

'My parents have given me six months, then I have to get back and study to become a doctor or an accountant or something stupid like that.'

'Which one? They are quite different things.'

'They don't care, as long as it's one of those professions,' she said, putting on a posh English voice.

'Why don't you say, *bugger off* and do your own thing?'

'It doesn't work like that, Ceri, not with my family. It's ingrained in me to obey my parents and do the right thing as they see it. It's them first, then me later. If I did go off and become a lowly aid worker or whatever, I would never rest knowing that they would be heart broken.'

'You know, Melita, I wish I had a family like yours.'

'Really?'

'Yes, someone who would care about me and what I did with my life. Isn't that strange?'

In the evenings Melita and I went to the Sunset Lounge, to look like innocent virgins and get people to buy us stupid green *Sex on the Beach* cocktails, which I learned was just coloured water with syrup. We began to get quite skilled at disappearing at the right moments, to allow Karina's girls to take over the chat and pampering of male guests. Scorpion seemed to be pleased and he handed us both a bundle of scruffy, hundred-rupee notes at the end of the week.

We learned fast that everything was negotiable here in Goa, you just had to have your price and stick to your guns, but the most difficult negotiations were with the police on the beach, who were probably the most corrupt in the world. Strictly speaking, we were breaking the law by doing our business dealings on the beach without a license, but everybody did. You just had to bribe the man in uniform. The going rate was thirty rupees a day and that was him taken care of.

But us girls were different. We had something else to offer that the men in khaki couldn't get elsewhere. The constables were negotiable, and we got away with a few smiles and another twenty rupees, but the head honcho, the CID chap, wanted his cut. Inspector Denzil Braganza was his name. He would come looking for me when he was drunk, mostly in the evenings and try and fondle my tits, his breath smelling of liquor and cheap fags. Disgusting. No one in the Sunset Lounge would step in to stop him and I just had to laugh it off every time.

'I want to fuck her, but she say *No*. Why? Why?' he would ask Melita.

'We don't fuck anyone, Inspector, we're virgins and it's illegal in our country to have sex with anyone under sixteen,' Melita would remind Braganza.

'Hey guys, hear that? They're fucking virgins!' he would shout across at the bar and everyone would respond with mock laughter, including Jaz.

They were all afraid of the inspector, because he could have

55

anyone locked up on the slightest charge and nobody seemed to want to do anything about him, not even Scorpion. A night in a Panjim jail would take years off you. If the inmates wouldn't take on the challenge of giving you an initiation, worthy of the shittiest jails in the world, then it was the rats that got you.

'Ah, it's all bravado Ceri. Just ignore him.'

'But it's my fucking body he's touching, not yours!'

'He'll go away and find someone else soon. You'll see.'

But, in spite of the few slime balls, I was having a lot of fun discovering how to survive in my new world. I felt I had to call Mam and tell her my news. 'Hi, Ma, it's Ceri.'

'How's it with you, *Cariad*?'

'*Ya*, I'm fine.'

'Got to Pune after a very long journey and eventually found the centre,' Mam told me. 'Bloody fut-fut driver tried to rip me off. No way was I going to pay five hundred rupees for a ten-minute ride, now was I?'

'Are you on your own, Ma?' I already knew she'd been bumming around India for a few weeks with some waster who sang Bob Dylan covers.

'Just me, *Cariad*, and the Bhagwan. It's so cool. Just can't describe the vibe down here in Pune.

'I've just been for a swim, to wake up.'

'Have a hard night then?'

'No, nothing special really.'

Just stay away from the low life, *Cariad*. Those tossers at the Sunset Lounge. Keep clear of that greasy Jaz and his mate that ugly bastard Denzil, they're bad news, *Cariad*. Ask Scorpion to keep a special watch on you.'

Chapter 5

Lounge banter

M elita and I continued to get *hwyl* out of each other's company. The Welsh word *hwyl*, meaning something a bit deeper than just *fun*, and pronounced 'hooyl', hit our relationship off exactly. There was a kind of solace in being together. She was a couple of years older and better educated, but she didn't look down on me, a girl from a council house in Fishguard. I taught her to drink bitter with a lemonade top, and a few Welsh words and expressions. She'd not been allowed to have boyfriends, as her father said it would mess with her studies, so I had to fill her in on all the sordid details of my affairs with the low-life back home. I'd say in a scoring match of *Worldwise*, I'd score nine and she'd struggle to get five, whilst in the *Cleverclogs* category she'd be a nine and I'd get four.

The Sunset Lounge was beginning to get busy that evening. Jaz, the bartender, dressed in a Hawaiian shirt, sporting a garland of marigolds, juggled tumblers as he mixed cocktails. A distorted noise, pretending to be music, blared from cheap speakers. Dusk was half-an-hour old and the red glow over the Arabian Sea was giving way to a dark crimson-blue night sky, interrupted by a single, flickering evening star. A star, I was to discover every evening, that came out like an old friend to greet me after a long hot day.

We had the same star back in West Wales that came out in the morning and at night. Shepherds called it the Workers' Star. Wasn't it funny that although everything else around me was so very different, I still had the moon and the stars to remind me of home.

Melita and I went over to the bar and she pulled up a bar stool for me, steadying it in the sand. I perched on top of it, crossing my very white legs, which stuck out of my cut-off jeans. Jaz the bartender stared at them and then I caught him staring at my tank top, which showed off my boobs, which were the envy of every girl in my year.

'Welcome to the Sunset again,' he smiled. I nodded.

'Where in Wales are you from, Ceri?' asked Jaz.

'Fishguard, ever hear of it?'

'Oh ya, cool. Never heard of it. Can I come and stay with you when I get to England one day?'

'It'll cost you mega.'

Over the next few days, I started to notice how the Beachboys dominated most of the business on the beach. Although Jaz managed the Lounge, he also acted as head honcho. He was Scorpion's eyes and ears, listening and looking out for anyone else trying to muscle in, discussing things to do with drugs, selling flesh, or the occasional whacking. Karina organised the most amazing parties and raves on the beach, giving Scorpion's bar fame with visitors far and wide. The Internet was packed with references to the Sunset Lounge as the essential place to visit on your trip to Anjuna, and Jaz topped up the comments with fictitious accounts from women who had met a handsome dude and danced till they dropped. That's the way things were done out here. You scratch my back and I'll scratch yours. You could get away with murder, literally, if you knew the right people.

'Scorpion seems like quite a fun guy,' I remarked to Melita.

'Don't be fooled by all that smiling,' she warned. 'I think the Beachboys are really hard, nasty dudes, who operate the beach, selling drugs and pimping. On Anjuna they've collared the market in Ukrainian women, who are tall and really stunning. As well as local young Goan boys, who are handsome, dark, lean, and under orders to satisfy the lust of the white *ferenghi* women. He is the hardest of them all. Just don't cross him whatever you do.'

Perhaps because she was older, or because she understood how things worked out here in Goa, Melita seemed to have her ear to the ground better than me. My concept of *hard* in Fishguard was limited to bust-ups in the High Street on a Friday night. I was yet to discover what *hard* really meant.

There was the sound of scuffling and two of the Beachboys came in, manhandling a short guy with greased back hair. 'Call the boss!' one of them told Jaz. The bartender punched in some numbers and mumbled something about a bloke going off on his own. Minutes later, Scorpion was in the bar.

'Caught him dealing on the beach, Boss.'

Scorpion narrowed his eyes, took one look at us and ordered, 'Take him behind the toilets.'

For the next two or three minutes we heard a series of screams, pleading for mercy, thuds, thumps, swearing in several languages, and then quiet. 'Get rid of him,' I heard Scorpion say. Jaz smiled throughout the encounter, as if he was listening to a comedy slapstick routine, and whispered

59

'The boss is pissed off, ha ha.'

Both of us girls sat in stunned silence.

We never found out what happened to the man who displeased Scorpion. Whatever it was, it couldn't have been good.

Almost on cue, in walked a couple of blondes who were obviously from Australia, with their fake jewellery, clean-cut hair and tight blouses, displaying bulges in all the wrong places. They had come for their sundowners and had been seduced into staying over for the end of the Happy Hour, which Jaz seemed to advertise only to tourists that looked like spending serious money.

'So, what's it to be, girls, a Straight up against the Wall, a Sex on the Beach, or the guaranteed Club Legover?'

The Aussies giggled like teens. I'd later discover that Jaz unashamedly, trotted out the same old gags time and again.

'I'll have another Against the Wall, Jaz,' said the plump pink one, beaming.

'You know what, Donna,' said the other, 'I'm going to swap the Wall for Sex on the Beach.'

'Good for you. Best way forward, ha?' said Jaz, grabbing a bottle of White Mischief Indian vodka and pouring it with a flourish from an arm's length height.

The giggling and the banter continued until their drinks were prepared, and then Jaz turned his attention towards us.

'Now then, a nice drink?' he asked, with a hint that it might be his treat, but this was unlikely. Jaz was a mean bugger.

'I'm a lager with a lemonade top sort of girl,' I responded.

'Bloody heck! That's big money, ha? Who's your sugar daddy?'

'And mine's the same. We can go elsewhere if it's a problem?' added Melita.

'Sure, that's what I always say… give them what they want,' Jaz winked to the Aussies.

'Hey, you've got us on a fun-packed evening with Dab Danny knocking out his grooves.' He turned to us, 'You staying then? It's a big night tonight. We're expecting a crazy party over from the Taj Hotel, so Scorpion's gonna want you on top form, moving to Danny's grooves.'

'We're not sure, not after what we just saw happen. We could be next.'

Just then the DJ Dab Danny played Beyoncé, his first track of the evening. I began to move to the Queen of Music on my bar stool. 'I love this!' I shouted, and Melita and I did a bar stool dance, messing around to the rhythm of 'If I were a Boy'.

The Aussies didn't know how to take us and smiled nervously into their coloured mushy drinks. We smiled back at them. That was when Scorpion turned up and took up his position near the pinkies. 'Good evening ladies.'

'*Namasté*,' the one called Donna greeted him.

'Ah, you speak Hindi?'

'No, not really, just one or two words.'

'*Namasté*, my name is Scorpion.' He held his palms together, smiling and nodding, the smarmy psycho git.

'Scorpion? That's an unusual name,' said Donna, the pinker of the two.

Scorpion didn't look like he'd just pulverised some poor guy to death at all. He wore a shiny red sports jacket, with an open collarless white shirt and a solid gold cross hanging from a short chain around his tree-trunk thick neck. Had it not been for the deep cut scar on his right cheek, he might have been mistaken for a travel representative.

'I'm Donna and this is Judy.

'*Aré yar*, like Punch and Judy.' The women looked confused.

And what do you do here, Scorpion? Relaxing after a hard day?' asked Donna.

'I have a firm. Blokes work for me looking after the security of this beach and to keep such lovely people like you happy.'

'Oh, that's cool.'

'If you want someone to look after you, just say. They're good, strong, nice Goan boys from my church, ya know.

'Oooh, that's nice work,' chipped in Judy, the less plump of the two.

'Just all in an honest day's work you know,' said Scorpion, turning his attention to us.

'So, how are our two new hotties doing tonight?'

'We've had a good day, Scorp.' I don't know why I abbreviated his name, but he didn't seem to object. 'Sales are good, people love buying dross.' I wanted him to hear good news.

'If you need anything, you know, come and see me,' he offered, stroking me on the face. I just continued to smile as innocently as I could, but inside, it felt like Alwyn Hughes was touching me.

'Anyone tries to mess you around, remember, Scorpion is right here to protect you beauts,' he assured us. And I believed him.

'Well, so far so good. Melita and I are just having a ball!' I laughed, and Scorpion grinned, showing off his golden tooth, so I thought I'd test him with a little challenge.

'Some of the men in khaki have been harassing us a bit. We mentioned we were working for you, but they just laughed.'

'Bloody buggers. I'll have a word with their boss Braganza the next time I see him. Don't you worry.'

'Thanks, Scorp, we'll rely on you.'

'Look after the girls, ha?' he said to Jaz. 'One good turn deserves another, okay? We'll speak again soon,' and he went off to talk to the Aussies again.

Dab Danny stepped up his grooves, with more action from his desk and we both leapt off the bar stools and began to dance. Melita was a great dancer and I kept following her moves from my very basic knowledge of Salsa on the telly.

'You're a lush dancer, Mel. Where did you learn?'

'At home, my mam taught me. She's the guru.'

Melita and I stuck close together every evening, not just for safety, but because we felt a sense of *hiraeth,* that drew us together. *Hiraeth* is what we Welsh feel for our homeland. A sense of longing to get back there, and now we were feeling it for our roots in India. We were both sure that way back in the past, we had common ancestors from somewhere here in India. Mam had talked a lot about Northern India, where the gypsies had come from, but Mam hadn't got much further than Goa.

As time went on, I liked being here because it felt like the real world. Don't get me wrong. I love the land of my birth, but back home I sort of felt trapped. Each day came and went. Same old, same old. Here, I was free of teachers telling me off for not handing in homework, social workers asking me stupid questions about my family, and pubs refusing to serve me a drink. Here, I was a businesswoman doing deals all day, making a good living without any support from my mam. All that and I'm still not even sixteen, when most of my mates back in Fishguard were at home puking up after a pint of cider at the Bell.

In 2010 there were loads of people like us in Goa, who were escaping something or the other back home, and yet any Goan here would have gladly exchanged their lives for what we had. There wasn't a lot here except for the sea, sun, and hope for better times.

I had almost forgotten about Harpo, my husband-to-be, when a nice little surprise arrived for me in the form of an email from him.

Hey toots, it's me your betrothed. Just been released for good behaviour.

Now is that a surprise, me the gentleman? Anyway, the rumour out here is that you're away in India. Aren't you the lucky one! I'd love to be with you, but lack of dosh prevents it, unless I rob a bank or something. Don't worry, that's only a joke! Look up a few of our gypsy relos if you can and record some poongi tunes on your phone for me to play when you get back. Stay cool toots. I love you lots.
XXXX

Chapter 6

The rumble

Thanks to Jaz's fakery, Scorpion's online presence was superb. People anywhere in the world knew the Sunset Lounge and arrived in large numbers for the promise of an adult party. The hundreds of visitor reviews said it all: 'Best nite of my life. 100 rupees a line must be the best value in the world.' It was only the stiff entrance fees that kept the backpackers and the locals out.

The best parties were at the end of the week when the Sunset Lounge hosted its Naughty Nighters. It was a weekly rave the club staged to get the weekend going. Scorpion had sent out his best looking Beachboys, leafleting the area in and around Anjuna and the more exclusive resorts further north.

Their target was single, white foreign women, who had come to Goa for a holiday of uninhibited sex and drugs in the sun. The boys spoke confidently, offering a party to remember. Their bright white teeth created smiles, which radiated excitement and the promise of fun for the night ahead.

'I'm Kenny, I'll look forward to seeing you tonight. Don't forget, first drink's on me!' was the opening line of one of the boys to a group of thirty-somethings from Swansea. I'd seen them working the beach all week.

'Hi! Wanna party tonight, girls? I'm Elvis, yes the real thing. Are you lonesome tonight? I have other talents too, hah. Hope to see you tonight at the Lounge,' a Presley lookalike invited a couple of middle-aged women from Adelaide.

At the same time, Karina was packing off her Ukrainian all-women workforce to conduct their own promo campaign. Dressed stylishly in nearly transparent cotton paisley dresses, they too promised a night that would surpass a man's wildest dreams. The men in their sights were wealthy Indians, who had also come to Goa to see what the fuss was all about.

The Ukrainian women were well-practiced at picking only those that were serious party animals and not the roving groups of young men who came just to get drunk and gawp at foreign women, and have their picture taken with them. They would choose a spot to sunbathe next to their targets, whenever they spotted men on sun loungers, wearing expensive watches or designer swimwear. Indians love to show off their wealth. In would come the girls, wearing their tiny dresses that revealed their stunning bikinis.

'Is this place free for me?' was the opener and they would lie down briefly, pretending to soak up the sun, turning over from time to time to smile and engage the men in conversation.

Their moves were highly effective. Invitations were issued and excuses made to go somewhere else. This was a proven art and the result was that, if everything went to plan, from ten o'clock onwards there would only be standing room at the Sunset Lounge.

Scorpion called his 'workforce' to turn up for the team

briefing before the doors opened. Karina, who wore a black one-piece sleeveless cat suit, reclined at the end of the bar. She exhaled a long plume of cigarette smoke and ambled over to speak to me. 'Boss says that he'd like you to do him a favour tonight.'

'Oh, and what…?'

Just look hot with your friend and dance around to DJ Danny's grooves. You're part of the show tonight.'

'We came to chill…'

'I wouldn't disappoint the boss if he's asking nicely, just to dance a bit you know,' warned Jaz with his rare serious face. 'You know you owe the boss big time, remember. It's only to dance and look hot. He may not ask so nicely the next time. Scorpion's not a nice guy when he's disobeyed. I've seen guys get their legs broken for less.'

Melita nodded her approval on behalf of both of us.

'I've seen most of these dudes in church,' I remarked, slightly confused.

'*Yar*, St Anthony's is the boss's recruiting ground. Their parents think he is the dog's bollocks, because he puts cash in their pockets. Nobody asks questions in St Anthony's when there is cash involved. You just get respect and plenty of it, when everyone else is unemployed.'

'And Karina?' asked Melita.

'Ha ha, you ask too many questions. She rocked up in Goa and very quickly identified Scorpion as the perfect business partner to help her develop her gentlemen's services, with lots of girls from Kiev waiting to join her. Guess they're all unemployed in Kiev too, hah?'

'Like us in Fishguard.'

'So just be thankful that you nice girls have the boss to look after you.'

'Now listen everyone, it's going to be a great show tonight. Everybody feeling good?' shouted Scorpion.

'Yar!' the yell went up.

'You're all looking good, too. It's a great night to have fun, make money, and give people a time to remember. Just a few things. Tonight, we've got tabs, ganja, and some very nice powder, just in. Hundred a line. Try to sell the *combo package*, we'll throw in the hits for free and give them real value. Tonight's a special price, fifteen thousand for the *combo*. Girls, give the men a happy ending to remember and boys, go fill those milk bottles right to the top. Remember we keep half your tips.'

There was laughter. Karina put her arms around Scorpion and purred, 'And I save one big long kiss for the boss, yes?' He gave an uncomfortable smile, showing a hint of his immaculate white Goan teeth.

'Hey chief,' a hand went up from Jaz. 'There's a bit of rumbling that there are some Ukes recently arrived from Kiev, who are putting it about that they're the new gang in control of things.'

'*Yar*, I heard that, too, from one of the guys who hires out canoes on the beach,' added one of the Beachboys.

'Yes, some of my girls have been threatened by them, with promises that they will end up as fish food if they don't work for them,' complained Karina, 'but these guys are just vermin. There only a few of them. They're in your country, so you can kick their balls into their heads if you want!'

'Okay, we're always going to have to watch our backs, but you guys are a special force that can deal with anything. Let's always be prepared. Don't take on anyone single-handed,' warned Scorpion. 'Make sure you have help around. We've got to make this place look like a place to have fun in safety.'

Like clockwork the show kicked into gear. The lasers lit up the black sky, techno was the mood music to get things going from Dab Danny, who looked on top form. He'd pulled in a couple of minor Bollywood stars and some of the revellers were getting selfies taken with them.

The bars were manned by sharp, well-dressed staff, who moved in time with the music. Karina frequently gave out image guidance to the staff. 'You guys must have good hair, yah?' They all had perfect, well-cut hair. No dreads or long ragged locks were permitted. 'And hot shoes. No Nike nonsense.'

'Girls, special privileges if you dance on the bar for a bit. It's always great.'

'The bar?' I objected. 'No fuckin' way!'

'C'mon, let's give it a go. Free booze all night. Do anything for that!' shouted Melita. She stepped up on the bar stool and pulled me up with her and we were soon getting it up on the wooden-topped bar, which was slippery and dangerous as hell. Men gawped. One tried to join us, but one of the boys took him down. 'Ladies only, sir,' was his polite response. Dab Danny went wild on the sound system and announced that the dancing girls were accepting drinks at the bar. People could show their appreciation by buying them a couple of Pina Coladas from Jaz the barman. I hated Pina Colada, but quickly realised that each drink totted up hundreds of rupees for the Sunset.

In a strange way, we both felt protected up here on the bar from the scum on the dance floor, and I was paying back Scorpion for being our Goan Knight when we arrived penniless. But then again, I didn't have a choice. I was getting sucked in up to my eyeballs.

The entrances were guarded by bulging, bearded doormen, who looked like wrestlers at a wedding. They wore close-fitting suits that seemed to be one size too small, stressing their well-developed six-packs, and their black beards just amplified their fiery looks.

'Do you have an invitation, sir? Thank you. That'll be three thousand rupees. Please ask for the *combo pack* later on in the evening. Well worth it. First drink's on us by the way. Have fun now, okay? You're only young once. Hah.'

The guests wandered in, heading straight for the bar to pick up their first drink. The Sunset Lounge was vast, some of it extending over the beach dunes. A huge crimson Buddha was in the middle of the dancing area, giving its blessing to everyone enjoying Scorpion's temple of pleasure. It carried some words about forgetting your inhibitions and leaving guilt at the door. Had Karina made that up? Incense sticks glowed in fancy holders, giving off a heady perfume of sandalwood, large crimson cushions were strewn in dark corners for couples to lie on, while the trance-inducing music pumped through giant speakers from above. You couldn't talk, so everyone just moved in time with the beat. Melita and I danced easily with Pina Coladas in our hands. Expensive cars dropped off guests, while ordinary mortals just stood outside the enclosure, with their cheap cameras, flashing pictures of someone they thought they'd seen in the movies.

Scorpion was in full view everywhere, as he greeted guests and gave them the thumbs up. So too were Karina's women, who danced with glasses of something bubbly and expensive in their hands, inviting the men to join them in their gyrations.

The Beachboys were active with their women guests, dancing closer, with more touching, doing exactly what the boss had told them to do. They seemed to be enjoying it, with frequent shouts of hysterical laughter heard above the sound of the music.

Karina shouted out over the noise waving her hands in a dance move 'This is the new India. As good as Ibiza, Magaluf, or any of Europe's hottest beach clubs. Also, we have the full service here. Anything at a price, *yar*?'

The *hwyl* was suddenly interrupted. At the entrance the much-anticipated group of Ukes had arrived. They were all white men. Well stacked. Scorpion was quick to get to the entrance to make sure his guests were welcomed in his smarmy fashion to show he was unconcerned by any threat to his position. There was a younger guy, looking a bit like he was embarrassed by his older companions, who were being loud and poking fun at the bouncers. The eldest man, who could have been the younger one's father, was built like a gorilla. He was twice the size of any of the doormen both in height and width. Scorpion tried hard not to look nervous, judging by the way he kept waving his hands around, calling his men to attention and to stand aside for the newly arrived guests. He called for Karina to come and meet them. These

71

important tourists needed to be handled carefully.

'You're welcome here, Mister, please have a great time. Lots of booze and girls for you,' he greeted them, forcing his best fake smile.

'We just want to party like these other nice people,' said the big guy in a voice that sounded scornful and superior. 'We heard you have hot girls here.'

I counted five of them as they moved past Scorpion brushing him aside. Karina spotted her fellow countrymen instantly, very much like we were able to pinpoint the Brits from a mile off on the beach. She put out her fag and moved in to greet the new guests.

'*Dobre*, welcome to the Sunset Lounge,' she said coolly, extending her hand in greeting.

None of them acknowledged her.

They walked past to the bar, where I was grooving with Melita. 'A bottle of vodka and five glasses,' barked the daddy of the bunch. Jaz almost clicked his heels to attention, as he reached for a bottle of Stoly and set it out on the bar with the five glasses. 'Ice?' he asked.

'Ha, ha, no you fuckin' idiot man, we don't have ice with our vodka. You need some education!' came the reply from one of the thuggish-looking guys.

'It's not a problem,' said the youngest one. I quite liked the look of him. He stood out from the others, with his Rasta hair. He came up to Melita and me. 'Hello, my name is Igor and I come from Kiev. Please excuse my friends. Their mood is a bit high since this afternoon. Too much vodka in the hotel bar. Your name is please?'

'I'm Ceri and this is Melita. I'm from Wales and she is from

England' I answered, trying to be heard above Dab Danny's music.

'I work for my father Vlad,' he said, pointing to the eldest of the group. 'We're all from Kiev, you know, in the Ukraine. Are you here on holiday?'

'Not quite, I'm here to find my family roots in India and we're working for a charity that supports *Banjara* homeless children,' Melita explained.

'Ah, *Banjara*, I love them. I've been studying their gypsy music for a few years.'

I was beginning to like this guy Igor.

'My father is gypsy,' I told him.

'So, this is very interesting then I must say. All of us having so much in common.'

For the next half hour we talked or shouted at each other over the music, until Igor suggested we dance. Scorpion's instructions were that we should stay together all evening, so it was a sort of threesome dance, with Melita leading the Bollywood moves, while Igor and I just followed.

The Kiev contingent was getting noisier and one of them made a grab for one of Karina's girls, as she happened to be passing. The girl yelled and kicked and pulled herself free. Jaz called Scorpion with the aim of restoring order.

A Beachboys scrum had by now formed a tight cordon to stop the men from breaking free. There were guests arriving all the time and Scorpion had to get rid of the problem quickly. I could see him talking to Igor's father and their bodies showed a less than friendly exchange. Scorpion's arms were flailing, whilst the Ukes were jeering at him.

'You'll be deported in a couple of days and your time in the sun will be over.'

'We can pay those guys too, you know. More money than you,' snarled Vlad the gorilla, spitting on the ground. One of the Beachboys tried to take a swing at the big guy. He was easily blocked and took a blow to his right eye.

It flattened him instantly.

This started a chain reaction of the scrum piling in to attack.

I heard the smashing of glass and saw the Ukes holding the stems of broken bottles, instantly converting innocent beer bottles into menacing lethal weapons. Jaz got slashed across the face and at least another of Scorpion's protectors had blood all over himself. Then bar stools, glasses, and bits of furniture started to fly through the air as the commotion spread.

Another Uke came through the entrance carrying a can of fluid, which he poured over the coir matting at the centre of what once was the dance floor.

The middle of the tent exploded into an orange hue.

I felt a heat bomb hitting me in the face from several feet away and a solid wall of fire shot up to the top of the tent. We saw two of the punters emerge from the fire, flames leaping off them. They headed for the exit, waving their hands wildly like demented men.

'Come on, you need to get out of here!' warned Igor, staying very close to us. Melita grabbed my hand and we ran outside through a gap in the tenting behind DJ Danny's music desk. He'd given up on his grooves, but his music kept blaring and the strobe lights flashing.

The men on fire were now rolling around on the sand

outside to put out the flames. They yelled for help. I'm not sure what happened next, but soon there were police sirens outside, and Danny's music finally stopped. The Ukes legged it out into the darkness and others followed. The men who had been on fire were howling in pain, as we watched the Sunset Lounge, engulfed in flames, crumble to the ground like a groaning monster slain to death. The incident had hit like an earthquake from nowhere.

The Ukes were going to pay for this. Scorpion's face glowed with anger in the light of the flames and I'm sure he wanted to rub the Ukes off the face of Anjuna while he began clearing up the debris.

'Took ten years to build up this business from nothing!' I heard Jaz moan. 'Just an hour ago this was a place of fun and pleasure. Now look, a wreck of broken glass and trashed furniture, with bloodied people lying around. Just hope nobody dies.'

Karina nodded 'It's crazy, just crazy. All the other surrounding Indian states are getting drier through their ban on alcohol. Goa is now even more popular, as it's one of the few places where drinking is still allowed. The Ukes and every other idiot want some of the action.'

'Of course, the Boss showed the way by throwing in sex and substances and they think they can do the same,' Jaz complained.

Karina went over to Scorpion, gave him a hug and kissed him on the cheek. Her bright red lipstick left its mark. 'Don't worry *darlingski*, those nasty men are worse than pigs. You can eliminate them, I'm sure.'

But Scorpion was not interested in Karina.

This incident was just a blip.

The Ukes had thrown down a challenge to his empire and he would not rest until they were neutralised, but for now he just sat waiting for the firemen to put out the flames.

The Beachboys had begun to disappear into the darkness. The blue strobe flash of the fire engine's lights punctuated our surroundings. We sat on the sand outside the wreckage, still dazed. I began to wonder if Scorpion was for the first time losing his grip on the gang. That's when I noticed this guy in a T-shirt that said, *I'll Love you when I'm older.* The blue light flashed on his white T-shirt. He waved one of those royal queenie waves, with a slight movement of the palm of his right hand. I smiled and he came over.

'Hi, can I get you girls a drink somewhere?' he drawled.

'Mmm, were you not here for the rumble? This isn't a great time,' I replied.

'Sure, I was here all along. Happens all the time out here. Place gets successful then someone wants to pull it down and take it over. That's competition, but you girls don't need to hang around here do you? What can you do now?'

The boy felt like he was settling in for the night. He had respectable stubble, shoulder-length black hair, a pair of denims, and some fancy looking pointed shoes. This dude was not short on the moolah and was definitely one of the well-heeled Bombay set.

'How long are you girls here on holiday for?' he asked. 'Oh just a few days.' I said, with boredom in my voice. It seemed a *tup* question. Dumb.'

'English?'

'No bloody way, man! Welsh.'

Do you know where that is?' piped in Melita.

'Sure! Tom Jones, Gareth Bale.'

'Go on, sit with us, here on the sand,' Melita invited, thinking the boy was cute, She patted the ground next to her. 'What's a boy like you doing in a place like this?'

'Coolest place on TripAdvisor!'

'What do they call you?' I asked.

'Roki.'

'I'm Ceri and that's Melita.'

'Great, where are you staying?' asked Roki.

'Oh, in town at a small place. You won't know it.'

Roki had been educated in St Xaviers in Bombay, where the rich sent their kids, and he'd dropped out at some stage or been expelled, probably for doing drugs. No surprise then that he had found this place.

'I love this beach, it's the best in India. I've been coming here since I was twelve.

Used to come with my parents to the hotel up there, The Taj,' Roki told us.

'You must know it very well,' Melita replied.

'Yes. I've seen it get busier and busier, year by year. Once only hippies and palm trees, now *chokras – low-lifes* - from all over the place, with their cheap cameras, pestering nice girls like you, and now this fire has destroyed one of the jewels on Anjuna.'

'And you, what do you do?' You don't seem like a *chokra*, not with those fancy shoes,' I asked.

'Oh, I'm a struggling journalist, trying to make my way from the very bottom rung.'

'Hanging out here for a big scoop?' suggested Melita.

'Yes, I'd heard there might be a bit of *garbar* here tonight. *Trouble.* Hey, tonight must've been hard for you. Can I get you a drink? Maybe somewhere more comfortable? The hotel down the beach has a nice bar, let's go there,' he suggested.

'If they let us *low-lifes* in?'

'You guys look cool. It won't be a problem.'

'Oh, thanks for asking, but we've had a hundred Pina Coladas already, and we don't have any scoops for you, other than the fact that these Ukes just wreaked havoc on a Goan business, in an attempt to take it over. How about that?'

I didn't think that Roki was really interested in a scoop at this stage, he just wanted to pull for the night. He was clearly loaded compared to us poor unfortunates. Daddy probably dropped him a few *lakhs* every year to keep his son in good shoes and fund his trips to the beach. I had no problem with that. I thought that if this was the beginning of a war for control with the Ukes, then Scorpion could do with some media support.

I seemed to have a weird sense of loyalty to Scorpion and Karina that night and hadn't felt like leaving them with the Lounge burned to the ground and Scorpion deep in the agony of his loss. But Melita was looking at me hard. I could tell she wanted to sample a posh bar and hang out more with Roki but didn't want to be with him on her own, so we said goodbye to Karina and Jaz.

'You watch, he'll be after a threesome in those huge hotel beds,' jeered Jaz. Roki pretended he didn't hear that remark.

The Taj Hotel was the sort of place where one night would have cost us the price of our flights here to Goa. I'd never been anywhere like it. Marbled floors, chandeliers, really tidy looking staff, who made the Beachboys look like dossers. Most of them seemed to know Roki, as he breezed in off the beach with us in tow.

'Let me get you a glass of champagne, we make it here in India. It's very good,' he offered, as we sank into a set of very comfy sofas. Three bubbling frosted glasses arrived. Roki raised a glass and the two of us girls took a long gulp at the bubbly. Oh, how I'd begun to love the stuff! I could drink it all day, if I'd been able to afford it. I sipped from the glass at first, but then the blood lust of bubbly got to me and I downed the whole lot in a few gulps.

'Hey, take it easy!' warned Melita. 'That's not lemonade.'

'Another one?' asked Roki. How could I turn down such an offer? Roki poured me another glass and it tasted better than the last. Total nectar.

Both Melita and I had stacked a few that night and we were getting cheekier with our boy Roki, who seemed quite chilled by the attention he was receiving. 'I know I said I didn't come here for any scoops, but it looks like I've got two beauties.' Roki said smiling all the time.

'Ah, and would you two scoops like to come back to my place for a bit of late night relaxation?' Roki suggested.

I was seriously pissed now, but Melita was more in control of the situation. 'We've got work in the morning, mate. Need a clear head.'

'You speaking for the two of you?'

'Yep, we're joined at the hip. Aren't we, Ceri?'

I nodded silently and Roki didn't pursue the invitation.

But tell you what, we'll see you again if you tell your readers what's happening with this Uke invasion trying to destroy a Goan business.'

'You really believe in this gang of bad boys?

'We're family now. They protect us from the police,' explained Melita, who I thought was doing a good job at promoting Scorpion's cause.

'Okay, I'll try and file a story tonight and see if my editor approves it. He just might.'

Part Two

Chapter 7

The kind rasta

R oki's champagne was wonderful, but my head was at bursting point the next morning. Melita looked like the inside of my aching head, so we decided that we'd only work for a few hours, as we had promised to manage a sports day with the orphans that afternoon. Scorpion's infrequent handouts of dosh was an unreliable source of income, so we had decided to continue with our jewellery business, especially given last night's attack on the Sunset Lounge. We set up in our usual spot by the Taj hotel at nine o'clock, but business was slow. There were the usual power walkers taking their morning exercises, some fishermen bringing in the last of the night's catch, and it reminded us that Saturday mornings at nine o'clock was a waste of time. Then Melita whispered to me excitedly 'It's those Uke dudes from last night, in the water.'

A couple of bleached white men walked out of the sea towards us. When they caught sight of us, I knew we were staring trouble right in the face.

'Hello, now what are we having here? It's the birds from the Sunset Lounge working for that brown monkey Scorpion,' one jeered.

The other came up right close to me rubbing his disgusting

wet body against my front and tried to pull my hair, so that my face was touching his. I tried to wriggle free, but he pulled harder. I was too close to him to give him my Alwyn Hughes special head-nutting move. No one seemed to be coming to our rescue. Then Melita screamed with a high pitch yell that could have broken glass and was probably heard all over Anjuna. The Yuke let go and said something that sounded like swearing, whilst his friend kicked our little jewellery stand, spreading all our trinkets over the sand, and they calmly walked off. 'That was just a taster of what is to come for you, bitches. Tell that to your boss, ya?'

We stood there in silence for at least a minute.

And then began to pick up the bits and pieces from the sand and place them back in their trays. It wasn't long before we had company. Igor had also been swimming. He had heard Melita's yells for help.

'Can I help you? I heard your screams. I will speak to my father and get you compensation.'

'We don't need your fuck'n compensation! Just get the hell out of our sight. You and your lot of shits!' I yelled.

'I am really sorry, please accept my apology for this and for last night too.'

'It's not just us that you're attacking, it's our friends the Beachboys. That's their living that you and your scumbags just took away,' Melita fumed.

'I'm truly ashamed of my father, his assistant Aleks, all of them. They are not very nice when drunk. Could we be friends? I enjoyed our meeting last night and I'm very interested in what you're doing for the *Banjara* children. Very nice jewellery. You made it?'

'Just fuck off, will you?' I shrieked and Igor slowly walked away with a slight limp to his left side. Whilst the Ukes seemed to all have a sort of swagger, with their bowed arms that didn't swing much in time with their steps, Igor walked differently. I noticed things like that. He didn't look the hard type with his dreads. He had an overall gentler quality. Was I feeling sorry for him after my outburst?

It took a good half hour to pick up all the bits of fakery strewn across a wide area of sand. We worked quietly, each of us thinking about the future of our enterprise, If the Ukes kept up their harassment, we couldn't pretend that Scorpion could protect us.

We'd just finished putting the last pair of earrings in the trays when Igor returned. This time fully clothed, sporting a baseball cap over his Rasta hair and a satchel. We ignored him. He held out his right hand clutching a roll of cash.

'Okay, I give you hundred dollars for your poor children as a donation and compensation for the problem caused by my father's men.' The children can eat cake this afternoon and maybe I can get on my knees to beg of your forgiveness? How do you say, cool?' He knelt on the sand with his palms together in a pleading gesture.

A hundred dollars! Frigging hell, I thought. That was more than we would expect to take in a whole month of walking up and down Anjuna. I was struck with a sudden bout of dumbness.

'Okay, that sounds like a deal!' agreed Melita, quickly. Now leave the money and just go. We don't want your guilt or anything. What happened earlier was just unforgiveable and anyway, she has a boyfriend and my husband expects me back to make his lunch.'

That was Melita at her best. Quick to strike a bargain and build in all sorts of get-out clauses in case the deal went sour. I'd learned so much from her. Here in Anjuna money converts any sceptic into becoming a believer. It draws smiles and insincere greetings and we were falling right into local customs.

'This is warfare, Ceri,' Melita reflected, tuning her back on Igor. 'We're on the home side and these Ukes are the foreign invaders. We're still under the protection of the Beachboys if we ever get hassled. In India it's very black and white, you have to take sides.'

Igor pulled a strange bulbous instrument out of his satchel and began to play. I'd seen Harpo play one like it before. The reedy, nasal sound at first stuttered and then began to flow smoothly. A minute later he stopped 'See, the *poongi,* it's the instrument of the gypsies. I can come and play it to your children, and they will be entertained.'

I wasn't sure if it was the hundred dollars or that he reminded me of Harpo, but I couldn't help liking this guy. Was he real? Why were his fellow Ukes the complete opposite? Roughnecks, bullies, probably rapists and murderers, too?

'Ha ha, are all the girls in Wales looking good and as clever as you?'

I laughed nervously. I don't know why, as I'd heard nearly every bloody chat-up line ever invented, but never in a heavy foreign Uke accent. It sounded very sexy and almost genuine. I must have blushed deep red and he knew he'd scored a direct hit.

'Hey, maybe we can meet later, ha?

'Look we're busy today. Business has been slow,' Melita refused, 'and we have to be somewhere else this afternoon.'

'Please let this donation be my private gift, yes? No one to know. Can I come to your orphan party this afternoon? I can teach them to play football, too. In Ukraine I was playing for the special hospital team in Kiev.'

'The children would love a bit of footie, wouldn't they Melita?' I begged.

'Scorpion is going to go apeshit if he finds out we're chilling with the opposition,' warned Melita. But Igor continued with his pleading and another tune on the *poongi*. It eventually won Melita around, 'Okay come to the west side of the beach at four o'clock and they will be there. Bring a ball, too.'

'How come you were playing for the Kiev hospital?' I asked.

'Oh, that's a very long story. I can tell you about it someday,' Igor hedged, smiling faintly.

We talked about nothing much that I can remember from there on. He said he was helping his father with his business, I'm not sure exactly how. He'd travelled from Kiev only a few weeks earlier to join his father, Vlad, who had been here for a few months.

Then there was an angry shout, which sounded like someone calling his name, and Igor swung around, his eyes widened, and he stiffened. 'It's my father, I must go. See you later,' and he slipped away in that limping walk.

Chapter 8

Charitable acts

We were big fans of Father Michael, the priest at St Anthony's. Melita kept banging on about how cool and liberated he was and how amazing that he'd started this charity for *Banjara* orphans. In reality, it was more than just orphans he catered for, homeless and some disabled kids also got enrolled.

You didn't have to be Catholic or even a Christian to get a place in the St Anthony's School for Disadvantaged Children. The only unfortunate thing was the abbreviation, which was SADS, but it did attract attention and people made generous donations from all over. Every month collections would be made throughout the parishes of Goa to support his cause. Our efforts at selling jewellery were one of those small fundraising steps that helped feed those kids.

Back in Wales I would have thought this priest was secretly fingering up children and the charity was just a front to satisfy his evil urges, but here not so. This guy was the genuine article do-gooder, with a mission to put his parish on the map for helping the poor. Amidst the gang culture and massive police corruption, he was one of the few lone voices standing out against it. As a result, he had a long line of admiring middle-aged female parishioners who adored him.

Melita had taken on the task of organising a sports event for around twenty kids of varying ages, from eight to fifteen. We had to get them from St Anthony's to the beach at Anjuna, where there was plenty of open space for them to run around. We marched them in single file, with Michael at the front, Melita in the middle, and me at the rear.

When we arrived at the beach, true to his word, I saw Igor kicking a ball around doing those kick-ups that the professionals do before a match to warm up. He was good. The kids all ran up to him and we had suddenly lost control to this barefooted Uke, draped in dreadlocks, who tottered around with an odd shuffle in his step.

'Hey, let's play a game of football, ya?' he shouted out. There were yells of approval. 'Okay, we have two teams, girls versus boys, ya?' There were more screams of delight. 'I play for the girls?' he asked, and the girls all shouted, as did Melita and I. 'You, Mister,' he said pointing at Michael, 'you play for the boys, ya? In goal.'

Michael and Igor drew out a pitch and there were roughly ten a side. I stood in goal, something I'd never done in my life and the game started, with everybody trying to catch up with Igor's ball, which he seemed to have in possession for as long as he wanted. Every now and then, he'd let one of the boys get the ball away and they'd kick it past me, into our goal. I was useless. And then Igor would get the ball and equalise. Michael was worse than me at being a goalie.

The kids were having a great time and when we called a halt to the game twenty minutes later, the girls had won by ten goals to nine. Melita nudged me. 'This guy is a natural, Ceri, they're loving it.'

We fed and watered the kids with meat patties and water from plastic glasses filled from a bowser, which I carried on my back. Igor dominated the excited chatter of the little ones. Unlike other adults that talk down to kids, Igor was on their level and they loved him for it. When he said he had to go and work, they pulled him back and refused to let him go. He signalled to me to come and rescue him.

'Could we meet tonight?' he asked.

'I've promised to go out with Melita.'

'She can come, too.'

'I'll call you.'

Then he was gone, without my number, but I knew that wouldn't be the last we'd hear of him. He'd be back, sniffing around us, either trying to wangle his way in or stopping off on the beach to bribe us to have a drink with him. But Scorpion finding out about our friendship would be risking Igor's life and ours. There was a lot about him that reminded me of Harpo. Wasn't it strange how attractive forbidden things were? The more that I was told about how dangerous it was for me to be with Igor, the more I wanted him. The more my mam had told me how bad Harpo was, the more I had longed to be with him.

Everything was negotiable here in Goa, you just had to have your price and stick to your guns, but the most difficult dealings were with the police, who were probably the most corrupt in the world. Inspector Braganza, the head honcho, demanded bribes that were way above what we could afford. Scorpion, with Karina's help, took very good care of him. After the Sunset burned down, Scorpion and Karina set up temporarily at the Palms Guest House, hidden away in the back streets that ran parallel to Anjuna.

Scorpion hated the idea of being in exile at the Palms, but kept telling everyone that this was just a temporary arrangement, until the Sunset could be restored to its former glory.

Like clockwork, on Friday evenings, Braganza would come knocking for his dues. That's when Karina would always appear at the bar, dressed to kill in her Grecian dress. 'Hello, boys,' she'd say, 'Oh, and girls,' looking at us. 'I see I'm having some competition, hah?'

And Braganza would add, 'No, you're the best girl in the world for me, you know that. Now I need to see you about something before that bloke of yours, Scorpion, gets here,' he would pretend to whisper and she would giggle like one of us girls, despite being twice our age.

So, the inspector was getting his cut to keep Karina and her other Uke girls in Business, proving that everything was possible if you paid your dues to the right people. And the half dozen or more Uke women, who plied their trade under the protection of the Beachboys, ensured that Inspector Denzil got his cut as frequently as he wished.

Whenever I saw the inspector, he'd catch my eye and call out to us mockingly, 'Hello little virgins, hah, hah, hah.' There'd be fake laughter from Jaz and Melita and I went along with it.

He was a thick-set, tall, pork-eating Goan Catholic, who looked intimidating to most locals when he stood up to his full height. 'My job is to make people scared when they see me. I'm not a nice guy. Nice guys finish last in my world,' he would bray, like a neutered mule.

There was always a tumbler of rum and coke for him on the bar from Jaz, with an envelope passed discreetly underneath it, unless of course he got his end away with Karina, I guess. His hallmark *dunda,* his ever-present police truncheon, was always tucked under his arm, ready to dole out instant punishment to those that he felt needed it.

Jaz told us that Denzil ran The Foreigners' CID, which was specifically there to ensure that tourists from abroad were protected from the criminals that had begun to prey on visitors. Isn't that ridiculous? Every year, nearly a million visitors came to Goa and they brought money with them in search of pleasure, which provided the opportunity for both legal and illegal trade. 'Where there's money, there's nasty *gundas,*' was Inspector Denzil's motto.

The police gave Denzil the legal permission to mete out violence and he had established a formidable reputation for extracting confessions and intelligence from suspects. No one wanted to be hauled off to the *Thana,* the jail, to be interrogated by Denzil.

'That's the way it works here in Goa.' explained Jaz. 'You have to be frightened of the police or else they're no fuckin' use.'

I remember one evening before the fire at the Lounge, the curtains to Karina's head office parted. The Inspector emerged without looking at us and departed without saying anything, just like a naughty boy walking away from the scene of his dodgy antics, hoping not to be seen. What a farce!

Then Karina emerged, looking as sexy as ever, in her war paint and that white Grecian dress and shook her head to remove a curl from the front of her forehead. She came to join us and pulled up a bar stool.

'One happy policeman,' she congratulated herself, pleased that she'd done a good job for the firm like the professional she probably was. 'What you girls think of me, tell me, really?'

I wasn't used to such direct questions. Maybe it was her Slavic way, open, honest about what she did, no holds barred. I looked at Melita to help me out, but she was equally schtum.

'It's a job, you see,' she reflected. 'Do it good, be proud that you do it good. If you're a rubbish collector, doctor, or even sex worker like me, be proud of what you do, and carry your head up high as the mountain. Through good times and bad.'

'But Karina, aren't our bodies for giving pleasure to ourselves and people we love?' asked Melita, showing her Goan Catholic upbringing.

'That's what they teach you, sure, but how many women are really doing that, tell me? Not many I tell you. Always about pleasing men, so why not make money at it?'

She began to tell us her story and over the next few evenings I began to really like this woman and sympathise with her. She was born in Kiev and I guessed she was in her mid-forties.

She had started her working career in a Kiev clothing factory, until someone offered her an evening job as a pole dancer to make a bit of money on the side. After a couple of years, she dropped the factory job and took up erotic dancing as a full-time occupation. But when one of her friends was strangled by the bouncer of the club, she decided it was time to leave town for a safer working environment.

She'd come to Goa three years earlier, having first arrived in Bombay to try her luck in films. With most of Europe having difficult immigration laws, she was told by a male friend that a white face in Bombay's Bollywood would be highly valued. English

Page Three models had found their way on to the Bollywood screen and there was no reason why Karina shouldn't have a go.

Life in Kiev was hard, with little opportunity for work and six months of some of the coldest weather in Central Europe. Bombay was a very different story. Her first success as an extra came early in a minor movie, but she had to sleep with the producer to get the part, which paid just enough to clear her expenses for one night's accommodation in a cheap hotel.

There followed a few other parts in minor roles, but they all came at a cost and she found she was accidently becoming a sex worker. One of the film crew was off to Goa for a week's holiday and invited her to come with him, as he needed female company, and that was her first introduction to Anjuna.

Whilst Bombay had been a culture shock compared to Kiev, Goa was like paradise. There was room to breathe, each rupee went three times as far, and the people were far more friendly, but the bloke she came with made too many demands on Karina. 'He was a dirty one, I tell you. Wanting me to suck his cock many times a day.

After two days I dumped him. Then I found myself at the Sunset Lounge, wearing the one dress I had acquired whilst on set in Bombay, playing a Greek siren, and the rest was good for me.'

Scorpion found her a beachfront apartment, paid the rent for three months, and offered her free accommodation, in exchange for being his head of hospitality. In just a couple of weeks, Karina had begun to look after Scorpion and his clients and had reached out to Kiev to recruit half a dozen other women to join her in Goa.

When the Ukes arrived in Goa, they told her guy, but Karina had left Kiev to avoid people like them and was changing her loyalties. Gradually, she became aware that beneath the tranquility of the sandy beaches and coconut trees, lay an ugly underworld that was just about as seedy and dangerous as the life she had left behind in Kiev. The only difference was the thirty degrees of regular daytime temperatures, which she found much more acceptable than the minus twenty back home.

Chapter 9

Hari and me

A njuna was a surprisingly clean beach, considering the rubbish that got dumped on it during the day by visiting youths, who didn't seem to mind leaving their junk lying around. Or picnickers who might descend in a large family party and leave an unpleasant pile of plastic and leftovers. Magically, all this crap got cleared up every evening, not by the government or by some green do-gooders, but by the *Banjara* gypsies, who were probably the brothers and sisters of the children at the orphanage.

I only slowly began to notice these invisible people. They would be singing softly to themselves, whilst Melita and I were busy packing up our little stall under one of the few surviving coconut trees on Anjuna. The Banjara were picking up plastic bottles and other litter from the beach and putting them into large gunny sacks.

This was the odd thing about Goa and probably the whole of India.

Everybody had their place in the system, as if someone had carefully planned the whole thing over many centuries. The *ferenghis* coming from abroad and leaving their crap for gypsies and the gypsies selling it on for a few *paisa*, was part of the whole elaborate game of keeping everyone in their place. I'm sure people like Igor and me, coming from elsewhere and selling tat jewellery, drinking their rubbish beer, doing drugs and selling sex, kept other industries alive, with everyone picking up their share of the booty.

These *Banjara* had probably been bottom of the pile for centuries past. They were relied upon to clear up all the mess that everybody left behind. So lowly was their position, that they weren't allowed to go anywhere near any of the other higher caste people.

Amongst the beach cleaning party there was this guy, a little older than us, sporting torn jeans and a spotless T-shirt, which said, '*I'm too sexy for myself*'.

'Unbelievable really,' Melita remarked. 'A fit bloke like him, stuck with picking up litter or dead dogs from the beach for the rest of his short miserable life. It stinks, doesn't it?'

The guy looked at us, paused, the young women with him giggled, and they moved on, continuing their litter-picking and leaving a spotless beach behind them. The next day at the same time they had returned and Fitboy was there again. I couldn't resist the urge to wave. He waved back and began to walk over to us. The women with him continued on their way, yelling at him to get back and continue his work.

I managed a '*Namasté.*'

'Good night,' was his reply.

'Hi,' said Melita, 'you like our jewellery?' pointing at the trays we were just about to put away.

'Ha, ha, I *Banjara* family. We make this. You want to buy? Very cheap!' He spoke confidently.

'We have a lot of these already. We need to sell to tourists,' I said.

97

'How much you sell for?' he asked

When I told him, he burst out laughing. 'Very funny, very funny. You very rich?'

'No, no, we give the money to help the school for the children at St Anthony,' Melita explained patiently.

He nodded without smiling, as if only half believing us, then he turned to walk back to his group of women. I couldn't help staring at the slogan on his T-shirt, which was a little dirtier today. Did he know what it meant? Then Melita did something we hadn't planned.

'Come and help us sell this stuff tomorrow. It's mostly for your people,' she offered.

What she said stopped him in his tracks. He looked back. 'I speaking no English. It is not possible.'

'We can fix that,' shot back Melita.

She held out her hand very professionally and shook his. I don't think he'd ever shaken anyone's hand before, let alone a woman's. He wiped his hands on his white T-shirt. Then I did the same and I felt the callouses on his palm. He wasn't sure if he should let go, so I pulled my hand away and smiled, so as not to offend him.

'Tomorrow come back here at ten o'clock,' said Melita, holding up her fingers on both hands. He nodded and left.

'Hope you know what you're doing,' I objected. 'He is an unknown quantity.'

'He has such a nice smile,' Melita responded. 'Trust me a little.'

'I think you just fancy a bit of rough now, don't you?'

'Look it's you that came to find your gypsy roots. Now here they are, all nine yards of them, completely untouched by the West.'

'Don't worry, Mel. I'm really quite excited,' I assured her. 'It's him I'm thinking of. What if he thinks we really want him to bang us? That sort of stuff is happening all around us.'

'You're getting a bit ahead of yourself, Ceri. He brought up the bit about the jewellery. I think he'd like to share in some of our loot. Look, the *ferenghis* who buy our stuff don't care, in fact they'll feel sorry for the chap and think they're helping him out.'

'Tidy, we could even write a handout in English that says *All sales to the rehabilitation charity for disabled gypsy children.* That will give their sentimental, liberal souls such pleasure.'

With that brilliant idea, we enlisted Hari to sell our bits and pieces at twenty percent less than our prices, so that the punters would genuinely believe they were getting a good deal, by buying from a local down-and-out gypsy. How good was that?

The next morning Hari arrived with a clean T-shirt which said, *'Buy me and stop one.'* We both laughed and he smiled too, completely unaware of its meaning.

'Hari, you're going to be a hit.' I held up my right hand for a high five and he seemed to know what to do. Now he needed a bit of sales training from us the experts, who had honed the art of the quick easy sale. The secret, we found, was to identify the nationality of the punters. We had pictures of them on our mobile phones, as we'd taken their photograph after every sale to make them feel special. The sweetest sound anyone can hear in a foreign land is their own language and we found it always got us off to a great start.

'Now Hari, see this picture, this is a French woman,' I said, pointing at a photo. 'See hair, nice hair, and slim. When you see someone like this, you say "Bonjour". It means good morning.'

Hari repeated the word in perfect French, 'Bonjour!' This boy was going to be big. 'If you see one of these,' continued Melita, pointing out a photo of an English woman, 'you say, "Hullo, good morning."'

'Hah, I see, hair like *Fakir*, bit fat, hah?' Hari was catching on fast. 'Ruskie, this is Ruskie, fat face, not like us,' he reacted to another of our photos, getting ten out of ten for accuracy.

Gradually we tested out half a dozen races for Hari to practice his opening lines on and soon he had them licked.

Hari was now a member of our mobile sales force. He plied the beach away from the Taj Hotel, whilst we concentrated on the southern end around the Taj. In a matter of days, we had doubled our sales! Hari looked so amazingly sorry for himself, with his hilarious vest and filthy shorts that he kept pulling in the sympathy of the mainly European visitors. He'd even mastered a few more sentences in English and Spanish with help from Melita, to impress them.

'Hello, Madam', '*Buenas*', 'Thanks' and '*Gracias*' were his stock phrases. The rest was conveyed with lots of smiling, nodding and laughing as though he was slightly off his rocker.

At sunset he would disappear, handing back our stuff and the proceeds of a day's work and we'd give him fifteen percent of the proceeds. I suppose we should have given him more but then I was a businesswoman and not a charity worker.

Hari felt he was doing well at his new job, so he changed his litter-picking shift to nights when he would pick up rubbish by the light of the moon. God knows when he slept.

What a boy was our Hari!

Of course, our brilliant plan couldn't work forever without a hitch. Not here in Anjuna. Into his second week, we saw Hari running towards us being pursued by two policemen and one of them was lunging out at his head and body with a *lathi*. It was a good thing that Hari was fast, or else he would have been floored. Despite having to carry a satchel of our booty he managed to outrun the men in khaki, dodging here and there on the soft sand, which is harder to run on. One of them, the plumper man with a pot belly was lagging behind, waving his arms and by the time Hari got to us, he had created quite a distance between himself and his pursuers.

He hid behind us two *ferenghi* girls for protection. Pathetic really that it worked, and the policemen stopped short when they came to us waifs.

'This man is working for us,' I stated, standing defiantly between Hari and the policemen. Me, a fifteen-year-old reject, excluded from a crappy school in Wales.

No, it is not allowed,' said the paunchy one. 'No license.'

'I have the permission of Inspector Denzil Braganza.' They looked at each other.

'You can call him now, from my phone over here. I have his number.'

This was pushing my luck, but I knew that public servants here in India are frightened of higher ups, especially when the boss is likely to be on some sort of backhand deal. They'd be given a kicking for displeasing the head of the underlings.

It's highly illegal in Goa to have a business as a foreigner without a license, but nobody I knew had one.

The policemen shouted something to Hari in Konkani that

didn't sound friendly, and then walked away. Hari had blood on his face now. We discovered that he'd suffered a blow to the head, which had burst a vein somewhere and it had begun to bleed slowly. I took one of the cotton scarves from Hari's bag and began to wipe his face, then got him to hold the cloth on the wound to stop the bleeding.

He just smiled through all of this, as if it was all in a day's work. I was beginning to like this boy even more.

'Look at my finger,' Melita told Hari, as she moved it right and left in front of his eyes, watching his pupils follow the movement.

'No concussion then,' she said confidently.

'Where did you get that trick, Mel? Good knowledge from my business partner.'

'Just something they did when my brother fell off a horse.'

'Okay, Hari, you're good to go then,' I said, pulling out a hundred rupees note and giving it to him, with a comforting stroke to his face. 'Just take the rest of the day off and get some sleep.'

His eyes lit up like neons.

The next day Hari was back on the job. The wound had healed, he'd shaved and put on a clean T-shirt which said simply, *Have a Nice Day*. Really tidy. Hari looked puffed up, confident now that he not only had a job, but also our protection. Sort of.

Days passed and Hari began to score big time. I'm not sure if it was his T-shirt collection or the way he put himself out there.

'Hari,' said Melita one Friday after sunset, 'come and have a drink with us, Hari *bhai*. Bit of fun, ha?'

'Not possible.' He shook his head in a way that suggested he really wanted to but felt he mustn't. 'Much rubbish to pick up tonight.'

Hari never took up the offer to get closer to us. Despite me giving him a hug every now and then, he'd stiffen up when I did so. We both kinda grew closer to him. This very low, rubbish-collecting gypsy guy, who was smart as hell, fascinated us. Were we feeling sorry for him and wanting to look after him, or was it that we always want what we can't have?

'I think he might be scared of being seen with foreigners,' thought Melita.

'No, I think his caste has had too many centuries of being told they are dirty, inferior people, and that's the way he's made. Like our Welsh Collies have had rounding up sheep bred into them for yonks and now they just do it without thinking.'

Hari had stirred quite a lot in both of us, so that evening I felt I wanted to tell Harpo all about it.

Shwti babe, something quite special has happened out here on the beach. You won't believe it, but I've met a real original gypsy who is a proper boy I can tell you. Just think babe, we both share in his genes going back centuries and I can tell there is a special bond between us. Nothing sexual or anything, so don't be jealous. He's just a special guy. Just like us back home, his tribe are a downtrodden lot and have to put up with a lot of jip, but they're always happy and play amazing music. It's okay babe, I'm not falling in love with Hari or anything. We're like brother and sister…

It's all very exciting back here, with my business blooming with my friend Melita. You'd love it here babe. Take lots of care of yourself. I dream of you most nights. XXX.

Chapter 10

Ingos market

With the Sunset Lounge no longer in operation, Melita and I no longer had to go there every night. It was Karina's idea for us to go to Ingos. The night market was such a good chance to escape from Dab Danny's grooves, Scorpion, the Beachboys, and Jaz. You could suffocate sometimes in the unrelenting atmosphere of the Lounge and the smell of sleaze, especially when you knew what went on behind the scenes.

Ingos announced itself long before it came into view. Firstly the music from a live band playing sixties sounds, then the throb of motorbikes in convoy, and lastly you're hit by a wall of strong aromas of sandalwood incense, spices, freshly-cut leather, and roasting chickens, all mixed in. And then you see it - men with beards, women in paisley pyjamas, and brightly lit stalls selling stuff that would be a third of the price at charity shops back home.

Ingos was set up by a German guy of the same name and became an overnight success with its mixture of live music, bars, and all types of retail. But when he went back to Germany, his permission to re-enter India was refused and local Goans took on the business. It continued to be unstoppable in its success. Melita had tried to get a stall there, but was told there was a three-year waiting list. Without the ready dosh to bribe our way up, we decided to stick to Anjuna.

Melita's eyes lit up when she saw Roki the journo, sporting the same T-shirt from the night of the fire and presumably still looking for scoops. 'Hey, girls, new territory for you?' he smiled.

'Yes, we're exploring,' I said. 'Still looking for the big story? Did your boss like your exclusive from the bust-up the other night?'

'Ah, he wasn't convinced that another scare story about foreigners would be good for the paper. But I still am interested in something, like an arrest, or a mysterious murder perhaps? I hear they're trying to take over Ingos night market and make everyone pay a cut. Any more goss for me to rake up here, any scandalous story, let me know.'

'Well,' Melita joked, 'buy us one of those really expensive glasses of bubbly and we may have one.' Roki and Melita were getting on brilliantly, so I decided to slope off and leave them alone.

The area around the bar was quite crowded now and I was lost in the mass of swaying bodies caught up in 70s rock hits, that I'd heard my mam play on her CD collection. Then someone tapped me on the shoulder, and I turned around to see Igor's dreads swinging in time with the music. My heart beat faster. I waved and he took my hand and swirled me around. We continued until the song was over.

'Fancy meeting you here,' I said.

'I'm coming here all the time. I love this place.'

'Isn't it good?'

'Let's get a drink.'

He got me another one of those blue drinks that I'd quite taken a liking to.

'Hey, you were a hit with the kids last week. All they have been talking about is Igor and footie.'

'I enjoyed it. They were so happy. I've been happy too, you know, about meeting you. You're... how do they say? What you see is what you get, spells WYSIWYG. It's computer jargon. In Kiev we are using the term all time for someone who is natural.'

'Well, as long as it's nice.'

We seemed to go on talking forever. I told him all about living in Wales, and he told me about his life in Kiev, how he'd become a computer game developer at the age of fifteen and wanted to come to London to work for a company there. How his father had sucked him into his business dealings by getting him to build a website, which ran on some secret web network that the government couldn't tap into.

'So, you're helping your father trade innocent girls like sex slaves,' I objected.

'It's not like that.'

'It definitely is. Karina told me. She's from your country.'

'But she is a whore. She is exploiting women from my country, too.'

'They're free to go if they want.'

Just then I saw Melita and Karina milling through the crowd, probably looking for me. I waved to them to attract their attention. Their expressions changed when they saw Igor. Karina said something angrily in Russian, to which Igor didn't respond.

'Ceri, we are going now. You must come with us. The company here is polluting.'

'I'm staying, you guys go without me,' I refused. You should have seen Karina's face. If looks could kill, I'd be dead long before I actually died and my frozen body would be left in a mortuary and fiddled abut, for someone to work out the cause of my death.

'What did she say to you?' I asked Igor.

'Oh, it wasn't very nice. Now let's talk about you and me.'

'How did you know I was here?'

'It's my job to know. I'm a digital geek. I can find out most things. Your phone was on and I knew exactly where you were. I spend most of my days on the dark web tracking movements and finding out what people want.'

'You're breaking the law?'

'There's a whole different world going on down there. It's like the ocean deep below. Just because you can't see what's below the surface, doesn't mean it's not interesting and full of action and life.'

'But it's people engaged in illegal stuff like drugs, terrorism and human trafficking.'

'That's what the politicians tell you, but they're trying to control us all. In my country, where there are few freedoms, we use it to talk and share the truth with each other.'

'Sounds a bit geeky and scary. I'm not sure.' I wasn't convinced by Igor's interpretation of the dark web.

'Anyway, tell me more about your country, this place Waal-ess.'

'It's pronounced WAYELS.'

'Ah, like the big sea animal?'

'Correct. It's a very beautiful country with lots of hills and sheep and farms.'

'Ah, so why do you come here?'

'To get a break from some people. My mam loves it here, so I came with her.'

'And do you like it here?'

'I'm learning a lot, about survival mainly. I think everyone from my town should come here, to see how hard it is to live and survive. And you?'

'People think I'm... how do you say, weird, in Kiev. Here I feel more normal, even if I'm white and people are brown.'

I smiled at him. 'Are we going to keep seeing each other?' I asked.

'What is this seeing each other mean? Yes, of course, I keep seeing you, I have eyes.'

I laughed. It was funny trying to explain simple expressions that I just took for granted. 'You know, keep meeting like two people of the opposite sex.'

'Of course, of course. I'm very attracted to you, even maybe for sex if you would agree.'

'Your father would go apeshit. I mean like crazy. Scorpion would, too. I owe him and Melita my friend. I couldn't let her down.'

'But Scorpion is a bad man. He will eventually try to sell you like a white slave. He is only being nice to you at the moment. Later he will get you hooked on free drugs, then drag you into his control. Grooming they are calling it.'

'I'm not stupid, I can control my space.'

We talked for what seemed like hours and found we shared the same ideas. In a way, we had both been excluded from the

109

places we came from. We walked around the market many times lost in our conversation, and the people around us were all a blur, like a merry-go-round that spins, making you want to hang on tight. Then we heard the haunting sound of women singing in unison and clapping a steady rhythm.

'Ah my friends, the *Banjara*,' said Igor, 'You must listen to them, they're singing about the goddess *Kali*.'

We'd stopped by a stall selling weird blouses with mirrors stitched into them and long red and black skirts with gold braids. The women's faces looked really craggy, with tattoos and ear lobes that had been disfigured. Their singing was loud and shrill, and it pierced through my rib cage to somewhere deep inside me.

'The who?' I said.

'*Banjara*, gypsies from across the border in Karnataka. This is something else really, isn't it?'

'I'm half gypsy, they could be my people,' I exclaimed, and Igor looked like I was pulling his leg. 'Yes, the blonde hair doesn't look like I'm a gypo, I know.'

'But that is crazy, I'm in total love with the whole gypsy thing,' he stated.

'You?'

'Yes, we have many thousand Roma in my country and they make the best music known to this earth. They're singing the same type of songs I have heard back in Odessa.'

'Unbelievable. How did you get to know so much about gypsy music?'

'I had a terrible experience when I was ten. I saw some Roma gypsies being beaten by policemen, for making their music in a square in Kiev. It hurt me, really it did, and I just wanted to hear more of the music. I went back to the same square every week to hear more. When I was fourteen, I got an old fiddle from a used furniture shop and went back to the square to get them to show me how to play.'

'They taught you to play the fiddle?'

'Yes, basically yes. I practiced for many hours every day. In a year, I was playing their mazurkas and polkas. They said I was good.'

One of the women without any teeth and a cluster of bright yellow-gold jewellery around her neck, smiled at us, clapping and singing all the time. Gradually, I could feel myself being pulled towards Igor like a falling tide that drags you towards a distant island. I liked this man more and more as I got to hear his stories. The market was beginning to get quieter around three in the morning, when two of Scorpion's Beachboys came up to us.

'Okay, you come with us. The Boss wants you,' growled the thickset one of them.

'She's with me, please leave us alone,' said Igor politely.

'Shut the fuck up, you Kiev Cunt.'

Igor was pushed in the chest. He staggered to regain control. Then the other leaner one pushed him from the back, as if to drop him to the ground. Igor stumbled again and I knew that if he fell, he'd be kicked black and blue by Scorpion's two thugs. Igor was not a street fighter, but I knew he wouldn't run and leave me. To the people around, this seemed just like another late-night brawl, brought about by excess drinking. So I yelled at the two Beachboys at the top of my voice to stop. In seconds another Uke was on the scene to defend Igor and he was able to stand up straighter.

'Leave, come on, let me go!' I said to the Beachboys. They made sure they held both my hands. No one bothered to help stop me from being carted away and bundled into a Maruti van.

They took me to what looked like Scorpion's temporary 'office' at the Diva Centre and told me to wait there on a smelly sofa which reeked of stale tobacco and strong perfume. Scorpion entered soon after, looking flustered. 'I'm not sure if you're mega stupid or just wanting to die young. Do you know what it means, prick teasing that Uke Rasta fellow Igor?'

'I was just having a drink with him. He's not like the rest of them, really.' I tried to make my case.

'You really are stupid then. Do you know what will happen, if that shithead's father finds out that you're shagging his own sweet son?'

'I'm shagging no one.'

'Look, you're one of us now. You work for me, remember. He's gonna come and get his guys to gang bang you, to teach his boy a lesson.'

'You're making a mountain out of nothing.'

'Just leave that hairy-headed dope head alone. I'm warning you. Think of who is making a nice life for you here on Anjuna.' He came right up to my face with a demonic expression. All I could see was his bloodshot eyes. 'Make this the last warning. You don't wanna be upsetting me again, I'm telling you.'

And that was Scorpion's parting shot as he left his office.

I went back to my shack to find Melita had already fallen asleep. It was four o'clock in the morning and I was still wide awake, partly still thinking of Igor and strangely quite excited at the chance of meeting him again. So, to try and get to sleep, I wrote in my little black notebook as the glimmer of dawn lit up the Arabian Sea.

If I were queen of Wales and were going to design a school for teenagers like me to really learn something about life, I'd make sure they came to Goa for their last year, to see how people learn to survive in Anjuna. If you can manage it here, anywhere else in Wales is going to be a doddle. People like me and my mates would never be bored. No way.

I know I made a few mistakes and might just run out of luck by taking a few too many chances. They say a cat has nine lives, I must have used a few by now. You take a wrong turn here or there and get back to recover yourself to safety, but after a while you start thinking you're invincible and then, bang! You end up in the gutter.

I guess I was quite fearless after my time with Harpo, my slightly nutty fiancée, who I still love and some of the other crazies at Fishguard Secondary. And now in Anjuna, I may not see all the dangers that are hanging around staring me in the face, because I'm blinded by people smiling at me, wanting to know where I came from, asking my name and wanting to take a selfie with me in it. Melita, my Brummie friend, doesn't get asked so much, because she's not white, probably like their sister.

Am I just ploughing right through thinking I am special and invincible? I actually feel I could stand up to Scorpion and tell him to go fuck himself. I feel like I can handle these Goans, because they're like the boys back home, only brown. They like the same music, like getting hammered and letching after girls. But, I haven't really got a hold on the Ukes. Apart from Igor, they are different. Really hard, can't smile and don't respond to our usual charms. It's as if they are on autopilot to achieve a mission and we are just pawns, to help them get to wherever they are going. I wish I knew.

Chapter 11

Cemetery deal

The Catholic cemetery at Bencula was a memorial to Goa's colonial past. Ornate graves, with elaborate marble carvings, dated back centuries to a time when rich Portuguese traders had made Goa their home. There were family graves, which had held the bones of family members for at least three centuries.

Some were simple affairs with wooden crosses and a concrete slab, whilst others were mausoleums that contained multiple chambers, a resting place for limitless deceased relatives. Once, these were immaculately tended monuments, but in recent times they had fallen into disrepair, the result of vandalism and neglect.

But it was a peaceful place today, a sanctuary for wildlife and for people who needed somewhere to get away from the scramble of cars, incessant beeping of horns, and the noise of the surrounding neighbourhood. The silence was only periodically broken by parakeets arguing over something or other in the thick, ancient banyan trees which surrounded the site.

Under one of those trees sat Denzil Braganza, leaning against its gnarled trunk, the remnants of a Corona smouldering between the fingers of his left hand. His aviator shades, T-shirt, and jeans would have anyone convinced that he was a rich tourist resting in this graveyard of his ancestors. Denzil was soon joined by Scorpion, rather more decorated in tattoos with a large golden cross dangling from his neck.

They acknowledged each other with a greeting that was part way to a handshake and high five. Scorpion took a seat next to the policeman, who offered him a cigar. He declined.

'They kill you,' Scorpion objected.

'You have to die eventually, if the cigar doesn't, then those Ukes will. Ha ha!' laughed Denzil in a wheezing sound, that seemed to indicate that his lungs were full of fluid from years of smoking strong, Indian tobacco.

'Yes, *bhai*, but I have my boys to look after and right now they're not feeling too good with these bloody Ukes.'

'Yes, they're getting everywhere.'

'First the women, who I personally welcomed of course. Good for business.

Really good! But now these guys who come here and want to take us out, hah?'

'Hah, hah,' nodded Denzil.

'But we gotta stop the fuckers, Denzil, now! Right now! They've already destroyed my pride and joy, the Sunset Lounge and set off a war with my boys. Come on now, we go to the same church, we're fellow Goans, we're proud of our heritage and our land. I need your help.'

'Hold on, hold on. I can pick up the odd ones and harass them. Or take them to the Thana for a night, but some big move on these guys is outside my power.'

'Denzil, I'm paying you a good ten per cent of my take, man. That was wiped out last Friday, when the sister fuckers came and broke up the party. That ten per cent, is looking like zero right now.'

'Something you gotta know, *bhai*, they've been dropping a few ten per cents in the pockets of the chief, my boss.'

'Oh fuckin' 'ell. This country is so fucked up,' gasped Scorpion. 'How did you find that out?'

'I've been screwing his P.A. and she told me. She saw the dollar bills in his top drawer. Bundles of them.'

'I can't believe it, I really can't.'

'These guys are the professionals at this sort of thing. They go to the top. I wouldn't be surprised if they've also been topping up the chief minister.'

'That slimy son of a bitch?'

'Yes, one of my constables says he saw the chief's car dropping off one of those Nepali girls that the Ukes have been pimping out here.'

'Fuck! What is the place coming to?'

'Anyway, what's this big plan of yours?' asked Denzil.

'I want to blow the guys out of the sky. Wipe them out totally. Kaboom!'

'What do you mean? With a bomb?'

'Yes, of course. Big enough to do a lot of damage.'

'Holy shit, have you been on the *bhang*?'

'No, if we do a job, we do it well.'

'Where are you going to get that from? Make one?'

'I know people.'

'This is terrorist talk, way above my level,' objected the policemen, who was looking fidgety.

'No, you just need to do the looking out, surveillance, that sort of deal, and I'll take care of the rest. They sometimes go to that shack that you rent in Calangute. The Uke uses it as a shag pad and his gang meet there sometimes.'

'You seem to have that covered then. But if you bomb a bunch of Ukes, the government will be all over this with their Special Forces and CID guys from Delhi and it will be all out of control. We'll both be in dog-shit up to our eyeballs. You need to just make them disappear. The Indian way, quietly, like by *jadu* magic.'

When it came to a balance of brains versus brawn, Scorpion had an abundance of the latter and not very much of the former. 'I don't understand what *jadu* has to do with this.'

'You know Vlad the boss is into diving, particularly for salvage of contraband and the occasional haul of arms? They get their information from the fishermen, who tip them off when they catch something of interest in their nets. Then the Ukes go off and dive to find out more. One of my constables reported that a fisherman had showed him part of a prop from a plane that had come up in his net. He said he was going to sell it and the coordinates to some foreigners, who were interested in diving for salvage.'

'So, they go diving and we get someone to tamper with the air?' suggested Scorpion, finally getting to understand what magic looked like.

'Totally correct, now easy ha? We take out the lynchpin and then all the fuckin' wheels come off. We'll get these bloody buggers to hang themselves one way or another. Can't have foreigners running our country again.'

A Cessna Caravan single-prop, eight-seater plane had indeed gone missing over the Arabian Sea, but it had been flying under the radar and air traffic flight control systems. It would almost certainly have been carrying an illegal shipment of drugs or arms, destined for a dealer operating somewhere along the coast of Goa.

Vlad had been a contract diver for a company constructing pipelines and oil platforms in the Caspian, before he discovered that his talents could be put to better use recovering contraband drugs from the Arabian Sea. The expanse of water off the coast of Goa, was a convenient place to dump packages of cocaine and other drugs for collection and distribution to the punters that flocked to this hedonistic party-going state.

He would use the equipment and facilities of a small diving school at Pigeon Island, about ninety minutes sailing time from the port of Panjim. The sailing school was run by a former police diver, who had given up recovering dead bodies and taken to the more lucrative tourist industry, handing out PADI certificates to people who came to explore the depths of the Indian Ocean.

'I know a man…' Denzil continued, casually tipping some ash out of his cigar.

'A man?'

'Yes, who can fix things, you know. He'll do me a favour if I ask him nicely.'

'What, see off the Uke head honcho?' asked Scorpion, his eyes bulging up with intrigue.

'Ha, of course. You know what I'm saying?'

'*Yar*, *yar*, that will be great, but how?'

'Hey, leave that to him, there are ways. But it's going to cost.'

'What like a contract job? How much?' Scorpion's eyes

were literally bulging out of their sockets now.'

'Look, you'll be doing us both a favour. He is an evil *badmash* who gets on my tits, and it'll eliminate your competition.'

'Where there's money, there's nasty *gundas*,' was Inspector Denzil's motto.

'I can see that. So, it'll be good for us both and we can get back to normal.'

'Yes, so let's split the cost then hah? Let's make it a *lakh* each, okay?'

'A *lakh*? Fuckin' shit man, no way. I don't make that in a year. It's costing me a fortune to rebuild the Sunset.'

'Look, do you want to be in business or not?'

'I'm going to have to think about that.'

'Think? What's there to think about man? Do you want to save your Beachboys business or not?'

A *lakh* was a shed load of money for Scorpion. He'd already had to empty out the contents of at least one mattress stuffed with money, to bring his bar back to life and he was fast reaching the point when money was becoming scarce. He had tried to make it stretch by renovating only the front part of the Sunset Lounge. The vast area behind the mahogany bar that stretched up into the sand dunes was still a total wreck. Clever lighting and screens that shut off the mess of charred remains created the illusion that the Sunset was back to normal, but the area it covered was greatly reduced, as were the profits. It wouldn't be long before he'd have to take up Braganza's deal.

A few days later Vlad called on Madam Marina's, a discrete brothel that masqueraded as a guest house, to tell her that the

Ukes would be taking over her protection. When the seventy-year-old Marina, who was born and bred in Goa, tried to show him the door, Vlad told her he would return in a couple of days to see if she had reconsidered his request.

Scorpion put two of the Beachboys on twenty-four-hour guard inside Marina's front reception room, but when Vlad returned, he came in force at midnight, with three Ukes armed with an axe and baseball bats, and smashed through the front door. Marina's protectors were sound asleep and no match for the assault. One had his skull cracked open and the other had the axe partially sever his right hand. Vlad tied Marina to a chair with wire and threatened to strangle her, until she was prepared to agree to their demands for control of her business.

In the same week they struck a deal with the head of the local taxi union, to control the fleet of radio cars operating around Anjuna. In the deal, drivers would be offered generous commissions for selling any of the services the Ukes had on offer.

Karina told Scorpion that Vlad had to be eliminated at all costs, if he was to maintain the authority of the Beachboys. He returned to Denzil Braganza to strike the deal, in which the policeman stood to make a few hundred thousand rupees out of the transaction. Vlad would disappear somewhere under the sea, still tied to his leaden weights, after an apparent fault with his air system. He would become food for the sharks and other flesh-eating sea creatures.

With Vlad out of the way, his fledgling business would quickly melt away and the Beachboys could return to their activities, unchallenged for the foreseeable future.

Chapter 12

Job done

Pigeon Island is an unremarkable island. A rocky outcrop of wild goats and a few sea birds. Denzil Braganza's contact, Bibi, ran the diving school there. He'd discovered that the police force limited his ability to get wealthy quickly and that diving was where the richer pickings were to be made.

Bibi charged wealthy Indian tourists' extortionate rates for dives, claiming that he was a qualified PADI instructor, when, in reality, he had a fake certificate that a Bombay forger had made for him. With Bibi, you were literally thrown in at the deep end and it was a wonder that his students had not drowned on his watch, given the pathetically poor level of instruction he meted out.

But Bibi's biggest money spinner was taking people out to recover submerged contraband, just a few kilometres off Pigeon Island, which was a popular drop spot for drug traffickers. He chose to do this after four o'clock in the afternoons, when most of his tourist customers had gone back to their hotels on the mainland. His commercial customers would then arrive in their speedboats and Bibi would accompany them to the designated drop zone, which was about a kilometre away from the island. There, he would dive to depths of forty metres to recover twenty or thirty kilos of drugs that had been deposited earlier that night by a passing ship, skirting Indian territorial waters.

Bibi only accepted payment in hard cash and his customers departed happy with their payload.

'So, Bibi *bhai*,' said Denzil, who paid him a special visit one afternoon. 'I've got a question for you.'

'Fire away, Chief, but I can't tell you anything about my customers because I don't know who they are, nor do I wish to know.'

'No, actually I know most of your customers. They're friends of mine, so to speak. My question is really one about diving,' Denzil continued. 'How would you tamper with someone's air, so that he suffocates forty metres deep?'

'What? Make someone vanish down there?' asked Bibi, raising his eyebrows.

'Well, yes.'

'It's quite difficult really, because people dive in pairs, so if someone's air ran out, his partner would give him enough air to rise to the top safely. It's part of the safety drill, you know.'

'But you don't dive with anyone?' observed Denzil.

'Yes, but I'm a James Bond kind of fellow. I break the rules, I can't expose anyone else to the trickery that I get up to down there.'

'I understand. So, there is no one else who dives solo?'

'No, not really. Hang on, yes! There is that foreigner, Ukrainian, I think. He used to be a professional diver.'

'That's the fellow. I want him vanished.' Bibi's eyes widened. His jaw dropped an inch.

'Hey, boss, he's got connections. He could survive, or his

side kick will come after me and that'll be my time up.'

'I could make it worth your while. You see, he's being a real pain in the *gharr* with his *gundas,* causing trouble and trying to take over from our boys.'

'What are we talking about?'

'Oh, about half a lakh, say.'

Bibi's went silent at the mention of half a lakh. It was a lot of money, more than he'd earn in the entire tourist season. Denzil had definitely piqued his curiosity.

'Okay, let's say I'm interested, when are we talking about?'

'When he calls next.'

'That's tomorrow.'

'Yep.'

'Shit. Holy shit no. His boys would burn me if they found out.'

'Look Bibi, if you take out the Uke, his guys will melt away, believe me. He has no succession plan, it's either him or no one else.'

Getting rid of Vlad would solve a lot of problems for Denzil. The Ukrainian now had the Minister in his pocket, allowing him to act with impunity. It would be only a matter of time before he was running every racket in town. Half the taxi drivers had begun to drive cars financed by the Ukes, nearly all the beach shacks paid them some sort of protection money and forty percent of the drugs that were consumed emanated from Vlad's ocean haul. The Beachboys would soon be slaves to the foreigners in their own country. Vlad relied on Bibi to supply him with the diving equipment he needed every Friday evening. He paid in US dollar bills each time, which was well above the odds for the standard of Bibi's diving equipment. Bibi kept aside a regulator, a set of tanks and a mask, especially for his most valued customer. Now suddenly someone had offered a sum of money that would pay for a decade's worth of equipment hire, all in one lump sum.

'Hello there, Bibi,' was Vlad's greeting, as he sailed up to the diving centre at Pigeon Island, the following day, after Denzil had given his execution orders. 'Today, I'm diving for something slightly different than the usual packages.'

'Oh yes boss, a big ship of whiskey? Ha, ha,' chuckled Bibi nervously.

'Actually no, I'm searching for a plane that went down at night about twenty kilometres from here. I think there will be interesting things to explore on board, hah?

Maybe we can share the salvage.'

Bibi was naturally surprised by the offer of a share. 'Hey boss, that sounds interesting.'

'Yes, the usual deal then. You take a little and I take the rest? Ha, ha. Okay?'

Bibi couldn't argue with his best customer, whom he was about to execute for half a *lakh*. 'Sure then, the usual deal,' he agreed.

Bibi handed Vlad his kit, which he carried to the diving boat. Bibi took his equipment from the workshop at the rear of the diving centre, whilst Vlad keyed in the coordinates of the diving point into his GPS.

'Head north for forty minute,' he ordered.

Bibi started the engines and roared off the jetty, creating a white foamy wake with his twin fifty-horsepower Yamaha engines.

'Nice week of business Bibi?' asked Vlad. 'Yes, not too bad, boss.'

'You seen that prick the Chief Inspector recently?'

'No, not really. He doesn't come by here anymore. I think he gave us up as a bad job. We're just too quick for him and his inspectors.'

The sea was flat and the boat skimmed across the surface effortlessly. Vlad sat back to enjoy the short trip. He took a cigarette from his pocket and fumbled about to find his lighter.

'Look on the back seat, I've got one in my jacket,' Bibi told him.

Vlad reached out to the back to fumble around for a lighter. That's when he saw Bibi's mobile phone on the back seat light up with a message:

'Good luck. Scorpion.'

Vlad found the lighter and lit his cigarette. 'Would you like one?' he asked Bibi.

'Well yes, thanks. Been a long hard day. I could do with one. Been trying to give up.'

Vlad gave Bibi a cigarette and passed him the lighter. He noticed a slight tremor in Bibi's hand as he took it and flicked the lighter a few times to accomplish the simple task. Vlad knew how to identify *cool, calm and collected*, but also knew how to recognise *nervy, jumpy and panicky* and his diving assistant was distinctly the latter this evening. Years of dealing in the underworld had tuned his senses into highly sensitive antennae to pick up danger signals and that very moment Vlad was on high alert.

'You need to get that trembling right hand seen to by a

doctor. It could be the early signs of something serious, a nervous illness maybe?'

'Oh, I don't think so. I'm not ill, just a bit stressed maybe.'

The couple were silent for the rest of the journey and the only sound that broke the silence was the occasional chatter on the marine radio, interrupting the purr of the engines.

'Okay, we're near the spot now, cut the engines. I think we're in about forty metres of water, so let out the anchor for around sixty metres,' Vlad ordered, getting out of his seat to peer down into the water.

Bibi cut the engines and circled around until the boat had virtually become motionless, then let out the anchor. The boat gave a little tug when the anchor finally made it to the bottom and established a hold on the ocean floor. He switched off the engine and proceeded to prepare the boat for the dive.

'Let's get our kit on then, we've got about an hour till sunset,' said Vlad. 'Better check your phone, there were some messages for you earlier.'

He watched Bibi as he read the short message. The two men glanced at each other.

Bibi's eyes yelled out the silent bells of alarm. 'Okay?' asked Vlad.

'Ya, boss.'

'You know Bibi, I've not been happy with this bloody regulator for the last couple of dives. Could I try yours?'

'No boss, it should be okay. I only serviced it last week. Mine's much worse, made in India, no good.'

'No, I want to try it,' Vlad insisted, forcibly snatching the breather from Bibi. 'Now, you go first, and I'll follow after.'

'Boss, my equipment is not very good, not safe for you. Please let me use mine and you take your regulator. I have serviced it today. It's better for you.'

'You lying cunt...' growled Vlad. 'You've fucked up my regulator, I know.

Someone is trying to get you to whack me, ha? And I think I know who it is.'

'Boss, no, no. Not correct!'

'Let me check that kit then!' demanded Vlad, picking up his regulator. He began to connect it to one of the tanks and bent over the side of the boat to submerge it in the sea water to check if there were any bubbles escaping from the connections. Bibi took his opportunity, grabbing a boat hook heavy enough to crack Vlad's skull open, but the Ukrainian had expected Bibi to attack and had watched him from the corner of his left eye.

He dodged the blow.

Vlad was on his feet immediately, looking for something to defend himself with. Both men froze for a second or two. The Uke was the bigger man and probably the stronger of the two. He grabbed a gas tank and flung the ten-kilo steel projectile towards Bibi at the speed of light. The tank reached its target, throwing Bibi off balance, and he lost his grip of the boat hook. Vlad grabbed it, while his attacker was trying to regain control and struck Bibi once, then twice, then again and again. There were screams for mercy from the onetime assailant, who was now his victim, but Vlad was not listening.

'Whose idea was this, you mother fucker?' snarled Vlad with the boat hook still firmly in his grasp. There was another thwack and more screams of pain. Then another. 'Braganza...

Branga...' His answer was interrupted by another blow, which must have broken his skull, for there was the distinct sound of a crack as Vlad brought down the heavy wooden hook.

The Uke surveyed the motionless body, covered in blood, and sat down to contemplate his next move.

He helped himself to a cigarette, lit it, and began to regain his breath after exhaling a long plume of smoke. The sun would be down in half an hour and it would take at least another hour to get back to the mainland.

He dragged Bibi's body to the bathing platform at the back of the boat and kicked it into the water. It floated off slowly, head down, and the water turned reddish brown for an instant at the back of the boat. Vlad turned on the engines and headed back for the mainland. He picked up Bibi's phone, punched in 0000, then 1234, to see the last message from Denzil Braganza.

Job done he replied and slipped the phone into his top pocket. He rummaged around in Bibi's bag and found a large bundle of dollars stuffed into a side pocket, which he put into his own bag. When he was half a kilometre off the mainland, Vlad turned the boat around to head it back out to sea the back of the boat to swim back to land.

The boat continued its journey to oblivion.

Chapter 13

Tit for tat

Scorpion first found out about the aborted attempt on Vlad and Bibi's fate when Denzil Braganza called him.

'That idiot Bibi fucked up. Sunk without a trace and that Uke bugger had the cheek to send me a text message to say, *job done.*

'Fuckin' 'ell!' shouted Scorpion down the phone. 'Now what does that mean for me, my money, and my boys. We're going to be the laughing stock of Anjuna when the Uke puts the message around that we screwed up in such a bad way.'

Such are the ways of gangster wars, that tit for tat reprisals never produce a clear victor. Vlad had no option but to strike back immediately to confirm he had emerged victorious from the bungled attempt on his life. Scorpion's new flagship Diva Centre would be where Vlad would attack next to show that he was indestructible. So far, Scorpion had dominated the control of spas and massage clinics in Anjuna. Some of these offered genuine ayurvedic cures, but many were run by fakes and a few offered sex services, masquerading as ancient Indian massage centres. Single men came here for sexual gratification and the police allowed the businesses to openly trade and tout their services. With the Ukes into trafficking girls from Nepal and elsewhere, these businesses were prime sites for them to extend their trade.

Their takeover tactics usually began with a disruptive customer complaining about the service he received, accompanied by threats of violence. This would be followed up by one of the Ukes offering protection to allow the business to run peacefully. A few months later, they would force the owner to hand over his assets with threats of violence.

The Diva Massage Centre was a business that had been around for at least a decade and its owner, Anil Sharma, ran it well. He had come to Goa in the nineties to set up his legitimate business, offering ayurvedic massages to both men and women. He had trained in the philosophy of this ancient art of medicine in Kerala and had run a successful business until the Ukes called round.

Sharma didn't look like a fighter with his mild-mannered ways, but years of being a masseur had meant he was all muscle and bone. When a couple of Ukes went around to see him about payment for protection, he had given them a good kicking. They had promised to come back in strength and burn him out of his premises and he had dutifully informed Scorpion.

Vlad had decided to take his revenge on the Diva Centre as a demonstration of his power. Sharma woke up early one morning to perform his meditation and was confronted by Vlad and three other Ukes, armed with knives and a gun, sitting in his front room.

'Good morning,' growled Vlad, as Sharma turned quickly to try and escape back out to his bedroom. One of the Ukes blocked his escape route. Sharma, still drowsy from sleep, tried to fling a kick at him in the face and missed.

'You fight like a drunken dog,' Vlad insulted Sharma, once they had pinned him to the floor.

'The curse of Kali be on you,' groaned Sharma, as his face was pushed down.

'May all of you burn to death very soon.'

Vlad sneered, 'Now let's see if any of your fake remedies, chants or mantras will save you this time or if that dick-sucking faggot Scorpion will come to the rescue.'

Vlad's henchman Aleks used his dagger to cut off Sharma's *loongi*, the only garment that he wore, and used the cloth to tie his naked body at the feet and hands. There was a bowl of oranges in the room and Vlad took one of them and stuffed it in Sharma's mouth, as he spluttered and tried to resist having his mouth full of the citrus fruit.

By the picture window, that overlooked the pavement where Sharma's masseurs would sit from ten o'clock to show that they were available for sessions, there was a ceiling fan, which kept them cool in the humid heat of the day. Vlad instructed his men to hang Sharma by his feet from the fan, which he then turned on at its lowest rotation. He then pulled back the curtains to produce a bizarre and frightening spectacle.

It was still early and the street outside was deserted, but soon passers-by would witness the grotesque tableau of the human rotisserie. An upside-down man, with an orange stuffed in his mouth, and his long hair just brushing the floor, as he revolved at forty revolutions per minute. At first Sharma had tried to wriggle free, but his strength began to slip away.

And finally lost consciousness.

Later that morning, as the bright sunshine began to stream through the Diva Centre's picture window, the shopkeeper from next door was the first to notice Sharma hanging inverted from the ceiling. He raised the alarm and others began to congregate outside the shop, creating a huge hullabaloo, as Sharma's body continued to rotate. Someone called the police and Inspector Braganza was on the scene just before midmorning, about the time Scorpion arrived at his office. They cut down the lifeless body and closed the curtains on the window.

'This is a bloody mess! I thought you were taking care of that bastard,' howled Scorpion as Braganza emerged from the shop, leaving a forensics officer to prepare her report. 'I'm now not only a *lakh* of rupees down, I've lost the respect of these people, which took me years to build up.'

'Fear more than respect. Now someone else is being more fearful than you.'

'We're in this together remember.'

'I can call the Uke in for questioning, and see if forensics find anything. I doubt it very much. We're playing with fire here.'

'So, what are we going to do? Just lie back and get fucked, hah? What sort of police big shot are you?'

'I'll find out where his gang are having their next boozy leg over party. I mentioned this before, they hang out in a shack just by the North end of the beach. You can attack them there and perhaps wipe them out in one go. Perfect way to get your own retribution.'

'I'd heard about that. I'm going to need your help with good intelligence on when they are there and explosives, that sort of thing.'

'I've already told you how that will get the anti-terror people involved.'

'Handle it. We're both up to our eyes in shit.'

The Beachboys scrambled their gang in force, thinking that the beach hut confrontation would be their Waterloo moment, a battle which they had to win. The shack was set to become a battleground, with gang warfare conducted with machetes, baseball bats, and a few guns. The Beachboys had a couple of guns smuggled into Goa by a hustler, who acted as an arms dealer for small time criminals, but they were mainly for show and had never been used to actually shoot, kill, or maim anyone. Scorpion didn't believe in wasting expensive ammunition and, apart from the odd occasion that he used a gun for target practice, the weapons were simply to terrorise his enemies. This job needed something that would blow Vlad and his guys out of the sky and dynamite was going to be the only answer.

Two and a half hours after sunset on Saturday evening, a column of Beachboys began to converge on the beach to ensure that this was the final showdown with their enemy. There was going to be a devastating battle for control of Anjuna and, on the basis of numbers, it looked like the Beachboys would almost certainly be the winners.

These were two firms with one common goal to exterminate the other and take over all commerce on Anjuna. The Ukes were from the relatively rich world, better financed, well fed, and well-armed. The Beachboys from the poorer local world, underfunded, but with the key advantage of defending their own territory. Anjuna was about to experience these two opposites entering a new realm in their war for supremacy.

Braganza had confirmed that the Ukes had been spotted driving together to the beach hut on Saturday evening. They'd stocked up on cases of vodka and beer and a couple of Nepali girls were seen being escorted to the venue by Aleks in Vlad's pick-up truck.

'Here is the plan,' explained Scorpion to his men. 'I want an advanced group of you guys with me for the first attack and the rest of you lot in the dunes, to polish off the buggers that try and get away. We're going to use surprise as our first weapon and then just brute force.'

'What are we doing boss? Are we killing them, hurting them, castrating them?' They all laughed.

'Do what you need to do, so that they learn a lesson. But you guys know how to teach someone a lesson, so we never see them here again, *yar*?'

It was Karina who took a couple of Beachboys with her to lead the attack, while Scorpion stayed with the others to watch the bang go off. The idea was to blow the shack sky high and rid Anjuna of the Uke menace. They crawled on their bellies up to the rear of the shack. Karina lit a stick of dynamite and threw it under the wooden building. There was music playing inside, which sounded like Abba in Russian. The stick fizzed and Karina ran back to the group of Beachboys to await the big bang, but after a few seconds it was quite clear that the bang they had expected wasn't going to happen. The dynamite must have been too old or too damp. They'd have to find another way. Perhaps charge the front door.

While they were mulling over their options, they noticed the music being played in the hut had got stuck in a loop. 'Boys, something's wrong here,' Scorpion said. 'Listen to that music. It's playing over and over. We've been duped. The place is empty. Then, unexpectedly, the bang went off and blew up the shack. Bits flew everywhere. 'Nothing there, boss. Totally clean,' someone pronounced. 'We've been conned by the bastards. No Ukes and no Nepali girls.

Scorpion's mobile buzzed.

He looked at the message on his screen.

'Fucked up again? Our turn next.'

Chapter 14

Abduction

St Jude's church in Anjuna, had long since ceased to hold Mass and its white façade was beginning to crumble with decay. It was on the tourist trail, as an example of one of the oldest churches in India. The pavement outside was awash with floodlights well past midnight, like a lighthouse guiding lost travellers to safe places. On her own, draped in her Grecian white dress, stood Karina. Her long blonde hair folded over her left shoulder and she was holding a cigarette in a Felliniesque movie setting.

Parked in a car, just within sight of her, was Scorpion, ready to follow whoever she might entice to spend time with her. Street prostitution was not new in Goa, but the sight of a white woman offering herself for sex, standing by a decaying Portuguese church, piqued the interest of several cars that drove around the block a few times to take a closer look.

They were generally men in expensive chauffeured cars, not particularly looking for a night out with an expensive Ukrainian woman, but wanting to linger and observe this unusual spectacle. Eventually one stopped and wound his window down, 'Hello, lady,' said the chauffeur. 'My boss wants to know how much?'

'One *lakh* to a man in a car like that would be my starting price. The rest depends on what he wants, heh?' She looked through the window and blew the passenger a kiss.

'*Chullo,*' replied the passenger and the car drove off, leaving Karina standing alone.

The night had started well with a Marwari businessman inviting her into his

Mercedes for quick sex in the back of his car in exchange for fifty thousand rupees, all under the watchful gaze of Scorpion around the corner. There'd been a few time-wasters later on, who had just stopped by to poke fun, and three men in a little Honda wanted to negotiate a group discount. Times were harder without the Sunset Lounge in full operation and Karina and Scorpion were having to get back onto the street to bring in a reasonable living.

Scorpion sat thinking about the Uke's next possible retaliatory move on the Beachboys and how he had been tricked into believing that Vlad and his men had been in the beach hut the previous night. Braganza swore that he was acting on reliable information and that the Ukes must have been tipped off by someone in the Beachboys' camp. So far, he had been sure of the loyalty of his men, but with all the setbacks lately, could it be possible that one of them had turned towards the enemy?

He had begun to doze off and it was only the sound of Karina's screams that woke him from his partial slumber. By the time he came fully to his senses, he saw her being dragged into a Maruti by two men and the car accelerating away. His own aged Ambassador, once the sedan of the Indian upper classes, took a little while to fire up, and in the slight delay the faster Maruti's rear red lights had disappeared into the distance. He thought he saw Karina struggling in the back seat. He tried to follow, but the empty streets now gave no clue as to where Karina's abductors had gone.

Karina was his recruiter-in-chief for women from the Ukraine. She was the lynchpin of his firm.

He had to get her back.

'Where are we going, what do you want from me?' asked Karina of the man holding her captive.

'Shut up, slag, and stay still if you don't want to get hurt!' one of them growled in Russian.

'Where do you come from?' asked the other.

'Kiev, what's it to you?'

'You're a bit fat and ugly for a woman from Kiev.'

'You're going to be in big trouble, you know,' Karina courageously threatened. 'I'd recommend you let me go now!'

'Hah, hah, trouble? From that black monkey of yours out there somewhere? Don't be ridiculous. Now shut your mouth while I put this plaster on your face' said the man in the back of the car taping her up around the mouth and then tying her hands behind her back.

They'd travelled for thirty minutes or so before the car arrived at iron gates, which were opened by a man in khakis. She was blindfolded, taken to a room, and thrown down on a floor mattress. She heard someone else come into the room and the clanging of metal. She then felt two men holding her down. They grabbed her hand, and then suddenly there was excruciating pain and her finger was gone. She tried to yell through her taped-up face, but there was just a muffled sound.

She felt a female pair of hands bandaging up her hand and then she was left to lie on the mattress. 'We'll be back in the morning,' one of the men told her in Russian. He took off her blindfold and clanged the door shut. The place was silent again. Karina's mouth was parched, and she tried to shout for water, but no one heard. Her hand burned with pain.

She suspected that these were hardened men from her native country, who had been apprenticed in the tough training ground of Arena City, where Chechens, Armenians, and the Russian mafia competed for the tourist business. She'd had plenty of experience of them back in Kiev in the lap-dancing cocktail bars, where they controlled considerable empires, reaching back to Odessa on the Black Sea coast.

Karina lay awake, beginning to believe that Scorpion and the Beachboys would eventually have to relinquish their business to the Ukrainians because of the Ukes' ruthless, methodical way of controlling everything from drugs, to arms, to human trafficking. Goa had not woken up yet to the full extent of the threat. Her kidnapping was just one small step in Vlad's mission to grab control from Scorpion, on his way towards total domination of the underworld in Goa.

Her hand continued to throb with searing pain mercilessly throughout the night. Tiredness had given way to brief moments of sleep, as she lay bound and gagged on a mattress that smelled of stale urine and cigarettes. Now, the darkened room was being lit by fine shafts of daylight coming through the cracks in the heavy wooden door, raising the temperature, which made it stifling.

Apart from a mattress on the floor, there was little else in the way of furniture. Only a bare lightbulb and a bucket. She still wore her dress, in which she felt sticky and uncomfortable, with mosquitoes feasting freely on her bare arms.

While daylight was breaking, Scorpion was about to receive a shoe box. It contained an amputated forefinger with a ring, which he had given her. A bloodstained note in the box read, 'Let's talk if you want her back.'

Several hours must have passed. Then there was an unlocking sound outside and the door opened, letting in a huge flash of bright sunlight. The diminutive figure of a young girl stood in the doorway, dressed in a long *kurta*, holding a plate of food and a plastic bottle of water. Once inside, she put on the light and shut the door again.

'You want water? Some *dal bhat* to eat?' she asked softly. Karina nodded. 'Maybe I can open the tape on your face. But no noise hah? Or they will beat me and you.' Karina nodded again, and the girl ripped off the plaster from her mouth, making her wince in pain. 'Very sorry,' she said. 'I have to feed and drink you. Cannot open your hands.'

'I'm not going to run away,' said Karina.' I know the rules.'

'Very sorry but can't. Take water first,' the girl said putting the plastic bottle to her lips and tilting it upwards as Karina drank solidly to quench her thirst.

'You Nepali?' asked Karina. 'I can see light brown skin, hah?'

'Yes, me Nepali.'

'What is your name? Have you been here long?'

'Too many questions now, please eat *dal bhat*.' She held up a spoonful of the rice and lentils and put it in Karina's mouth. 'How is your hand?'

Karina swallowed. 'Oh very painful, do you have pills for pain?'

'I will see if I can get some, later maybe.'

Karina held up her hand and looked at the blotches of blood-stained bandage.

The hand had swollen up and continued to throb. 'Thank you for my food and water. My name is Karina. You have a very beautiful face, but you must be very young, hah, to be working here?'

The girl nodded. 'They say I must work here for two year before I can go home.

Then I see my parents again. Everyone will be happy.'

'What do you do here?'

'Too many questions. I come back later with pills, ya? Now you eat *dal bhat*.'

She funnelled in the food, then some more water, gesturing to Karina to keep her mouth shut as she left, shutting the door behind her.

Karina had heard of girls from Nepal being trafficked into Goa, kidnapped or sold by parents desperate for a few rupees to keep themselves from starvation, and now the Ukes were getting into child prostitution. She knew their ambitions were unbounded and would reach out to prey on the weakest and most vulnerable people, without any regard to ethics or social norms.

Time passed and now the room was extremely stifling, without circulating air. She thought she saw a rat scurry past through the shafts of light that fell on the floor. She hated vermin, more than snakes or other reptiles. Rats had once eaten alive someone's baby in her neighbourhood in Kiev and the thought of being attacked by rats while she lay bound on the mattress filled her with dread. Her eyes remained open like saucers, while several horrific scenarios drifted through her brain.

There was the sound of the door unlocking and the Nepali girl returned. 'I've brought you pill for hand and for head. Take it?'

She handed two white pills to Karina and helped her drink from the bottle of water to swallow them.

'It makes your hand better now,' she said.

'I come from Ukraine where it is very cold. Really hot here.'

'Ah, like the boss man and his friend?'

Karina nodded. 'Is it cold in Nepal?' she asked.

'Sometimes. Sometimes even snow.'

'Do you like Goa?'

The girl shook her head.

'The men are bad to you?' asked Karina.

She nodded. 'They ask me to do dirty things.' She screwed up her face. 'I don't like it. I cry much. Now they take my skin.'

'Skin?' asked Karina.

The girl unbuttoned the front of her *kurta,* exposing her stomach where there was a large pink scar. Other patches had been taped up with bandages round to her back.

Karina gasped. 'They did this?' She looked into the girl's face, trying to make a connection with her as she looked down at the ground. 'Open up my hands and I'll help you run away. I know a man who can help you.'

'No, gates outside locked. *Chowkidar* guards door. He is bad man.'

143

'Maybe tonight when dark?'

'No, no, they will hurt me, maybe kill me, no…'

'At least tell me your name.'

'Maya, my name is Maya, okay? Now I must go before they come for me.'

She shut the door and the room was back in semi darkness. Karina felt herself still trembling in a mixture of fear and anger over what she had just seen. This young woman being used not only as a sex slave, but as a skin farm for her fair skin, to service some cosmetic surgeon in far off Bombay or Delhi. The drugs, the arms trading and the brothels had been something Karina had got used to, but harvesting a young innocent human being's body for the gratification of someone rich was a new low.

Whilst the illegal trade in organs had begun to produce rich pickings for unscrupulous doctors in rural areas of India, where thousands of kidneys were procured from desperately poor peasants, skin harvesting was also beginning to supplement the illegal trade of gangsters. The Ukes had been quick to spot the opportunity seeing young vulnerable, fair-skinned Nepali girls as a source of healthy skin grafts to meet the rapacious demand for skin lightening amongst wealthy Indians.

Karina was no newcomer to living off the proceeds of crime, but the idea of harvesting an innocent girl's skin seemed to be mining deep recesses of misery. The horror took her mind off the throbbing pain in her hand for a while, as she lay on her back.

The pill she took must have had a powerful pain killer and she dozed off for a few minutes into a deep sleep. Someone put a hand on her forehead, and she awoke. The room was pitch black. She could not see a thing, but was sure it was a man's hand, large but soft to the touch. She heard a voice speak to her in Russian with a distinctive Kiev accent.

'In five minutes, I want you to make a run for freedom. I'm going to untie you. When you hear a cough, open the wooden door, and run outside through the courtyard and out of the front gate. Don't stop, keep running until you get to the beach.'

'Who are you, is this some sort of trap to kill me?'

'Just trust me, this is your only chance to survive.'

'What about the *chowkidar* at the gate?'

'He is taking a toilet break. Now or never.'

'Why are you doing this?'

'I'm doing this for someone I love.'

Karina felt the man cutting the ties that bound her and then he left. She heard the door close, but no click of the lock. Had he left it ajar? She slipped on her sandals, and she was up, running out into the fresh air outside, straight towards the single light that lit the entrance. The *chowkidar* had left the door unmanned, the butt of his *bidi* smouldered on the ledge. She opened the door and ran west down an alleyway, skipped over sleeping dogs and rubbish which littered part of her way. Her hand began to throb as her heart beat faster and harder and she began to get out of breath.

She had to keep running until she had reached the safety of the beach.

The five-minute dash for freedom seemed like an hour. Just when she thought she could hear the sound of the sea ahead and look forward to the prospect of freedom, there was a

Maruti, lights blaring, coming down the badly rutted road, which slowed down its progress.

She heard two shots fired.

Then a searing pain in her left shoulder.

There was a narrower alley to her left which she took, knowing the car could not follow her there.

Finally, Karina was into the open amongst the sand dunes, which provided good cover. She could see that the lights of Scorpion's guest house were still on and made a final dash for it, collapsing at the entrance.

Jaz was just about to go home when he saw Karina stumble in and fall. She was bleeding badly, her eyes rolled as if she was about to pass out. He lifted her on to one of the cushions and called Scorpion.

'Your woman's back. Nearly dead, I think. Get your doc friend here quickly!'

'Keep a look out for those *shaitans* in case they come looking for her,' said Scorpion. 'I'll be there as quick as I can.'

Jaz took the handgun that Scorpion kept locked in the safe and stuffed it in the back pocket of his jeans as a precaution. Things were beginning to spiral out of the Beachboys' control. First there was the attack on the Sunset Lounge a few weeks earlier, Scorpion's retaliation to try and obliterate Vlad, followed by the Ukes' slow murder of Sharma, then the Beachboys' failed attempt to blow up the Ukes in one single assault, and now finally the abduction of Karina. She would almost certainly have been used as bait to lure Scorpion into a trap, and that would have been the end of the gang. How much Jaz longed for the simplicity of the time when they were the elite that ruled the beach. Now the Beachboys had a continuing war on their hands, with no end in sight.

'What the fuck do you think you were up to, cutting that whore free?' Vlad yelled at Igor, when Aleks, his minder, told him that Karina had fled into the night.

'I thought she was going to die in that room all tied up,' mumbled Igor.

'Who cares, who the fuck cares? She's just a slut, brown nosing it with that monkey, destroying our chances of doing real business down here.'

'You can't keep killing people, and you can't go on ruining the lives of innocent young women. These Nepali girls. Really, how could you cut them? They're ruined forever.'

'Their lives were worthless anyway.'

'They're human beings. But perhaps you're not. Remember what Mother used to say about you?'

Vlad raised his fist, preparing to land a crushing blow on Igor's head, but held back. Instead he cursed and banged the table. 'Get out of here!'

Chapter 15

Friends and torturers

Of course, I'd missed all the *hwyl*. I'd been asked by Father Michael, the showbiz priest with unusual grey-green eyes, who always seemed to speak to me like I was his best friend, to help amuse the *Banjara* children that day. I'd got them to help me cook their lunch of rice and lentils which was awesome. The kids thought it was crazy to wash the rice and lentils before cooking them. 'Why waste all that water?' they wondered, and I just had to tell them, it was the way it had to be done. They dutifully helped light the wood fire with sticks they had gathered from the beach and soon we had two healthy pots of boiling water, one with lentils and the other with good healthy brown rice. Mam would have been proud.

Brown rice takes a long time to cook and they had to take it in turns to keep stirring the steaming pot for at least an hour, while we sang English nursery rhymes. How odd this was! Here was I teaching gypsy kids to sing *Ring a Ring a Roses* in Goa, when they probably had many dozens of their own songs to sing, but they found the song a lot of fun, especially when we got to the sneezing bit and falling down. It's odd how we communicated with each other in a combination of song, sign language, a bit of English, and also Lambadi, the gypsy language of which I had zero knowledge.

Just as my energy began to flag, Igor rocked up on his booming chrome steed, an Enfield motorbike, which got the kids very excited. I wanted to hug him but decided that it might send all the wrong signals. Harpo was my husband-to-be after all. 'Come and have a ride!' he shouted to the kids and they all rushed over to him, leaving me to do the washing up. So, we struck a deal that they had to wash up their white tin enamel plates before the fun ride with Igor.

It took quite a while for them all to go around the playground, riding pillion with Igor. Their beaming faces made me very happy and I took a few pictures with my phone. Father Michael offered to print them off on the school's printer. Each child got a picture that day of themselves riding a motor bike. What a treat!

I liked Igor's patience and enthusiasm, going round and round the playground. He appeared to get as much pleasure from the children's giggles and laughter as I did.

Sunset was upon us now and we'd milked the joy of the bike rides, so we took the children down to the dormitory, a modest wooden hut with bunk beds donated by Opus Dei, a Catholic charity. When they had settled in their beds, Igor reached into his satchel and pulled out his *poongi* to play them a tune.

'It's a lullaby,' said Igor. 'It will help them sleep.'

We both sat on the floor of the hut, as the high-pitched music swirled around the wooden hut and up through the windows. I could see in the light of the only oil lamp, that the children were closing their eyes. The trance effect made me want to rest my head somewhere and I did just that, on Igor's shoulder.

When I awoke the music had stopped and Igor's head leant against mine. There were voices of two men talking. I stared through the darkness and noticed Father Michael was speaking to someone outside, who was obscured behind the door. I arose.

'Ah, Ceri! Such bliss hah? This is Inspector Braganza,' Michael said. Braganza made himself visible.

'Ah yes, I've met Ceri before, yes, yes. Beautiful girl, hah?'

'And a beautiful heart, too,' Father Michael added. 'She is a volunteer here once a week and what a wonderful job she does! My dear, thanks to the Inspector's fabulous fund-raising efforts with Opus Dei, we're able to provide all this for the children. He, too, has a very good heart.' He paused. 'Your boyfriend, is he asleep?'

'Not my boyfriend Father. Igor has just come to give a helping hand.'

'Helping hand, yes, hah, hah.' Braganza laughed in his wheezy, sickly way, and he and the priest both walked away into the night. Then we heard two bangs in the distance and Igor remarked, 'Good party somewhere.'

'You're in the doggy-doos, Ceri,' warned Melita the next day, when she returned to our shack after getting a new consignment of jewellery.

'Oh?'

'You've been called to see Karina at Scorpion's guest house. Better go now. They think you've turned informer to the Ukes. That creepy cop Braganza has put the idea to Scorpion that he thinks you leaked the attack on the shack to your lover boy Igor.'

'No fuck'n way!'

I called in at the guest house. Karina gave me a nasty look. The sling that held her right arm had gone, and she had a small bandage around her right hand. I imagined they hadn't been able to save her forefinger, but Karina seemed to have brushed the whole abduction episode aside. What an amazing woman. She was dressed in combat trousers with an olive-green T-shirt, as if she had recently been stood down from an army training camp.

'You wait here, and I'll call the boss. Better have a good story. He's not feeling very happy. Go wait in the office.' I entered the windowless room and sat on a velvet sofa to await my interrogation. I still had no fear.

The failed attack on the Ukes' hideaway had been a blow to the morale of the Beachboys. The usual banter and high spirits had given way to grumpiness, which added to the general gloom at the guest house. I heard Scorpion arrive and he came immediately into the room with Karina. He had a bucket of filthy water, the sort they used at the bar to wash the floor.

'You know what you're here for, don't you?' he snarled.

'Melita said you think I grassed on your attack plans.'

'She did, did she? Well I don't *think* you grassed. I know you did. Do you know what we do to people like you, you fucking slut?'

'I don't know how you got that story but it's wrong, just plain wrong,' I answered without any fear in my voice.

'Don't fuck'n lie to me, bitch!' he yelled into my face, grabbing my hair with his hands.

They felt like a mechanical claw.

I was speechless by this sudden attack.

Karina looked on and threatened, 'There's no use lying. We'll get the truth out of you.' At that Scorpion yanked my head and stuffed it into the bucket of freezing water and held me down for what felt like an eternity. I struggled, kicking and trying to wriggle free. Was he really going to drown me? I could hold my breath easily for a couple of minutes, but with my struggle for survival I was desperate for breath after less than twenty seconds. Then he pulled me out of the bucket, and I gasped for the biggest gulp of air I can remember. It took me a long while to recover. 'You don't want to die by drowning, do you?' asked Karina calmly.

'I really didn't know anything about the attack, how could I?' Again, Scorpion dunked me into the bucket. This time I swallowed a load of water and nearly passed out. I was pulled out spluttering and spewing and given another chance to recover. I just couldn't go through that again.

'Braganza, Braganza!' I said between gasps of air.

'Braganza?' shouted Scorpion.

'He was at the orphanage last night. I saw him. Can't you see, he's lying to you. I was with Igor, we'd been there for most of the afternoon and evening. We heard the bangs go off.'

'Braganza was at the orphanage?' asked Karina.

'Yes, you can ask the priest. Can't you see, he'd tipped off the Ukes and thought he could pin the blame on Igor and me, although we hadn't been near the Ukes all day.' Scorpion let go of my hair and Karina threw me a towel. I began to breathe freely again. She spoke to Scorpion. 'Looks like you've been cheated on by that son-of-bitch policeman. Vlad must've known that Braganza had told Bibi to kill him and was looking for payback.'

There were no apologies for the sudden attack on me. Scorpion and Karina had turned suddenly from friendly, caring employers to evil torturers, because they thought I had switched my loyalty to the Ukes due to my friendship with Igor. In their world of black or white there was no grey and Igor couldn't be my friend.

I was told to leave.

Chapter 16

Fiddler on the beach

I hadn't seen Igor all week. Hari had begun to occupy much of my time, as he soaked up every bit of English I taught him, and questioned our sales techniques, often to improve what we were doing. At the end of each day Melita and I would collapse outside our shack and listen to the sound of the sea. I would pull out my little notebook and write random thoughts about the people we had seen over the day. Hari featured heavily in most of my writing.

I hadn't quite worked out how he kept so cheerful despite his miserable existence. How could someone who had to work all day and then most of the night look so happy? His mouth was permanently cracked open exposing those brilliant white teeth. Wasn't there anything that would piss him off? Melita kept working on improving her Hindi, practising it on me, as if I knew what she was saying.

Then on Friday evening, when we were at our hut for our end of the week wind down session with a couple of roll ups, my mam called my mobile.

'*Cariad*, how are you?' She sounded pissed.

'Oh I'm fine, working, doing stuff on the beach. What about you?'

'Brill! The people here are fantastic and the *Bhagwan* is

amazing. But I've got a problem, my love.'

I knew that the only problem Mam ever had was that she was out of ackers. Child support had funded her habit for several years and even now she was asking me to give her money. For Christ sake I was only fifteen, but she was my mam and I was earning reasonable money out here on the beach. It gave me a sense of power to be able to say to her, 'How much?'

'A few hundred would do it, *Cariad*. Really, I won't ask again.'

'When are you coming back, Mam?'

'Oh, just a couple of weeks and I'll be done with my meditation intensive workshops.' I heard the thunder of a motorbike engine revving up on the road, at the top of the hill above the dunes.

'Mam, I have to go. I'll get something to you at the *ashram* on Monday.' I hung up, pretty annoyed that the money I sent to Mam would help fund this spiritual centre's fakery. I'd heard enough about *ashrams* since coming to Goa. Some were genuine, but others were just another business for preying on gullible westerners like my mam.

Melita looked over her shoulder and said, 'There's that fuckin' Uke coming rutting for you.'

It was as if there was a mass murderer outside looking for me. Melita scowled at me, 'Mind how you go, girl. Fuck him, but don't get killed for it.'

I grabbed my satchel and ran out into the twilight evening towards the sound of the throbbing Enfield motorbike. It was the happiest sound I had heard all day and I flung my arms around Igor and kissed him on the mouth. I felt Melita's eyes piercing through me, as I jumped on behind my surprise date. We roared off along the potholed street to the accompaniment of barking pariah dogs and Igor's beeping horn.

'Where are we going?' I yelled from the back, but he either couldn't hear me or didn't wish to respond. The sea was to our right, so we were travelling south and we continued to do so for over half an hour, until we turned back towards the sea and into a quiet bay, which was quite unlike anywhere else in Goa that I'd seen.

The warm evening breeze swirled around my bare arms and legs and I looked up at the massive starlit sky. There was my old faithful friend, the Evening Star, blinking out a greeting, telling me I was in good hands tonight. *Tad-cu* called it the *Seren y Gweithwyr*, the Workers' Star as it was the first thing that farm workers saw in the morning and the last thing that guided them home at night.

The shore was ringed with coconut palms, there were fishing boats dragged on to the beach and there was a solitary bar, lit by a neon sign that said Kevin's Crabs. There were no *ferenghis* around except for us, and the Goan family of six at Kevin's were tucking into something that resembled a platter of crabs and chips. They ate in silence, interrupted by the slurping of straws protruding from their green coconut drinks.

We held hands like lovers, as Igor led me to a makeshift bar consisting of a plank of wood suspended on two tree stumps. The children stared. 'Where is this?' I asked.

'It could be heaven... don't you think so?' laughed Igor.

A guy in red shorts and a tatty vest, who was presumably

156

Kevin, came over and offered, 'Can I get you a drink?'

'What have you got?' I asked.

'Only beer and local rum,' he replied unapologetically. 'There's also a few of those coconuts left.'

'Okay, could you please bring two coconuts and two large glasses of rum?' Igor requested. Kevin raised his eyebrows and smiled. 'And one of your peppered crabs with chips.'

As Kevin disappeared behind the bar to get the order, I said quietly, 'I've never had coconuts with rum and crabs. This will be my first time.'

'So, there's a first time for everything. You will enjoy.'

'Back in Wales we're surrounded by sea and the boys catch crabs and lobsters every day, but I'd never eaten one. They're all exported to Spain or end up in expensive restaurants, where Mam and I could never go.'

'We have many nice fishes and crabs in the Black Sea. My grandfather lives in Odessa and I go there every year for my holidays.'

'You know, if I was rich, I'd just like to travel like a gypsy to all these places I've heard of, to see if they are like the way I think they are.'

'So how do you think of my country?'

'I don't know, but Kiev reminds me of funny, rubbery chicken, smelling of garlic, so I imagine the place smells like a KFC. Odessa sounds all mysterious and sinister. Paris, romantic with accordions playing, and Rome with fountains and noisy lambrettas.'

Igor burst out laughing. 'You are having an interesting mind. I see chess when I think of Kiev, crabs in Odessa, perfume in Paris, and Mafia in Rome.'

The coconuts and rum arrived. Igor poured a glass of rum into each coconut, swirled them around with the straws, and handed one to me. '*Na zdorovye,*' he toasted, raising his coconut, 'Good Health!' I replied with the same toast in Welsh, '*Iechyd da,*' Good Health! and took a long gulp of the nectar through the straw.

'Bleeding heck! This stuff is bloody strong. That's going straight to my head.' In fact, it was also reaching many other parts of me.

'It's good, yah?'

The crab arrived, steaming on a banana leaf. There was a heavy polished stone, to crack the claws open and we feasted on the white creamy flesh inside the shell. I'd never tasted anything as good before and the chips just added to the sense of yummy pleasure. 'You know how to whisk a girl away on a magic carpet, I'll tell you that,' I congratulated him, as I wiped the last of the peppery sauce from the banana leaf, with a solitary chip.

'Finish your drink and I'm going to teach you some gypsy dances that I learned from the Roma in Odessa.'

I slurped the last dregs of my coconut. The rum in it had now made me so light-headed, I felt like I could fly out to that Evening Star of mine on Igor's Enfield motorbike. I could have sworn it blinked out a code that signalled a bright future ahead for me, with this forbidden man who had swept me off my feet with crab, rum, coconut, and his gypsy stories.

Igor paid Kevin and we staggered out on to the sand in the dark, with the neon light from the bar illuminating the froth on the waves ahead of us. He pulled out a pair of earbuds, stuck one in my ear and the other in his. I saw the glow of his screen, as he scrolled through something, and then the sound of a fiddle began to play in my right ear.

'Listen to the music first and get the rhythm,' Igor clapped in time with the music, and soon I had the idea clapping along with him. He held me close and we moved together in time with the music as the violin played. First quickly, then slowly, as the tempo moved to a more romantic pace.

I could hear a violin in one ear and the sea in the other, as we shifted and swayed. I've no idea how long the track played for, but I didn't want it to stop. The rum had now taken full effect and when the music stopped, I dropped to the sandy floor and took Igor with me. What followed was unadulterated lust and passion in free fall, with the rum helping rid me of any doubts I might have about this bloke, who was bad news as far as my friends in Anjuna were concerned. Sometimes you have to follow your gut, and right now, it was only telling me one thing… that I had to have as much of Igor as I could take

And he seemed to be getting the same message about me. Our lovemaking continued for what seemed like hours. Kevin the Crab had long turned off his neon light and departed and we were still writhing in ecstasy on the sand, in darkness, as I groaned my way through with an insatiable desire for this man, who had literally carried me away beyond the Evening Star.

It was Igor who rolled off me finally, exhausted. 'You're unbelievable,' he groaned softly in my ear.

'I think it was the violin,' I whispered. 'What am I going to do with you?'

'Wrap me up and smuggle me into your shack so Melita

doesn't see,' he joked.

'If only such magic was possible. Perhaps a spell that would turn you into a toad that I could keep in my pocket?'

'No, we'd need a magic wand that would end this hate. There is a song in one of those Hollywood movies that says, 'they teach us to hate at seven or eight.' How true, ha?'

'Yes, that's about the time they started called me a gypo at school.'

'And they started calling me a Russian cripple. I had a twisted spine, caused by the radioactive dust from Chernobyl when I was in my mother's womb. There were a few kids like me, who were affected. I think I got off lightly.'

'And now you're okay?'

'Yes, mother worked hard to get me fixed up by a brilliant surgeon. I now have a lot of steel in my body, but my father still thinks of me as a freak. He's embarrassed having me as a son, when he is surrounded by all those tough guys.'

'You know, I like that little shuffle of yours. It marks you out as being different.'

'Ah, that's the nicest thing a girl has said to me.'

'Why do you stick with him? He traffics girls and treats people like dog shit.'

'My mother's last words to me before she died, was to be loyal to him. I don't know why, after all, she drank her life away thanks to him. Anyway, the gang is like my family.'

'Scorpion almost killed me, because he thought I told you about the plan to blow up the shack where your father was last week. Braganza told him he'd seen us together before the incident.'

'Ah yes, that policeman is taking money from my father

and from Scorpion, only we're paying him more. I overheard him telling my father about some plan to attack his men. They had set up the whole sham to trick Scorpion I'm sure.'

'We're doomed really, aren't we? You and me?'

'I can handle myself, I'm Ukrainian. I've got the big guns to fire off behind me. But you've got Scorpion and he won't be protecting you if he keeps seeing us together.'

'After what he did to me, I'm going to keep well away from the Beachboys.'

'You can't leave a gang when you want. It's like some crazy cult. We just have to be careful.'

'I was bullied at school and have learnt how to take care of myself, but this is a way different thing. Not quite like messing around in the playground.'

'You've got a wild spirit. I love it.'

'Let's do some more wild stuff again, heh?'

We both stripped off and ran into the sea to let the warm waters of the Arabian Sea sober us up and wash away the leftovers of our lovemaking. We swam towards my Evening Star, and I yelped for joy. Igor whooped back. If Kevin was asleep in the shack, he would have heard our shouts. Or perhaps he was deep in slumber after a hard day of cooking crabs.

We dried ourselves off in the warm night sea air and Igor kissed me, really tenderly. It was irresistible and we locked again into our lovemaking and repeated the whole thing over and over again, until we noticed an orange hue in the sky over the beach. In three hours Melita would be wanting me to go out selling jewellery with her.

We had to go.

On the journey back home, I held my arms around Igor tightly with the side of my face against his back, hearing the throb of the Enfield through his body. The warm night air blew through my wet hair and for those few minutes I suddenly felt like the happiest person on earth. None of the dangers that lay ahead seemed to matter. I was invincible anyway… wasn't I? A *gypo* Welsh girl from a council estate in Fishguard.

Melita kicked me out of bed the next morning, as I lay dreaming of Igor and myself drifting away, on a flower-laden canoe to paradise island in the distance. 'You total tart!' she sneered. 'Time to get real and get to work.'

'Oh Mel, my head is pounding like a blacksmith's hammer. Please! Just another half hour?'

'Come on, into the sea, that'll get you going.'

She tugged me by the arm and dragged me down to the waves and threw me into the water in my jammies, forcing me to swim against the foaming breakers that glistened in the morning sun. I was still exhausted from my exertions of the night before and only just managed to keep afloat, as the powerful waves crashed down on me.

Melita decided I'd had enough punishment and came to escort me back to shore, where we both lay on our backs, dripping in saltwater.

'Thanks Mel, that's a little better.'

'You still look terrible. What did you…?'

'Oh, it was all amazing, but my head. Do you have anything for pain?'

'Yes sure, but you've been drugged, gal. What did he give you?'

'Rum with coconut.'

'That's the oldest trick in the book out here, gal. You can't see what's in the coconut. That bastard spiked your drink and fucked you all over, literally.'

'And you know what? I had the greatest time of my life, ever.'

'Look, Ceri, can't you see it? Your darling lover is just another no-good slime ball Uke, just like his dad and all their beaver-busting gang mates. I don't want us to fall out over this stuff, but please just get some sense into that aching head of yours. Next thing you know he will be selling you to his dad, so the punters can bang you for a few hundred rupees a go.'

'You're being disgusting, Mel. I've never heard you talk like this,' I objected.

We went back to the shack and changed into dry clothes. Melita made me a cup of sweet tea, gave me a couple of Paracetamols, and we sat in silence looking out to sea. I waited for the painkillers to take effect. Melita felt she had pushed me hard enough on Igor, so chose to check up on her overnight messages.

Could she have been right about Igor? I couldn't see it. All that stuff about him loving gypsy music and being into their culture wasn't made up for me. I'm sure it wasn't. No, Melita was wrong. She hadn't experienced the warmth and the magnetism between us. How could she know?

We got our merch' together and made our way to our spot by the coconut palm. We were an hour later than normal and someone else had occupied our spot. It was Hari. 'Hey guys, I'm thinking you were taking the day off, so I came by to look

163

after the shop while the bosses were away.'

'Thanks, Hari.' I said.

'No problem. By the way look out for a Uke woman, she was asking about you.

Not in a very good mood. Very rude actually.'

I knew this was Karina. She must have heard from Jaz that I'd gone off with Igor the Uke and now she was on the warpath looking for me. You don't get over being kidnapped, held captive, and having your finger amputated too easily.

'She wants you to go over and see her as soon as possible. If you don't, she said, she'll send Scorpion after you. Ah ya ya, she was mad angry.'

'You'd better do as Hari says, Ceri, or you'll be in even hotter water. Tell her you were drugged. It started out as a laugh and a ride on a bike and then went from bad to worse. She'll take that and that will be the end of it,' advised Melita.

'No, I won't. I'm not going to make up some cock-and-bull story. It's just going to make things worse.'

'Is "cock and bull" what I think it is?' asked Hari.

'Not now Hari, I'll explain later,' Melita responded. 'Well, you better make yourself scarce, Ceri, before they come looking for you.'

'You know what, I've just about had enough of that tart and you're not helping much either.'

'Well you might as well know the truth. You're acting like a two-year-old.'

'I'm not going to stand here and take this shit from you.'

'Okay, then why don't you go and shack up with your lover boy?'

And that was it.

I had developed a new-found rage that made me want to defy Madam Karina. She didn't own me. Nobody did. The only place I could think of going now was St Anthony's with the orphans' project, where I could hang out like I did the night I came to Goa. I could just disappear there, until things were a little cooler. I loved the kids. We could play and I'd teach them hopscotch.

My phone rang. It was my mam. 'Hi, Ma.'

'*Cariad*, how's it with you?'

'Yeah, some good, some bad, when are you coming back?'

'Tidy, tidy, darling. Pune is lovely. I was wondering…'

She wasn't listening to me. This was always the precursor of something going wrong with Mam's life. It could be something difficult she wanted done. Or an excuse she wanted to convey to the school, or a neighbour.

'I've run a bit short of the spondulix again *Cariad* and wondered if you could send me some to the post office here.'

I don't think I'd ever heard anyone refer to money as 'spondulix' but my mam.

This was the last thing I wanted to do right now. 'Mam, I only wired you some cash a few days ago. I'm not making enough at the moment myself.'

'I just thought now you were in sales and all that, you'd be able to spare a few more quid for your old mam.'

'I work for charity Mam, it's fuck-all pay.'

'Don't swear at your mam, you know I've told you so many times.'

'How much do you want?'

'Oh, just a few thousand of the folding stuff.'

'That will clean me out completely.'

'I'll pay you back, *Cariad,* honest. As soon as I get back. The *Bhagwan* has put up his prices suddenly and I need to complete my meditation intensive by next week.' Then you'll have your nice peaceful Mam back to take you back home.'

She was pleading now over the phone. Just think how I felt. My own mam pleading for money from her fifteen-year-old daughter. It was like passing a beggar in the street, totally fit and healthy with an outstretched palm.' You would just pass him by, without a jot of sympathy.

I threw a few things in a bag when I got to the shack and didn't leave a note. I hadn't come with much and was intending to leave with even less. I softened towards my pleading Mam on the way to St Anthony's and stopped by the post office to send her a money order of a couple of thousand rupees, which wasn't much, but literally half of all the money I had left in my purse. I knew she would spend it easily on *ganja* or whatever they smoked out there in Pune, without a care for how much I'd slogged for it.

That was Mam and her generation of takers, who had lived off other people all their lives, and us lot were now having to suffer from the careless way they had spent their years. Just consuming, as though there was a huge unending store of everything they needed somewhere in the sky. They'd fucked our planet and our futures in their endless orgy of consumption.

When I got to St Anthony's I made for my old spot on the veranda I'd occupied a few weeks ago. I rolled out my *duree* and stretched out to make myself at home. I was back at square one, but free for the moment from the warring gangs and the people who were trying to rule my life. Father Michael was the first to notice me.

'Hello, couldn't keep away from us hah?'

'I've fallen out with my gang Father.' I told him. 'Just need some time away from them.'

'Yep, we all need that from time to time. Come in and have a *chai*. Tell me about your troubles, I'm good with them. I've had a few myself.'

He dispatched the children off to play and brought me a mug of steaming *chai*, which seemed to be constantly on the go somewhere inside the staff kitchen. He made himself comfortable on the floor.

'I was sixteen, about your age probably, when I announced to my parents that I wanted to be a priest. It was like I'd dropped a nuclear bomb. They wanted me to become a teacher or perhaps a civil servant and hey, you'll love this, my mates were most concerned that I'd never be able to have sex with the hottest convent girl they all lusted over.'

'And you never did?' I asked.

'That's another story for another time, but my most troubled time was just then. It was me versus my world. It's very lonely when you believe one thing and the rest of the universe is trying to convince you otherwise.'

'And you chose to do your own thing?'

'Yes, I put it down to prayer and asking God to give me strength.'

'You trying to convert me?'

'Not at all. You asked me how I overcame my darkness, so I told you. It's always worked.'

'But I don't believe in God and all that stuff.'

'Fair enough, but you must believe in something. What keeps you going? Why do you wake up in the morning?'

'I dunno, it's just instinct I suppose. You have to eat, so you do stuff to make that happen. You have urges so you act on them. That's me, plain and simple. What's wrong with that?'

'What's wrong is that, when you hit a dark patch, you've got nothing to turn to. If an animal can't find food or a mate, it just keeps on looking until it does. We're different. We think, and if we hit one of these periods of doubt and darkness, we need a higher purpose to help guide us.'

My cup had run dry. Michael offered me a refill. He poured the golden brown, milky, sugary liquid into my cup from high up, at arm's length. I sipped the sweet, hot liquid and began to think about what he'd said.

'I've never prayed. Always thought sad people prayed. No-hopers, people with fuck-all, sorry, not much to do.'

'Well, you don't have to recite anything to pray, although for some the chanting bit works.'

'Do I have to kneel? Not doing that.'

'No, you can sit right where you are, close your eyes and just ask whoever God might be to give you strength and to protect you. Want to try?'

'Yeh, okay. Close my eyes you said? I'd better turn my phone off.'

'Yes, take a deep breath in and breathe out slowly. Keep repeating that thought in your mind and then begin to think about how it feels to be looked after by that force out there. Think of all the times when you've been really happy, that helps a lot. Oh, and one final thing, open the palms of your hands upwards, that's very good, too.'

And then he was silent, and I went into a mental picture of happiness, undiluted pleasurable times, like when I was with

Igor, with Harpo, and when I nutted Alwyn Jones the PE teacher. It was soothing, like a bag of ice on an aching head. This God stuff looked like it was working on me. I must have fallen asleep after that, as when I opened my eyes it was getting dark. I'd been there for several hours, with the help of some force just straightening me out.

I felt calm and relieved. I was here on a veranda, outside a seventeenth-century church and not out on the beach at Anjuna. In fact, I wanted to be as far away from there as I could be. The sound of children chatting noisily in the refectory began to bring me right back to the present reality, that there were hungry mouths to be fed and that I should help out. I walked into the large room, where there must have been at least fifty children of all ages waiting at long wooden tables, all looking forward to their evening supper, which was the simplest meal of *dahl* and rice.

I offered to help and was told to ladle out spoonfuls of steaming brown rice onto banana leaves, which served as plates. Fifty eyes watched me go around with the serving spoon, but soon their attention was diverted by Father Michael, who came around with a ladle, pouring out the brown soupy *dahl*, which was to be the main nourishment that these kids would receive. They were joining hundreds of millions of people all over India who had eaten the same dish that day. *Dahl bhat*, the staple for the poor, the rich, and the middle classes.

The children watched and waited until everybody had been served, and then Michael said grace in Konkani and the eating frenzy began. In just a few minutes, the piles of rice and *dhal* on the banana leaves were gone and the children resumed their chatter.

There was no asking for more as there was none. The cook had saved me a plate of my own, which I ate with much joy, given that I hadn't eaten since the night before, when I sat down to eat peppered crab with Igor.

Before I went to sleep on the veranda there was something, I felt I had to do: write to Harpo.

'Shwti babe. I hate to start this email with saying I'm sorry, but it's true. I really am sorry that I have to call off our engagement. You see I've just fallen over totally bum over tit, for this Uke guy. I think I mentioned him in one of my previous emails. I'd hate to deceive you and keep you waiting for me babe, but this guy is the real thing. I can't get him outta my mind. Something has clicked in my head and after tonight I want him even more. Maybe if you were here, it would be different. I hope you find another wife very soon. I'm sure you will. Cariad.'

Chapter 17

Carnaval

P anjim was the capital of Goa. It had once occupied the status of a place of special splendour, the seat of the Portuguese mighty empire that spanned from the Americas to the East Indies. Apparently, this dossed-out city had once been described by Portuguese travellers as being 'better than Lisbon.'

Wherever you look in Panjim, there are rusty old cannons and other memorabilia that celebrated the Portuguese Navy and its control over its conquered islands in the Indian Ocean, as far away as the straits of Malacca. Many Portuguese became incredibly rich through the spice trade, which flowed from Goa out to Europe. They built grand houses and paved roads for their splendid carriages to support their extravagant lifestyle.

The Goan people today are the product of the union of Portuguese soldiers and local Indian women. The Goan people remained proud of their roots, well after the Portuguese left in 1962, which is when the Indian army marched into Goa and took control. But the Portuguese influence on the colony, in terms of relaxed attitudes towards dress and easy living, continued.

One of the customs that carried on was Carnaval, the

absolutely crazy partying that takes place before Lent. This is like Christmas without the turkey, but with sunshine and lots of semi-naked people in feathers, doing very suggestive dances, fuelled by masses of booze. The partying spills out everywhere onto the streets, accompanied by floats that are sponsored by local businesses and organisations like St Anthony's.

Father Michael saw Carnaval as one of the main events in the calendar to promote Goan culture. Whilst Hindus have their *holi*, the festival of colour, and Muslims observed *Eid*, for Goan Christians, Carnaval is the event that makes them stand out as the fun-loving people they believe they are. Carnaval is celebrated as a sense of pride in their belief that they are different to the other Indians, who have come to live in Goa from other parts of India.

I'd made the veranda my temporary hangout and Michael would stop by in the morning and bring me a hot sugary *chai*. I in turn, helped out with the children's meals and even in the school, teaching them cute phrases like, *How is the weather?* and *Would you like sugar in your tea?* I hadn't turned my phone on for days and had no intention of listening to endless messages from Igor, Melita, Karina, Jaz, or my mam. It was nice to shut out that world for now. Then on my third morning I was summoned to the planning meeting for the construction of the St Anthony's Carnaval float.

I'd remembered how to make things with paper and glue and found myself lumbered with the job of helping design the costume for King Momo. This was the mythical dude, who presided over the Carnaval. He was the benign old man, who gave his blessing for all the depravity to go on. Scorpion had been chosen as this year's King Momo, being the king of sex, drugs, and immorality. Not a choice that I relished, and I hoped he'd keep his hands to himself while he was King.

'But I've never designed anything in my life. All my clothes came from a cheapo Seconds shop in my town,' I protested to Father Michael.

'But you come from England where they have Kings and Queens, you're the best person for the job.'

'Wales, please, where we have a Prince that no one ever sees.'

'Well you know what I mean. The crown, the gown, that sort of thing. Scorpion loves to dress up. He'll love the idea of a personal dresser.'

'Yes, that's what I'm worried about.'

'Don't worry, you don't have to actually deal with him until the day. Use me as your mannequin. I'm about the same size.'

It's amazing how inventive you can be when you have to. I found a fluffy white bed cover that would be an excellent substitute for ermine, an old altar bearer's cassock, and I began to make a crown out of gold paper from the school art room. I had several goes at getting it right and the children acted as my consultants. They had far more ideas of what a King's crown should look like and applauded when I got Michael to don the whole outfit and parade up and down the room.

'Why Scorpion as Momo?' I asked Michael. 'If anyone, it should be you doing it.'

'Scorpion's got the money and the following, believe me. He's a sort of King for most of the youth around the parish. Ah, Melita was looking for you earlier. You should patch things up, now you're stronger.'

Melita was hanging around the veranda when I returned from the fitting. I didn't mind seeing her now.

'We've been trying to contact you for days. Everyone's worried sick that something might have happened to you,' she said, in a tone that seemed to express genuine concern. For once I didn't feel like snapping back a cynical reply. She held up her palm for me to return the high fives. Not a hug or embrace, so that was okay. I returned the gesture.

'So, what happens now?' she asked. 'I'd like you to come back with me to our shack. We're still your family and we want you back. Igor's been over every day wanting to know where you are. Look, I don't mind who you wish to go with, but I'd hate you to be sleeping rough out here for days on end. Where do you wash?'

'They've allowed me to use the children's toilets when they go to bed in the evenings. It's good of you to enquire after my personal hygiene.'

'Come back and let's go swimming every morning and evening.'

'I'm not going to sell any more of that tat, you and Hari can run that business on your own.'

'Okay, but you need some dosh to live, unless you sell your body.'

I didn't like that. 'If you think that's what I did with Igor, then let's end this conversation now.'

'No, I didn't mean it that way, honest,' she retreated.

'I'll help out here in the school and eat their *dhal bhat*. No harm in that.'

'Okay, fine, that's it then, Ceridwen.'

'That's the first time anyone's called me that.'

'It's what it says on your passport, which you carelessly left in the shack.' She handed me the document, looking at the picture inside. 'Nice piccy of you.'

'Thanks, what a twat I am!'

'Now if I said that, you'd bite my head off. Friends again hah?'

This time she held out her arms and we embraced. Not a fond holding hug, but a gentle meeting of our bosoms accompanied by a mutual patting of the back. I packed my plastic bag with the few things I had and told the kitchen staff that I'd be away for the rest of the day.

I'll admit it was good to be back on the beach again. That evening we went for a swim and Melita and I talked for hours sat outside our shack. I discovered how little we knew of each other and how much time we'd spent at the Sunset talking about nothing. Just rubbish. Now we were getting down to some serious things about ourselves, our fantasies, our fears.

'What sort of a name is Ceridwen anyway?' asked Melita.

'It's Welsh, a sort of combo word like most places in Wales. Literally it means Fair Poem. It sort of goes with my blonde hair.

'Mmm, interesting to be called a poem.' What about Melita?'

'Short for Carmelita. It's Spanish actually.'

'Do you get asked much about who you are? I mean, a Brummie accent, brown skin, and a name like Melita.'

'A lot. *Where are you from?* they ask, and I say *Brum*, and they say, *No, where are you really from?* and I feel like nutting them.'

175

'I get that about being called bloody English.' We laughed.

'Better get to bed now, it's Carnaval parade tomorrow. I'm dreading the moment I have to get Scorpion into that King's gown,' I sighed.

'No, he'll love it. The Boss loves to dress up. Jaz told me that he thinks Scorpion likes putting on women's clothes. I don't know what that actually means, but he seemed to be implying that he may bat for the other side, if you know what I mean.'

'Bet he's never told him that to his face.'

'No, he'd be history if he did.'

Chapter 18

Riot

The Carnaval was to start at Furtado House and process along the Mapusa Road, then turn left at the Happy Llama Café and proceed past St Anthony's, on its way to Sunset Point. There would be one hell of an all-night rave that would last well into the next day, until everyone was totally exhausted, or their livers had given up the fight.

All this would take place in the zoo of alcoholic excess, surrounded by some of the driest states in India.

By ten o'clock on Saturday morning, it seemed the entire community of Bencular parish and Anjuna had descended on Furtado House and spilled over along the Mapusa Road, leading to the beach. Traffic had been diverted away from the area and the only way you could get to Anjuna was on foot, or if you happened to be in an emergency vehicle.

The lead St Anthony's float was fronted by a huge golden mask, which must have been recycled from the year before. There were two large speakers, a sound system donated by Scorpion, and DJ Dab Danny was getting ready for his marathon session of music. Jaz had been over earlier to deposit several cases of rum, and two barrels of Kingfisher beer had been set up with a small bar. That was the booze sorted.

Scorpion arrived to take his role as King Momo with Karina, who I supposed was to be his queen. She had already dressed herself up in a long green dress and plaited her blonde hair. I had to take my hat off to Karina, she must have been the toughest woman I'd known. There was she, abducted recently, had her finger mutilated, having narrowly escaped with her life, and now looking like a queen in the most feminine costume, straight out of some posh dress shop. I kept my distance from them, until Father Michael sought me out from the crowd milling around the area.

'Salvador, you know Ceri, who has been working on your costume. She's going to fit you out.'

So, Scorpion was Salvador really. I had to suppress the urge to laugh out loud. I just did the girly thing of holding my hand to my mouth while the urge faded.

Scorpion noticed.

'Ah, yes we know each other. Good customer at the Sunset. How you doing girl?'

'Been busy with your gown, hope you like it. It took days to make and the children here have helped out, too. Come on children, let's help King Momo get dressed,' I shouted out to a couple of children hanging around the float. They were jumping up onto the trailer dancing around in seconds and I knew I'd be safe with Momo and the kids, with steely-eyed Karina eyeing me up suspiciously.

'Pass the cassock first, children,' I called out. 'Now, Salvador, please pass the cassock over your head. I have two sizes; in case this doesn't fit.' He didn't like me calling him Salvador. I guess it was like calling a bloke Ernest, after everyone had been calling him Spike or Biff or whatever.

178

'You can call me Scorpion now,' he allowed.

I smiled and nodded. 'Now it's time for the ermine coat, what do you think?'

'Mmm, I'd like a mirror to see myself,' he said, putting it on. 'Karina, does my bum look big in this, ha ha?' He twirled himself around like a model.

Karina was expressionless. 'My thought is that I like you better as plain normal Scorpion in jeans and T-shirt. You suddenly look like half man, half woman in that frocky cassock thing.'

'But it's the sense of occasion, Karina. Think of it, I'm saving centuries of our traditions.'

In fact, this idea of Carnaval was relatively new in Goa, mainly to ape the big Rio Carnival, with feathered dancers in thongs and wobbly buttocks to please the crowds. The Goa tourism guides plugged the event for weeks before it began and over the last fifty years it had grown huge.

Now we were climbing onto the Sunset float to join the start very soon.

Melita had found us. She jumped up on the float and clapped her hands in an expression of fake joy and everyone else did the same. Michael yelled, 'Three cheers for King Momo, hip hip…'

And the crowd responded three times, each time louder. A few of the other floats were now arriving to take up their position, drawn by rickety old tractors that were probably a hundred years old and shouldn't have been on the road. They belched out thick smoke, leaving a cloud of black smog for people to cough and splutter. Fortunately, we were in the front of the procession and didn't have to endure the deadly pollution.

'You look awesome, Melita, in that feathered outfit,' I complimented her, marvelling at the way this Brummie girl had transformed herself into a local Goan Carnaval dancer.

She posed for a selfie with me.

'You look terribly white, Ceri, up here. Let me put a bit of colour on your face and find you a headdress.' With a bit of help from Karina, who didn't say much to me, Melita painted something on my face and put a headband on me with ostrich feathers sticking vertically upwards. I thought I must have looked awful, but when Melita retook the selfie with us, I was quite pleased with my cattish face with whiskers, pug nose, and wide eyes. Not even Mam would have recognised me. I liked it this way.

A police jeep pushed through the crowd with Denzil Braganza and four tin- hatted constables all kitted out in their cleanest starched khaki, with *lathi* sticks protruding like spears over the top of the vehicles.

'Hail King Momo,' Braganza shouted to Scorpion, 'and of course the Queen. Have a good Fat Saturday.' One of his constables lifted a large plastic bucket of sweets on to the float. 'That should keep the crowds quiet. Hello girls, see you later, hah?'

The jeep then continued on its journey, presumably to check that the rest of the route had been kept clear, and Braganza winked back at Karina through his Ray-Bans, giving her a wave.

Jaz had hired a troupe of dancing girls from Panjim, who looked more like American cheerleaders with their frills, tinsel and short skirts than Carnaval dancers. They were to lead in front of the St Anthony's float, and he fussed over them, telling them exactly how far away from the float they had to be.

'Now girls, stay focused on your dancing and your moves and don't go off with any of the crowd. We're paying you to be part of this gig, right?'

They giggled. King Momo waved and blew kisses at them from on top of the float. He grabbed a megaphone and yelled, 'I declare the Anjuna Carnaval has begun, let's have fun.' Dab Danny gave him the thumbs up and began to pump out deafening beats from the two large speakers at the rear of the float. As the beat pounded all the way down the Mapusa Road, everyone standing around began to move with the rhythm, hips gyrating first, then the rest of their bodies.

The tinselled girls started well, but I wasn't sure how they'd keep up their enthusiastic moves for the hours that lay ahead. It's funny how Goans seemed to move their hips more than us. You could see the contrast in the crowd as the white *ferenghi* tourists awkwardly moved the top half of their bodies, whilst the locals were giving everything to the bottom half. Melita told me it was because Goans learned to dance from very young and didn't have hang-ups about moving the lower half of their bodies. I tried to do more of the Goan moves with the lower half of my body and shift my bum and pelvis side to side and to and fro. I felt like I was Rihanna. Bloody brilliant.

Our tractor started up happily, with a minimum of smoke, and began to inch forward. King Momo began to throw out sweets to the crowd and the excitement of getting something free drove them mad. Hands were stretched out in the air to catch a flying lollipop and some people began to scramble on

181

the ground to pick up the ones that were dropped.

As the procession continued, we seemed to gather more of a crowd, like hungry animals knowing there were some goodies to be had. In half an hour we came to our first stop, The Happy Llama café, where there was a reception committee on hand. They had their stalls of food and drink and a band to play us in.

Scorpion told Jaz to break open the rum and we began to fill up plastic glasses of beer. In minutes, hundreds of people were swilling back beer and neat rum, and I knew this was going to end in a riot. I hadn't touched a drink for days, but Melita poured me a beer and I couldn't resist the temptation any longer.

We continued on our journey, inching our way to St Anthony's, where Melita and I dropped off for a pee as the party continued. We'd picked up more of the Beachboys by then, who presumably were King Momo's bodyguards for the day. The tinsel girls took a rest, Karina lit a fag with her left hand and sat down to rest from the fatigue of waving and throwing sweets to the kids.

This was the last stop before Sunset Point, where the Carnaval would come to a halt and continue the Fat Saturday festivities into the night. More booze was piled on the float for the final run and we were joined by Roki, the smarmy journo, whom we'd met a few weeks earlier at the Sunset. I wasn't really sure about this boy. Was he just a smartarse spoiled rich kid or was he genuinely trying to expose corruption?

He kept taking a lot of pictures of Melita and I waving our hands around, and asking questions of everyone around him to the extent that he became a bit of a pain. Momo had to tell him to button it up, if he wanted to be on the float for much longer.

And then we were on the move again. In an hour we arrived at our final destination and I doubt there was a sober person anywhere around. The crowd was well behaved, and everyone seemed intent on enjoyment, both tourists and locals alike. Someone tried to touch up Melita, but she gave them a mouthful of abuse. My cat face didn't draw much attention and I was able to keep enjoying the day, without the constant harassment of being asked where I was from and having my picture taken.

There was a big central stage at Sunset Point and various local acts had been scheduled to appear. It started with a fanfare of colourful, traditional dancing which I think was Portuguese. It was quite unlike anything you'd see in India and I thought it was boring, like being back at school and forced to learn folk dancing.

Scorpion and Michael watched the dancers with pride, nodding all the time and looking so proud that their traditions were being preserved.

The sun had begun to set, and the sky turned a deep purple, as the orange ball began to get swallowed up by the sea. The crowd went silent, as if King Momo had instructed them to be quiet, and in the hushed murmurings of awe at nature's unfolding theatre, I heard the distinctive chant of *poongis*. There must have been at least two of them. It was the sound of the *Banjara* that I'd first heard from Harpo at St Non's in Wales, and then from Igor a few nights earlier. Now Igor and Hari came on, with their haunting music ringing all the way down Anjuna beach, just like Harpo's had done around the cliffs of St Non's. They were followed by gypsy dancers, presumably from Hari's family, who had come on stage to dance. They were dressed in their traditional elaborate flowing skirts and decked out in shiny ornaments that gleamed and glinted in the stage lights. They were young girls, most of them, and highly acrobatic. They leapt and literally flew across the stage as if gravity was not a problem.

Hari and Igor each took a position by a microphone on stage and the amplified music seemed to reach to heaven and all around the state.

Then the drummers came on with the pounding sound that made my ribcage vibrate in a way that felt electrified and transfixed to the music. People began to move to the rhythm of such awesome live music and Igor and Hari just swayed in time, lost in their own world. I was so proud of them both. How had they met? I had no idea they could play together.

Father Michael clapped in appreciation, but I was beginning to feel that this was about to end. The *Banjara* were untouchables and how long would it be before their pagan music at a Christian festival would be stopped? I noticed some of the Beachboys looking annoyed and beginning to move towards the stage. Braganza's *lathi*-carrying policemen had left the safety of their police jeep and also appeared to be intent on trying to stop the *Banjara* gypsy takeover.

'Bloody mother fuckers, who do they think they are?' I could hear Braganza shouting. 'Use your *lathis* to get them off the stage.'

'Someone's taken my wallet!' shouted another, 'Watch out

for those children, they're after your money.'

The Carnaval was beginning to descend into chaos, with hundreds of people still enjoying the gypsy music and the dancing, while others were intent on stopping it. There was a riot about to develop, all fuelled by booze, drugs and hate.

I had now jumped off our float and pushed my way towards the stage, dying to speak to Igor. As I pushed through, I could sense the tension rising and the pounding of the drums heightened the sense of trouble ahead. The sight of a lowly-caste *Banjara* in the limelight, making music with a foreigner, taking over this traditional Goan festival, was about to end the enjoyment and sense of fun. They had to be stopped. Jaz and two other Beachboys leapt on the stage, knocked over the microphone stands, and began attacking Hari initially with fists. The *poongis* went flying and the music stopped abruptly. Hari fought back and Igor tried to defend himself with a microphone stand. He swung it wildly holding the rod in both hands, then the heavy metal base of the stand struck Jaz on the head.

It felled him instantly.

I caught the horror on Igor's face, as he sensed he had connected a deadly blow on Jaz and saw him fall.

My heart stopped for a moment.

I knew what I was seeing would drive a hatchet right through the love that had developed between us.

Suddenly Vlad, accompanied by his hardman Aleks, was on the stage trying to defend Igor, who was about to be attacked with a knife by one of the Beachboys. Hari, now free of his attackers, fled the stage. I couldn't see Jaz now. He had not risen from the floor. The crowd began to jeer at the interruption. I managed to break free of the throng and pushed my way onto the already packed stage, suddenly feeling propelled by a renewed force to try and rescue Jaz. When I got up on the stage, one of the Beachboys was trying to revive Jaz, who lay motionless on the floor, a trickle of blood coming from his head.

Vlad and his thug Aleks dragged Igor away, disappearing into the crowd. Someone who said he was a doctor knelt over Jaz and tried to open his eyelids. 'Looks like major concussion,' he said, shaking his head. 'He needs to get to hospital.'

'Come on, Jaz!' I shouted into his ear. 'Hang on, hang on.' I tapped the side of his face, but the doctor pushed me away. 'That's not helping, please stand aside.' The doctor felt his pulse and kept shaking his head. 'Stand aside,' the doc repeated. 'His heart has stopped. I'm going to try and resuscitate him.'

He made several attempts to pump some life back into Jaz without success. 'Come on Jaz,' I kept saying to myself, 'Please try.' And then finally the doctor stood up, 'He's gone. I don't think there is much I can do now.'

'That fucking Uke is going to pay for this with his life!' yelled one of the Beachboys. 'Your lover boy, hah? How do you feel now, seeing one of our own killed by him?' No words came out. I watched in stunned silence.

I was tapped on the shoulder by Roki the journalist. 'Did you see what happened?' I just shrugged my shoulders. He took some pictures of Jaz with his phone. 'This was the guy from the Sunset Lounge, ya? Bit of a scoundrel?'

I shook my head and he took my picture.

Half an hour later, an ambulance did manage to get through with Braganza and some of his men. The medics checked Jaz's still, lifeless body and nodded their agreement with the doc that he was dead. They covered his body with a sheet and transferred him to a stretcher.

I stared dumbfounded at the shrouded profile of Jaz, like a death mask, just lying there. One moment he was with us, up to his roguish ways, and the next he was gone. Suddenly that white sheet separated life from death. It was the medics' final verdict that Jaz was no more.

'Clear this stage now, immediately!' shouted Braganza. 'This is now a crime scene.'

Karina had arrived and was behind me. I heard her say, 'I hope that's enough proof for you that your Uke lover is a murderer. All these people saw it. I hope one of the boys catches up with him and skins him alive.'

'He was just trying to defend himself. Jaz started it all,' I responded, knowing before I'd spoken that I was wasting my time defending Igor.

'You just don't see it do you. That boy is no different to his father. He tries to impress you to get into your knickers and you fall for it. They're all the same those guys. Don't risk your life anymore with him. We're not going to protect you anymore. We're going to get our revenge for Jaz, I can tell you now. Stay well away from him, or you will be dead as well.'

I turned around and left Karina without saying another word. I left the crowds behind and went back to my shack by the beach to be on my own. I knew Igor had not meant to kill Jaz. He was definitely not a murderer in my mind. But Jaz was dead, killed by my lover. In the court of rough beach gang justice, he was going to be enemy number one, and I would be guilty by association if I hung out with him.

Later that night my phone beeped, and I looked at the screen. There was a message from a mobile number.

'Darlingska, I love you...'

'Where R you? R U ok. I love you, too.'

'I'm not a murderer.'

'I know,' I texted back. 'You are going to be in great danger now. I'm sad that I can't see you.'

'We can find a way. I'm going away for a few days. Stay strong.

Part Three

Chapter 19

Father and son

J az was cremated the next day. The Beachboys wanted to make it quite a show, a real *tamasha*. His body, wrapped in white muslin, was carried on a stretcher by six smartly dressed Beachboys in black to the *ghats*, where the funeral pyres were lit. Scorpion's front man, was consumed by flames on his final journey. Karina, veiled in black, held Scorpion's hand as the flames and smoke arose to the heavens to the chants of '*Ram Ram Sita Ram.*' The local *Enquirer* ran Roki's exclusive article on the front page, about the brawl and the fatality. Ceri's picture was featured on the page with the caption, *British Girl Watches Horror of Carnaval.*

Braganza had quickly released the body from the hospital morgue, citing the cause of death as misadventure. He knew that neither one of the gangs was interested in the law delving further into their clandestine activities. Being in the pay of both of them, he had thought the incident was best kept out of the public eye. He knew, however, that scores would have to be settled, and that Jaz's death could be the start of a tit-for-tat war to get even.

Vlad decided that it might be a good idea to take Igor out of Goa for a few days, until the events of the Carnaval had cooled in people's memories. He drove across the state line to

Maharashtra that night in a Toyota pickup that was perfect for the distance to their destination in Bombay. Indians give a lot of respect to big foreign cars, as they are usually owned by the very rich or by big criminals, neither of whom are worth challenging.

The guard at the border almost stood to attention, opening up the barrier as he waved them on and Vlad smiled wryly. Igor retained his grimmest face throughout. He had just killed someone he hardly knew. The image of Jaz being struck and falling kept playing in his mind like a video that had got stuck in a loop. Even when he closed his eyes, the images flickered undiminished in his brain.

'There's no use you scowling at me that way,' Vlad countered to total silence from Igor. 'That dog was going to kill you, and you would have been the one in the morgue.' Still no response. They drove for another half hour while Igor pretended to sleep. The phone rang.

'*Da?*' growled Vlad. There was someone talking at the other end. Igor assumed it was Braganza. 'I don't fuckin' care what you think or what your boss wants. I pay you enough, don't I? The dickhead was going to stick a knife in my son! One less miserable cunt is nothing, another twenty to go. I'm not going to lose any sleep over him. Deal with it.' He hung up. Vlad pulled into a petrol station to get fuel for the gas-guzzling vehicle and left the cab to pay.

Igor pulled out his phone to send Ceri another message.

Father is taking me away for a few days to escape until things have settled down a bit. I'll miss you. I didn't mean to kill your guy by the way.

They continued their journey. 'Are you going to continue to ignore me for the rest of this journey, after I just saved your life?'

'I'm just ashamed that you are my father,' Igor finally answered.

'Ashamed? You ungrateful good-for-nothing boy. I work all my life to create a future for you and for what reason? You know what I feel like doing now? Ha?'

'Yes, kill me, stick electrodes on my genitals till I shout out in pain, break my ribs, something like that, I know. Like an animal, rather than a human being with a brain. My father is an animal.'

Igor couldn't believe what he was saying. The vitriol just began to spew out, as if someone had turned on a tap inside his brain. 'Do you have a brain or did Chernobyl fry it so bad, that now all you have is balls. Your brains are in your balls.'

And then it came. A left fist with Vlad's free hand that landed on Igor's right eye. He yelled out in pain, holding his right hand to protect his face from another blow. Vlad had slowed down, so Igor tried to open the passenger door and fall out of the moving vehicle, but Vlad braked immediately, locking the doors. He banged the plastic dashboard with his fist, which resounded with a thud, as it took the brunt of a blow that would have broken any man's jaw.

'You're going nowhere until I drive some sense into that skull of yours. This was all your mother's fault. I lost you to her.'

That comment was designed to stab right through Igor's heart and inflict the greatest pain. It succeeded. Igor couldn't counter with anything, as he absorbed the pain, taking a deep breath. Vlad continued on their journey through the night, banging his fist on some hard object in the car from time to time. In the dim reddish light of the cab, he would look at Igor, checking on the side of his face, which had begun to swell and puff up around his left eye. Despite his enormous rage, Vlad felt a tingle of remorse over attacking his son, although he felt that the boy needed a lesson and had deserved it.

When he saw the distinctive green cross of a pharmacy in the distance, he eased off on their speed as they passed by, noticing that it was open twenty-four hours. He reversed the truck and parked outside. 'Wake up, you've got to get that eye seen to.' At first Igor ignored him with his eyes closed. 'Come on, you don't want to lose an eye because of your stubbornness, do you?'

Vlad got out of the cab, opened the door on the passenger side, and pulled Igor out by the hand. Had it not been for the excruciating pain, Igor would have sat there to make his father continue to suffer the guilt of hitting him. He followed Vlad into the pharmacy, which had to be unlocked by speaking to the pharmacist through an intercom.

'Hello, Sir, ah ya, ya, that does look bad!' the pharmacist exclaimed from behind the counter.

'My son was attacked a few hours earlier and I need to have his eye looked at by a medically qualified person,' Vlad demanded.

'Oh Sir, very sorry to hear that. I can examine, I have many years of experience, plus I have a B.Pharm and six months internship in Bombay hospital.'

The pharmacist shone the torch from his mobile phone at Igor's face and asked him to open his right eye as much as he could. When he was satisfied, he put the phone away.

'Okay, your eye is fine, but you may need stitches, as there are quite deep cuts to your forehead. I can dress the wound now and give you painkillers, but you must go to a doctor in the morning.' He cleaned the wound, dressed it with sticking plaster and gave Igor some tablets to swallow. 'This will stop the pain and help you sleep. He should get to bed when you arrive at your destination. Are you going to the city?' Vlad nodded and pulled out a large amount of money without counting. He handed it to the man who seemed very pleased.

'Sir, I'm very sorry to say there are too many bad *gundas* around these days in my country and no police to catch them. Please excuse this unsatisfactory situation.'

Vlad thanked him with a grunt and walked outside, holding on to Igor who was by now quite unsteady on his feet. The pharmacist made a note of their number plate as they drove off into the night.

The pain had begun to ease, and Igor decided to continue to probe his father. 'Those Nepali girls. Look what you did to them. And my mother. She was dying while you couldn't care a fuck. Literally.'

'You're getting hysterical again. Calm down.'

'I'm really thirsty, do you have any water?'

'No, we'll have to stop again for some.'

They fell into silence briefly once more, until Igor broke it again.

'Father, you can't claim that all the things you do with those Nepali women, the brothels, the drugs, taking that woman's finger, the extortion, all those are just business?'

'You need to grow up son, all business is about some winning at the expense of others. The bigger the winners, the greater the losses and suffering on the other side. It's the law of the jungle, especially out here. Eat or be eaten.'

'I don't believe that. My experience here has been the reverse.'

'Your experience, really! Your experience has just landed you millimetres away from being killed or even worse, locked up in a stinking Indian jail for the rest of your life. Now shut up and keep quiet until we find a hotel.'

Vehicles were now passing with increasing frequency, as dawn began to break. Igor looked at his face in the mirror.

'Father?'

'What is it?'

'What made you take to crime or this type of business as you call it?' he asked, seizing the moment while he could play the vulnerable son to utilise the few precious hours while his father showed some remorse.

'You'll never understand what hunger means. That damned explosion in that Soviet reactor in Chernobyl was the ruin of our nation. Friends of mine lost their lives, saving us from total annihilation by turning off the deep underwater valves in radioactive water. But the nuclear fallout destroyed our agriculture and many towns and cities in the east of the country. Our economy collapsed. We had to do anything to survive. My night club *Secrets* was my baby. I set it up from scratch and I kept you and your mother with a great lifestyle thanks to its success.'

'But you were terrible to her when she was ill. Your rotten

trafficking business was more important than her.'

'As the Russian minority, we were treated as roadkill. We had to stand on our own feet. I look at life the way it is, I don't care what you think, but it's people like me that keep body and soul together. Even now, see, despite the fact that you hate what I do, you relied on me to come and save you from having one of those monkeys plunge a knife into you. Doesn't that prove my point?'

In all the years that Igor had known his father, this was the first time he had ever heard his father speak to him like an adult. It seemed that Vlad had always been embarrassed to have a son who was frail, and forever being seen by doctors. He had frequently only spoken to him through his mother.

Was it that he had just killed one of Vlad's enemies that had gained him some fatherly respect?

Or was he now not frightened to confront his father?

'Forget that English slut now, unless you too want to die,' warned Vlad. 'They will use her as bait to lure you into a trap. Believe me, I don't want to have to come and collect your body from the morgue. I can't keep on protecting you forever.'

'Don't worry about me. Anyway, she's trying to break away from the gang now.'

'Don't believe that. She's been groomed good and proper. Scorpion's not going to let her go.'

A brand-new hotel came into view, an America-style, neon-lit motel, perched right by the side of the road. Vlad pulled over. He booked two rooms, paying for them in bundles of dollars much to the manager's surprise. Igor spent the next day asleep in his own room.

Chapter 20

A walk on the wild side

Jaz's death and cremation were soon forgotten in the everyday life of Goa. He was just another member of a notorious gang. Bad things happened to people like him every day. The *Enquirer* would publish story after story about crime and how gang culture was destroying the place that had once been paradise on earth. None of this seemed to abate the insatiable appetite for lovers of sun, sea, sex, and cheap drugs in the party capital of India.

Tuesday evening before Lent would be the last evening that Goans would celebrate, before their more sober times ahead in the lead-up to Easter. The death of Jaz had shocked those in the community who had known the popular barman. Father Michael announced he would be taking confessions before Ash Wednesday, the first day of Lent.

There was a smattering of people waiting to see him, mostly regulars whom he'd once described in a sermon as 'repeat offenders.' Those who were addicted to committing the same misdemeanours, over and over again without any attempt to reform their lives. After hearing the last confession, Michael sat to reflect on his day for a few minutes. He was preparing to leave, when Scorpion arrived in the confessional.

Scorpion, like most other Goan Catholics, made Easter confession his annual act of contrition, when he would ask for forgiveness for all the terrible things he had done during the year. It's something he'd done since he was a child. It may have been superstition or just a mere Pavlovian act of wanting to cleanse himself, to feel better after the beatings he'd meted out, or the terror he had inflicted upon his enemies. Tonight, he had something else on his mind.

'Oh hello, Salvador, late evening at the office?' asked Father Michael.

'Bless me, Father...' asked Scorpion.

'Bless you, my son. Now I seem to remember you were in confession last year, about the same time?'

'Yes, yes. But now I'm troubled and I want to speak to you. I think I've sinned more by omission.'

'Yes, Salvador, that's a sin but I wouldn't call it a big one, hah? What is it now?'

'I've got a couple of things. Firstly, I want to confess one big one.'

'Yes?'

'I plotted to kill my enemy, the head Uke. I gave Denzil Braganza a lot of money to have him bumped off, but the plan failed.'

'Oh, that's serious, Salvador. You must show great remorse for a mortal sin like that. You know God's non-negotiable commandment, *Thou shall not kill.*'

'I do, Father, and I've been troubled by that a lot, but it was a sort of survival thing. I had to try and eliminate him, before he got me.'

'*Thou shall not kill,* Salvador. Remember the commandment.

It is quite unequivocal. Have you discussed this since with Denzil Braganza?'

'No, Father. He's not the sort to talk about such things. It just never happened.'

'Well you must try. I can only give you absolution if you promise to discuss your crime with him.'

'I'll try, Father.'

'You must. I know we are living in troubled, violent times. Last Saturday was so terrible, it has shocked us all.'

'There is something more that has been really troubling me.'

'Oh?'

'You know you've often spoken about the sins of Sodom and Gomorrah and how God punished their people with fire?'

'Yes.'

'I think I'm a homosexual.'

'You think you are?'

'I mean I am. I've had some physical contacts with men and it seems to come naturally to me. Girls just don't seem interesting. I know everyone would hate me for this, but I need to tell you as it's supposed to be a sin.'

'Thank you, Salvador, for confessing this. Yes, it is a sin. I'm not going to condemn you for it though. All I ask is that you pray to our Lord for the strength to suppress these urges. Being a leader of young men in our community is full of challenges and this is just one of them. I'm always here to help you talk about it, remember.'

'Thank you, Father.'

'I won't give you any penance for it, just a period of thoughtful reflection will do.'

Father Michael was troubled by this last confession. He'd had many people through his confessional since he'd been ordained a priest. Every now and then, one came along who was conflicted by his sexuality and Michael knew that there was very little that he could do about it. He also knew that his faithful came as repeat offenders, never really intending to change their ways, and it was just their Catholic guilt or need for talking therapy that brought them out once a year during Lent.

Scorpion would almost certainly stand to lose his position as gang leader of the Beachboys if there was any ambiguity about him being a one hundred per cent heterosexual male. Not only would he be ostracised by his own community, but the Ukes would take every opportunity to undermine and ridicule the Beachboys as being weak and effeminate.

Scorpion knew his secret was safe with Father Michael and he walked away feeling relieved that he had got a huge weight off his shoulders for another year.

Anjuna's stretch of sand was bounded on one side by the Arabian Sea and on the other by undulating dunes that shifted to and fro every year, with wind and weather changing the landscape. Once there were only dunes and a scattering of wooden boatbuilding businesses, but then in the sixties and seventies, tourism brought temporary huts and shacks to service the rapacious appetite of the newcomers.

The dunes stretched out inland for several hundred metres away from the beach, where there were only coconut palms and tufts of spiky grass which held the ecosystem together. Various species of wild sea birds used the area for nesting, as the dunes were an oasis of calm, undisturbed for most of the year.

Scorpion read a letter in the local *Enquirer* expressing disgust that the area had begun to be known as a place where gay men went for casual sex. The writer had described how he came upon two men in a 'compromising' position, while he was out for a walk amongst the dunes. Apparently, foreign men were going there expecting to meet young local men.

Scorpion thought about the idea for several days. If he was really gay, this would surely be a place to visit and find out once and for all. Apart from Father Michael, he had no one to consult or talk to about it and he kept awake at night thinking through the possibilities. Would he be caught by someone and discovered? Would he catch AIDS and die? And what if he enjoyed the encounter? What next?

He chose to visit the dunes on a Friday night, when Goans went for promenades on the beach until sunset. Scorpion decided he'd visit the dunes half an hour after the twilight began to fade and the birds in the dunes commenced their evening chorus. The bird chattering reached deafening proportions as darkness fell and they settled in for the night. A little shiver grabbed Scorpion, despite the warm evening air that blew over the dunes. He began to feel his stomach churn nervously about what he might be about to experience.

He noticed single men walking down below him, but none stopped to give any signal that he might act on. He was too afraid to approach anyone directly, for fear of having to talk to someone who was not on the lookout for gay sex. What if it happened to be someone from Inspector Denzil's constabulary, trying to trap people like him? He could face an extended jail sentence.

Two strangers appeared to meet up, exchange words, then

disappear somewhere in the dunes, and he was all alone again. The night had now become pitch black on a moonless evening. He waited. Then it occurred to him, that it was likely that no one would be able to see him in the dark, so he decided to take a stroll. It was not long after that a foreigner, a white man in shorts, walked up to him.

'You got a light, mate?' the man requested.

'No, no, sorry I don't smoke,' Scorpion stammered.

'Up for a bit of action then?' the man continued.

'I… I'm…' blurted Scorpion, not sure what to say.

'Okay, no worries, just looking, sure,' replied the stranger and walked away fast.

Scorpion realised too late that he'd just been propositioned.

He was scared.

Too scared to want to do anything about it. So, he continued to amble along in the dark, circumventing the perimeter of the dunes. He could hear music blaring out in the distance from one of the beach bars and was thinking of dropping into the bar and calling it a night on the dunes, when he noticed a man walking towards him, silhouetted by the lights from the beach bars. It was too dark to make absolutely sure who this stranger was, and anyway he relished the idea of an anonymous encounter.

'Hello, sir,' greeted the man, who sounded younger than Scorpion. The accent was foreign and in the dark, he would not have known who he was speaking to. The anonymity was exciting.

'Looking for a friend?' asked Scorpion, feeling a little more confident of himself. 'Hah sir, I be your friend for fifty rupees,' the young man responded.

'I pay you?' asked Scorpion to be sure.

'Yes sir, anything you want for fifty rupees. I have condom.'

'Oh okay, that's good, too.'

'Money first please, sir.'

Scorpion searched for a fifty-rupee note in his pocket. The man took his hand and led him away into the darkness of the dunes.

And that was it. Scorpion's first sexual encounter with his own sex. He walked back to the guest house, more confused than before he'd come out that evening.

Was it something he enjoyed? Probably not. Would he do it again? Almost certainly.

'Hello, Darlingski,' Karina greeted him. 'What have you been doing? You have sand all over you.'

'Oh yah, I took a snooze on the beach as it happens.'

'I can tell by your face, that you've been putting it about with one of those floozies from the Carnaval. There was a real hottie amongst them. The tall one with the big tits hah?'

'No way. Face like a pig.'

That was the beginning of a regular Friday encounter with the anonymous young man whom Scorpion met in the pitch-black night, by the southern perimeter of the dunes on the dot of ten-thirty. After every encounter his sense of guilt decreased and his confidence grew. Although he knew that it would destroy him and the Beachboys forever, he felt he could continue in this way for the foreseeable future.

It was helpful that he could share his burden with Father Michael and could trust his confidentiality, but where would it all end? He couldn't see this Friday night liaison ending soon. The anonymity seemed to suit both sides. The fifty rupees it cost him, seemed to make it a clinical transaction without any emotions or deep feelings. Who was this stranger anyway and was it just a commercial transaction for him?

Under the Indian criminal code, Section 377, same-sex liaison between consenting adults was defined as illegal. It was a law introduced by the British and was adhered to decades after Independence, despite the fact that homosexuality had been accepted in India for centuries, going by ancient sculptures and works of art from *Kujurao* to the *Karma Sutra*. The *Enquirer* published a feature in their Sunday Exclusive on the emerging gay-dating location in Anjuna and deplored the sexual depravity in the dunes right under the noses of the authorities. 'Is this another foreign import that we Goans have to live with?' the paper deplored.

The Minister for Tourism promised to stamp out the practice and ordered the police to take the strictest action against the 'miscreants introducing non-Indian ways to the country.' On the following Friday a group of constables, led by Denzil Braganza, descended on the dunes behind Anjuna to investigate the alleged sordid activities.

They came prepared with sniffer dogs and *lathis* at the ready, to winkle out the depravity that had infected their land.

Scorpion was at his usual secluded meeting place by the bottom of a large dune. His date knew where to find him. The place seemed unusually quiet tonight, with no signs of the usual window-shoppers that came by to check out what was on show. Then he thought he heard a dog whimper and some shuffling of feet in the soft sand.

The dark corner where he sat was suddenly punctuated by

flashlights and he decided that it was time to get up and leave. Suddenly there were people shouting, telling him to stop, and then a flashlight shone in his face, and a hand grabbed him from behind. '*Accha*, so this is where you hang out on your Friday nights hah?' Scorpion recognised the voice of Denzil Braganza.

'Hello, Den!'

'Don't Den me you fucking fag,' Braganza growled. The constables burst out laughing.

'Your friend, sir?' they guffawed.

'Shut up dammit, this shit burglar has nothing to do with me. 'You,' he shouted, grabbing Scorpion by the collar, 'What are you doing here in the dark?'

'I was just taking a walk.'

'You lying bastard, you're coming with me to the *Thanna*. I'll wring the truth out of you if it's the last thing I do!' Denzil threatened, putting Scorpion in handcuffs. 'You should be fucking ashamed of yourself, bringing shame on us Goans with your bumming ways.' He spat on him. 'I feel dirty even touching you.'

Scorpion kept silent, deciding that it was best for him to do so. He'd felt to be on equal terms with Braganza, he a gang leader and the latter a top cop, but now suddenly Scorpion felt subservient. They bundled him into a van and took him to the police station at Calangute, where he was held in a cell until Braganza came to visit him brandishing his *lathi*. Scorpion had never felt so ashamed of what had happened. The prospect of what lay in store with his gang and community made him want to lock himself away.

'Look I'm not going to torture you or hit you with this, I

just want you to confess to what goes on in those dunes on Friday nights. Just say and I'll let you go, I promise you, we're *bhai bhais* and I don't want to hurt you.'

'I go there to meet friends, just some people.' Scorpion was trembling.

'What, boyfriends like you?'

'Yes.'

'And you perform homosexual acts on each other, hah?'

'Yes,'

Scorpion nodded. 'Good, now we're getting somewhere. And you pay money for this?'

'Yes.'

'Does anyone know?'

'No.'

'Okay, do you know you've committed a serious offence according to the Indian Penal Code and I would normally have to charge you, but as you're from my church I'm going to let you go free with a caution, provided I have a chance to speak to Karina.'

'No way, man. That will be the end of everything.'

'It's that or the charge.'

'Look, you can tell Father Michael. I confessed my feelings to him last week. He knows.'

\'No, I want Karina to know. I think you know we have a thing going and she feels all guilty about it.'

'I also told Father Michael about my other sin.'

'What other sin?'

'That I paid you to bump off Vlad and how it went wrong.'

It took Braganza a couple of seconds for his expression to change from inquisitive to rage.

'You absolute bastard, you're going to regret this!' screamed Braganza. He left, storming out and keeping the prison door open.

A prison guard came in soon after, 'You're free to go now. We just need you to sign some paperwork before you go. Filth!' he spat at Scorpion.

Chapter 21

The *Enquirer*

The *Enquirer*, Goa's newspaper, was fervently supportive of a unique identity for the State. Although once a mighty publication of dozens of news-packed pages, it had struggled in recent times to stay afloat. The national dailies had begun to strangle it, threatening to rub it out of existence.

But its editor and his small team of committed journalists struggled on with the loyal base of Goans, who bought the paper daily to look at the world from their point of view. Roki Sequera had come to the paper fresh from the Jesuit College in Bombay. He had been covering weddings and funerals, the usual assignments that the editor gave young rookies. He also had to cover the late evening shifts, when the rest of the staff went home for the weekends.

Roki used this time on the Internet to look at some of the big stories of the day and marvel at the reportage of the world's press. He had come to the conclusion very early on that all media around the world catered specifically to their loyal audience rather than reporting the truth, whatever that might be. He longed to be given a scoop that would propel his name on a by-line around the world. Sadly, weddings and funerals didn't get him a mention, and no one outside the paper knew he even existed.

The phone rang at ten o'clock that Friday evening. Roki answered and heard a voice growl over the headset, 'This is the *thana* at Calangute. We're about to release a man, Salvador Fernandez, commonly known as Scorpion, the gang leader. He was apprehended on the Anjuna dunes at the homosexual meeting place, shortly after seven p.m. Six-foot-tall with a scar on his left cheek. Thought you should know.' The caller hung up.

Roki called the police station back, but no one knew who had called him, nor would they corroborate the story. Could this be his big chance? The fire at the Sunset Lounge had only made a few column inches and Jaz's murder had been buried in the mass of photos of the Carnaval. So far, Roki was just another journo looking for his big break. This was possibly something that would rock the foundations of the Goan establishment and would give him front-page prominence. He locked up the office on the first-floor building in Mapusa, got on his motorbike, and raced to the police station, nearly coming off at least a couple of times as he dodged cows, sleeping dogs, and potholes. In ten minutes he was pulling up to see a man on his mobile coming out of the police station, matching the description he'd been given. The man looked left, paused, then looked right and began to walk towards him.

Roki took out his phone and took a couple of pictures. 'Hey, what the fuck do you think you're doing?' the man objected.

'Scorpion?' asked Roki. 'Just wanted you to make a statement about your arrest this evening.'

'Get the fuck out of my way, man, before I punch your

head in.' Scorpion really meant it and Roki knew he did. This was one of the most notorious gang leaders Goa had known. The journalist backed away. They were still by the premises of the police station and a jeep was parked outside with a couple of men in it having a smoke, which made him believe he might have some scrap of protection.

Scorpion walked away. Roki did not follow. Instead he decided to go into the station. There was a constable at the desk. 'The guy who just came out of here. Was that the big *goonda* fellow?'

'Ha, ha, lucky bugger to be let off. Who're you, his bum chum?'

'No, I'm Press.'

'Go print that in your paper then, best way to bring down that villain. See how long he lasts when they know what he really does on Friday nights. He was picked up at seven p.m. tonight just by the dunes, brought here, and then the inspector let him go.'

'Is the inspector here, could I speak to him?'

'No, you won't get much out of him tonight. You'd better go now, we've got work to do.'

The paper was due to be printed at midnight. Roki still had time to file his story. He called his editor, who told him to delay the presses by half an hour, and by half past twelve that night, Roki had the first knockout by-line of his career. It was a front-page scoop on the gangster, who had been arrested on suspicion of cruising a famous gay scene at a time when the authorities were trying to clamp down on such depravities. Scorpion was pictured outside the police station in a grainy picture with the caption, 'Gang Leader in Gay Arrest.'

The news shook the fabric of Goan society at the weekend. If there was a hit parade of no-go areas in this Indo-Portuguese community, homosexuality would rank at the top with adultery, murder, and rape, and way above child abuse, theft, and violence towards women. The fact that one of their own was an accepted first-class thug, a drug dealer, and a pimp was all mildly excusable, but the discovery that he was suspected of being gay, was a totally disgusting sin that was only punishable by exclusion from the community. There was further analysis in the Sunday papers in the lead editorial mentioning the incident. 'Homosexuality, the disease of the West, has no place in fervent God-fearing Christian Goa,' it read. 'The bishop should pronounce on his explicit abhorrence to anyone taking part in such activities, to ensure that no other young impressionable minds decide to follow this abhorrent path.'

On Sunday evening Karina called Scorpion. 'Hey, the gang have called a meeting tonight to meet and discuss the way forward.'

'A meeting? Thought I called meetings.'

'I'm just the messenger. Come and meet your men. Six, on the beach opposite the Taj.'

Scorpion had been expecting the call. The news of his arrest was all over Goa and in the 'guilty until proven innocent' ferociously anti-gay world he lived in, he knew he had a big fight on his hands to defend his position as leader. Yes, he was stronger than most of the Beachboys and could have destroyed many of them in a clean fight, but the cards were stacked against him now. He'd stayed out of sight since his arrest, preferring to hide from taunts, stares from his neighbours, and any other forms of finger pointing.

The Beachboys had been his own invention. He had started the business up from the time Jaz ran a Rum-and-Coke cocktail bar at a roadside stall on the entrance to Anjuna.

Scorpion pimped a couple of Nepali women at the bar for men coming to Goa on cheap package holidays, throwing in the drugs for next to nothing. That was nearly a decade ago. He had since built up his current empire based on ruthless opportunism, taking every chance he could to exploit corrupt policemen and the burgeoning market for sex-and-drugs tourism.

He had thought long and hard about his current circumstances. He felt that he had the guile to survive and continue to run the Beachboys without loss of control. Karina would take charge in front, at least publicly, while he would lead with his iron fist from behind. None of them had the tenacity to work the system without him.

When Scorpion arrived at the beach a large group of Beachboys and Karina and her women had already assembled. They sat on the hull of a long-abandoned fishing boat, several plumes of cigarette smoke rising above their heads lit against the early evening light. They had been there for some time preparing for their meeting with Scorpion.

As he approached the assembly, a hush fell. Scorpion addressed the meeting, 'Hello, brothers and sisters,' he began confidently. No one acknowledged him. So, he continued. 'My thanks to Karina for calling this meeting today. We have a bit of a situation at the moment, with some false accusations about me being a fucking fag. Well, let me tell you, I'm going to be laying into Braganza big time with a lawyer, to bring a huge compensation case that will put him out of business forever. I'm so pleased that you came here this day.'

'They're laughing at us out there, boss,' Karina observed.

'I know, I know.' Scorpion clenched his right fist. 'But we're gonna return fire with fire, boys.'

'What, run a bar for fags?' shouted someone.

'Who said that?' Scorpion shot back. 'If any of you want to take me on, come up here and say something to my face, or just shut up and listen to my plans. I'm the guy who built this place up and no one's going to take it down without a fight.'

'We just want things to be normal again, boss,' Karina responded.

'They will be. Let me explain my plan of how we're going to do that.'

'The guys have been talking about what happened on Friday and we are concluding that you must stand aside as our leader.'

'What the fuck do you mean, stand aside?'

'Like, someone else take over from you. You are now damaged goods, I think you say, and the boys don't want to continue to be the laughing stock of Anjuna.'

'Damaged goods, hah…'

'No one wants to be led by a poofter!' shouted the same voice from the dark at the back.

'Who said that? Come up here and say that to me again, and I'll show you what a poofter can do to rearrange your face.' Scorpion paused to calm himself. 'I was just taking a walk through the dunes at sunset. I'm not charged with anything.'

'You know the law around here, *guilty until proved innocent.*'

'What do I have to do to prove to you that I'm not queer?'

'Bang one of the girls here, right now. Your moll, even, Karina?'

There was uproar. Karina shook her head. 'No, no need for that. He's never fucked me, boys, he's always been either too drunk, too busy, or too tired.'

Someone started handclapping, 'Go, go, go, fuck or go, go, go,' and Scorpion knew that his time as leader of Anjuna's most notorious gang was over. His plan to allow Karina to take notional control of things for a while was in tatters.

He should have known. The rules of the jungle would make his future tenure impossible.

Scorpion had been around for long enough to sense that he had lost the battle for control of his gang. There was little point in slugging it out and punishing someone to make a point. The once impregnable dam had developed cracks and it was only a matter of time before someone would take him down. He left quickly, and there was a cheer as he walked out. 'So, let's elect another leader,' he heard Karina say. 'I might be a woman, but I'm probably the only one who is going to help you beat those Ukes at their game.'

The blood rushed to Scorpion's brain and he felt his heart pumping hard, as he kept walking into the darkness of the night. It was as if someone had snatched his child and taken it over as theirs, because he was no longer a suitable father. He walked for hours aimlessly in the dark, his thoughts lurching from taking his life to taking someone else's, Braganza, or perhaps the head Uke Vlad. Scorpion was sure he could do a better job than the pathetic Bibi. He passed a row of parked cars, found one that was unlocked, and in under a minute had got it started.

He had chosen to leave Anjuna.

Back by the boat hull, Karina was making her leadership bid. 'I'm the best person for this job believe me. Why? Because I'm out for revenge to get back on Vlad for what he did to me. See this hand, I think you know what I mean. And then you know how I manipulate that crooked policeman Braganza. After the head I've given that son of a bitch, which is all on our secret camera which I personally salvaged from the fire at the Sunset, we'll have him eating out of the palm of our hand, hah? So whad'ya think?'

In the brief second of silence after Karina made her proposal, she nodded and confirmed, 'Okay guys, no objections, then I'm taking over. We're going to wage a war against those Ukes, a really nasty one, so prepare yourselves for a rough ride. I want Vlad, and that creepy son of his, to be quaking in their sandals at the news that the Beachboys have a new leader. So, what do we need to do to make them quake?'

'Strangle their blood line, the money they get from the extortion of the massage club owners,' someone shouted.

'Smash their dealers, the taxi drivers,' proposed another.

'Kidnap the son and cut off both fingers.'

'I like all those suggestions,' Karina smiled. 'But that will definitely make a big war happen a bit too soon.'

A young Nepali woman came to the front and stood waiting for her turn to speak. 'My idea is simple. We need to find a way to make government stop gangs buying and selling

Nepali girls like me. The Ukes make big money forcing us to fuck and they even sell our skin.' She pulled up her blouse, exposing the bruised parts of her upper body, where her skin had been harvested for markets in Mumbai. There were gasps from everyone.

Karina took advantage of the horrified reaction.

'I saw this with my own eyes when I was held by Vlad. Maya showed me her back. Such a terrible thing to do. I can't believe these people are from my country. I think I know how to begin,' she assured the Nepali woman. 'Let's get to work on the other ideas too. Let's make Vlad's life hell, here on Anjuna.'

Over the next few days the Beachboys went around the various known massage clubs and healing clinics in Anju scared of having their premises torched. Some had been given ultimatums by the Ukes to sell their premises, others were still paying protection money while knowing that they would be forced to sell out at some stage in the near future.

'If you guys want to save your businesses from these foreigners, then you're going to have to work together with our help,' was Karina's pitch, when she went visiting some of the Anjuna owners.

'But they're offering us money in cash,' a few owners objected, or words to that effect. 'How can we refuse, when we know our business will be destroyed or burnt down? These guys are animals.'

'Give me your CCTV images and my boys will form a protection force, to create an exclusion zone around this area once these dogs are identified.'

'And you'll be wanting your protection money, so what's the difference?'

'No, we want to drive them out, just like you. Can't you see, we have to work together to fight them. They're damaging our business as well.'

Karina was persuasive. Perhaps because she was a woman, she received a good hearing. In a few days her vigilante force of Beachboys was clearly visible. News had already got back to Vlad that the Beachboys were fighting back with Karina as their new leader. The fact that a woman was getting the better of Vlad was as bad for the morale of the Ukes, as being led by a gay gang leader had been for the opposition. Knife fights kept breaking out in the market. Braganza had to keep a patrol on constant duty while the shops stayed open during the day and early evening. Such was Karina's stranglehold on Braganza that she had managed to get him to give her personal protection from two armed policemen, while the confrontation continued.

But her greatest coup came early, when she contacted Roki Sequera to see if he would meet with Shakuntala, the Nepali girl, to hear her story about being trafficked into Goa and sold as a sex slave.

They met at the newspaper's office at Mapusa, a dusty old art deco building that had once been the beacon of hope for all Goans, with its curved glass windows and plush leather sofas. Now the windows were cracked, the sofas were dusty and scratched, but the editorial teams still beavered away on their computers preparing copy and advertising layouts.

Roki ordered two cups of *chai* for his guests and settled down with them on the sofas, which erupted in a cloud of dust. 'Tell me, Shakuntala, where were you born?'

'In village near border with India.'

'What age were you when you were taken across the border?'

'I fourteen, my friend same, same. We coming from school outside village. They took us and tied us up in truck with goats. I very scared.'

Over the next hour Shakuntala, in her faltering Hindi and English, told of her harrowing two-day trip in the back of a lorry with goats. They stopped by night to be given a drink and some bread and two nights later they were passed onto another truck, after some arguments about what they were worth.

Eventually they were housed in a brothel in Mumbai, where they were given a few days to rest and recuperate, after which the forced sex began. Initially only a few men, who paid top prices for their virginity, and then after a few weeks rising to an average twenty a day. They were told they would have to work their way to freedom.

The brothel appeared to be a clearing house for trafficked Nepali young women, and this was where Vlad first appeared and bought them for his Anjuna massage parlour and spa. The two Nepalis were by this stage traumatized. Vlad had to rest them for a few days, after which he offered them a deal, which entailed no more sex work in exchange for their skin.

Skin was being traded to support the burgeoning cosmetic surgery market in Mumbai and Vlad saw that the Nepali fair skin was worth a fortune in the right hands. He employed a specialist, who would come from Mumbai every week and take a layer from the girls' inner thigh, stomach, or back. These would then be used as grafts to beautify the rich and famous. Although the recovery from surgery was painful, the

219

girls preferred these procedures to the sex work, which brought them in contact with some highly unsavoury men.

Roki took notes and had a recorder on at the same time as back-up. The horror of what he had just heard was more than the young journalist could take, after having had to cover only Weddings and Engagements for weeks. He looked visibly sick, and had to excuse himself at least once, throwing up in the toilet next door. Karina sat calmly by the girl and held her hand as she told her story.

'Tell me,' Karina asked her when Roki was gone. 'I was freed that night of my captivity by someone. It was a man, he was Ukrainian, I know by the voice.'

'There was this guy. Always looking after us. He helped me to get out after I nearly died from cutting of my skin. He gave doctor money to give me medicine. But the bossman and his friend, they were really bad men.'

'Did you know his name?'

Shakuntala shook her head.

Roki filed his emotionally charged piece for review by the editor.

'I know this is a really big deal Roki, but I'm going to sit on it for a few days, until we can link it with something even bigger,' the editor told him.

'But I don't understand, how much bigger can this get?'

'We've got to wait until we can bag the really big fish, that crook Vlad. He's going to fall sooner or later like Scorpion, that's when we nail him properly with this story.'

The editor had killed Roki's hopes of global syndication and catapulting the *Enquirer* to international recognition. Trafficking women was fairly commonplace on the subcontinent, but the harvesting of the light-coloured skin of young Nepali girls was setting a new low, which the world needed to know about.

Chapter 22

The Bodega

In the meantime Scorpion was suffering the consequences of the publication of his temporary arrest on suspicion of soliciting sex from other men. Father Michael saw the piece and immediately contacted Scorpion. He called his number and unsurprisingly got no reply, so he sent him a message: *Hello, it's Michael here. There is much to talk about. Remember that's my job. Get strength from prayer.*

Michael's message was the first friendly contact Scorpion had received amidst a string of death threats and vile abuse. He replied, *Very shaken at the moment but thanks.*

Michael followed up with a call and this time Scorpion answered. 'Thanks for answering, I've been thinking of you a lot.'

'So has the rest of Goa, the hate mail I've received sets new standards in indecency.'

'God doesn't judge, and I'll be the last person to do that. Let's meet for a chat over *chai*. Don't come here, too many wagging tongues. The Bodega is usually quiet in the afternoons.'

The Bodega was a traditional café in an old colonial house with superb views of Panjim. The clientele were mainly middle-class Goans, who came to socialise with friends over an afternoon cup of tea and cake, continuing old fashioned customs that were witnessing a revival in recent times. The clients were dressed in Voguish casual clothing, bought from one of the fashionable outlets in Mumbai. Scorpion was not one to frequent anywhere as posh as this. He approached the establishment with the hesitancy of an intruder.

The patrons stared at Father Michael, and some recognised him and waved, but When Scorpion arrived, a hush descended. Normal conversations gave way to whisperings and stares directed at the café's latest visitor. His face had been in the newspapers only a few days earlier, making him instantly recognisable. Now it was as if he had grown multiple limbs like the goddess Durga and a trunk like Ganesh. The presence of a priest in a white cassock with him, just added to the intrigue. Michael overheard enough of the tittle tattle going around, while Scorpion's face morphed into a grim look of annoyance. The manager, busying herself with the minutiae of the day, noticed the change in the atmosphere in her establishment. Then suddenly Michael was standing up at the table and addressing the corner of the restaurant where he sat. It sounded like a sermon at St Anthony's..

'My friends, my brothers and my sisters, could I have your attention please?'

The murmuring stopped abruptly as Michael continued. 'My name is Father Michael and I'm the parish priest at St Anthony's.

Now all eyes were on him, with the occasional glance at Scorpion.

'We've just come here today to celebrate my friend's freedom. You see, he was wrongfully arrested the other day. It was a mistake. I suspect none of you have been locked away in a jail, but let me tell you, it is a terrible experience that none would like to go through. In my religion the Bible says, *Do not judge, or you, too, will be judged. For in the same way you judge others, you will be judged, and with the measure you use, it will be measured to you.* Some of you might be Christians, but whether you are or not, it doesn't matter. What it says, is simply please treat my friend here with respect as a human being and you will be blessed. That's it, end of sermon. Please enjoy your wonderful tea.' He sat down to pin-drop silence.

Michael was not an aggressive or pushy man and he was full of contradictions, but he was a long-term campaigner against injustice to fellow humans, usually by extracting a quote from the Bible. Scorpion, who had never had anyone stand up for him before in this way, felt like crawling under the table and disappearing.

'Now, Salvador, you must eat some of that cake and we can go and find Ethel who will order you some tea.'

Directly descended from a Portuguese family, the Bodega's owner, Ethel D'cruz, was one of the few who had not fled to Europe after the takeover of Goa by India in 1961. Now in her late seventies, Ethel always wore her dyed black hair up in a tight bun, revealing sharp features on her virtually wrinkle-free face. She was always dressed in the same dark-coloured skirt and white lace blouse when on duty, and was very much a part of the old-world attraction of the establishment. She described herself as a lapsed Catholic, and had never set foot in St Anthony's since Father Michael's tenure there as the parish priest.

'Good afternoon, Ethel,' Michael greeted her as she came over to the table. He knew that they weren't about to be evicted, as she had a little pad in her hand and a pencil.

'Good afternoon,' she welcomed the twosome with an air of cool efficiency. 'And what can I get you?'

'Oh, we're wondering about your velvety cakes,' asked Michael. 'They look so good and I've heard so much about them.'

'Certainly, two pieces and a pot of Nilgiri,' Ethel scribbled on her pad. 'We have not met, Father.' They shook hands. Scorpion continued to look down at the table, hoping that Ethel wasn't going to address him. 'And you sir, are the fellow that was in the papers?'

'Yes, that's me.' said Scorpion and they shook hands.

'I wasn't sure what the fuss was all about. Section 377 is a British law left over from colonial times. It should have no place in our Penal System,' Ethel declared.

'There you go.' said Michael, loud enough to be heard by the rest of those around him. 'There are good people amongst us.'

Ethel brought tea and her fabulous velvety cakes, which looked marvellous on a silver stand. 'Ethel you are a star,' Michael complimented her. Scorpion relaxed and even managed a smile when she poured the tea.

'Now I'll leave you two alone, but please let me know if you want anything else.' They were in a reasonably secluded corner of the room, which allowed them to conduct a conversation in private, despite the fact that Michael could sense that there were ears pinned back to try and catch their every word. A generously abundant money plant with trailing leaves provided additional cover.

Michael leaned over and asked Scorpion, 'So, how do you feel right now?'

'In short, terrible.'

'I've been thinking a lot about you.'

'Oh yeah?'

'I don't want to get too preachy or sanctimonious about things, but God has in a way saved you from a path which would not end well.'

'I built up that gang myself, from scratch.'

'But to do what? Make money from drugs, selling people's bodies, exploiting their vulnerabilities?'

'You're being very predictable. I was providing a service to the nation. Look at the hundreds of people that flocked to Anjuna because of it.'

'But can't you admit you damaged lives in the process, and that your way was not the best thing for us in the longer term? Someone out there would want a share of your action, the Ukes, the police or even one of your own upstarts like Jaz, and now Karina.'

'All a bunch of leaches.'

'Yes, and now thanks to the grace of God, you can put them all behind you. He has done you a favour. Did you ever sit back and think about the future of the Beachboys and how it might look in say… ten years, when you were middle aged, less strong and tough?'

'Never had time,' replied Scorpion and sat back in his chair. 'I can see where you're coming from, Father.'

'Michael, please call me Michael.'

'Michael, okay. But now I have nothing to achieve.'

'You do. You have many years ahead of you. Go to college. Do a business course or something and start up an honest profession. Do something that doesn't hurt people or exploit them, and you'll feel like a king.'

'I was a blooming *goonk* at school.'

'You're older now. You couldn't have built up your business, crooked though it is, if you were stupid. You've surely got a bit of loot stashed away under some mattress, so use it to get yourself a college education and if you've got a bit to spare, we could always use it here in the school.'

'Ah, never miss a trick do you, Michael.'

'What? No harm in asking and God will be more likely to answer your pleas for forgiveness, for those terrible things you've done.'

'Why don't you finish with Go in peace?'

'Eat your cake,' ordered Michael.

Part Four

Chapter 23

Take me away to the gypsies

After the disastrous end to the Carnaval, Melita and I had retreated to our shack by the beach. We were both in shock about the death of Jaz, but I was sure that Igor had not been responsible for his murder. The four-day celebrations had been cut short and Michael had called for his parishioners to pray for Jaz. We couldn't stop talking about him. We kept thinking about his presence, his regular attempts to get us drunk, and his terrible sense of humour, which he always thought was really funny. His short and tragic life made me feel so lucky to have been brought up in relative luxury, compared to Jaz's no-hoper wretched existence. I know my council estate in Fishguard was not exactly posh, but compared to most of the Beachboys our streets could have been paved with precious jewels. How amazing it was that, despite the slummy conditions he may have lived in, everyday Jaz came to the Sunset in a gleaming white shirt, starched and ironed to perfection.

After Jaz's speedy cremation, we heard about the misadventure verdict from the newspaper reports, which meant it was an accident. I hoped it was, because I'd have hated Igor to have been mixed up in a murder. I'm sure Karina, Melita, and the Beachboys believed that Igor had deliberately killed Jaz to impress his father Vlad. There couldn't be a more ridiculous suggestion. I knew Igor was the most loving, sensitive bloke I'd ever met. He was incapable of killing any living thing. Of course, any chance of us seeing each other would now become more dangerous than ever. The Beachboys would almost certainly be looking for revenge on Igor, and Vlad would assume that I'd be used as bait to lure his son into a trap. It was all too hard to get my head around. Then Hari came by on Monday morning, ready to commence his job as top salesman with a clean white T-shirt, the one saying '*Buy me and stop one*'. He was flanked by a couple of Beachboys with Karina.

'Here,' she said, 'you can have your top salesman back. I've just reminded him that he needs to do a little job for us.' For the first time I noticed that he wasn't his usual bouncy self. Hari and Igor played the *poongi* together, so I guessed they were marking his cards to find out his friend's whereabouts. The beach was filling up again with tourists, as if none of them had heard a thing about the horror of the weekend.

'Good morning,' he said dolefully. 'The show must go on, yes?'

'You okay Hari, you mourning with us?' Hari didn't reply.

However, I was so happy to see him again that I threw my arms around him and gave him a big hug. I didn't want to let him go. I sensed his discomfort. Of course, he was uncomfortable hugging a woman in public, let alone a *ferenghi* like me.

'Very sorry about the death of your friend Jaz, ya?' said Hari. 'It was accident I know.'

'Thank you, Hari, for saying that. I was sure it was,' I

replied, grateful that Hari agreed with me.

They don't like *Banjara* like me playing at Carnaval. We are too low, unclean people.'

'You play the *poongi* so well, Hari. How did you meet Igor?'

'Oh, he comes to our village many times to learn to play. Now he plays better than me.'

'It's so stupid really, all this hate that people hold of your people.'

'Yes. You know it's easy for my people to think that they are low, not good people. But now you show me that I can make money and be successful in your world. I know that you and your friend Melita are good people. It makes me very happy.'

'Is he hiding with you, Hari?'

'That I cannot say. But I know that woman Karina wants to know where he is. They have offered me much money to tell them.'

'Hari, I want to see Igor, too. Please tell him that, when you meet again. But I don't have any money to give you.'

Hari laughed. 'I'm just a poor Banjara living off rubbish on the beach. What do I know?'

Melita was observing our conversation and I caught her shaking her head at Hari from the corner of my eye. 'It is my life, I know what I'm doing,' I insisted, turning around to her. Hari was not going to get between us, so he went off in search of customers and I went to St Anthony's to continue my kitchen duties making *dhal bhat*.

Dhal-making was a simple, but mind-numbing activity. I had to chop lots of ginger into fine slices, grind several pods of turmeric together with tons of garlic, using a stone grinder, whilst squatting on the floor. As I sat pounding the mixture and pushing the stone back and forth, I began to think of Harpo. It didn't occur to me at the time, but he had a sense of freedom about the way he lived. No matter how often they sent him away for correction, he refused to change. I wanted to be like Harpo. You had to follow your heart, rather than do what others believed you should do.

Karina thought Igor was rotten to the core like all the other Ukes, but he was almost certainly the one who had freed her, otherwise she would have been rubbed out like all the others who got in Vlad's way. Igor was like Harpo and me, fighting against people who thought they knew better.

I ground the stone harder with the determination I felt to follow the message coming from deep inside me, which was to run away and live with the *Banjara* somewhere far away from here. Maybe it was the pungency of the garlic and ginger, which I had begun to make into a smooth paste, or the power of my emotions fighting to get through, but I began to do something I hadn't done much of in my life. I began to cry. I couldn't wipe my eyes because of the spices on my hands, so I just let the tears roll off my cheeks on to the grinding stone. I kept moving the mixture with the stone and the trickle turned into a flood and just kept coming.

The job was now done. I collected up the paste and put it into a large pan with a little oil to fry, before adding the lentils and water. Then I set the stove alight to boil the mixture for an hour. I dried my eyes with the sleeve of my T-shirt and sent a text to the last number I had for Igor, as the mixture heated up to boil under the yellow-blue flame of the gas cooker.

Darlingski, I want you to take me away to the gypsies. Xxxx

I sat on the kitchen floor, which was cooler than standing up, crossed my legs, closed my eyes, and took a few moments to think about all the nice things that could happen. Michael's tips on prayer were beginning to have an effect on me. I began to imagine this force out there which wasn't God or anything in particular, but definitely bigger than any of us.

Tomorrow was my birthday. What a nice treat it would be to spend the day with Igor, celebrating the sixteenth anniversary of my arriving on this planet earth. I imagined a fun-filled day, being carried off on his bike to that beautiful beach in South Goa, drinking rum and coconut water, crunching through mouthfuls of peppered crab, and making love on the beach, all day long. Perhaps in the daylight we could sneak behind Kevin's shack, or just fuck under water like the dolphins in Cardigan Bay. The thought of it all made me tingle all over. Then I heard the water bubbling and knew I had to get up and give it a stir before it burnt the bottom of the pan. Look, I was taking my new duties seriously.

I got up, gave the mixture a stir, and Michael came in to check on me, 'Ah you're back with us and learning to make *dhal.* Thank you, the children will be very grateful.'

'And thanks for teaching me to pray Michael. I've just been doing that while cooking.'

'Brilliant, and have your prayers been answered?'

'I don't know, I'll have to see. It's my big birthday tomorrow and I prayed that I might spend the day with my boyfriend, you know the one who people are accusing of killing Jaz.'

'Oh, well, nothing is too impossible when you pray, but sometimes God may not answer your prayers because he thinks it's better that way.'

'You think Igor is bad for me?'

'I can't judge that, only you can. I think you know the answers to all your doubts about him. Can I invite you to St Anthony's parish supper tonight? It's going to be the last bit of real fun before Lent? We've decided to come out of mourning for Jaz, just for tonight.'

I hesitated.

'Go on, treat yourself.' And I did.

I first helped serve supper for the children. Melita arrived when we were clearing away. The kids seemed to love my *dhal*. They dutifully mopped up every morsel of food on their banana leaves in silence before they resumed their chatter.

'Good day at the office then, Mel?' I asked.

'Interesting. Hari has developed a new sales technique, using his *poongi* to attract the punters. He's become a bit of a Pied Piper, enchanting people from all over Anjuna's beach to check him out. I just move in, with a bit of explanation of how his *Banjara* people need their help to maintain their craft traditions and improve their life.

'But the stuff is made in China!'

'I know, but it doesn't say so on any of the goods and we've doubled our sales in one day. People are just giving us money without even wanting the jewellery.'

'I hope you're coming to the end-of-Carnaval supper tonight?' I asked.

'No, I'm seeing someone tonight.'

'Now I am interested, who is he?'

'Oh, I can't say.'

'Go on Mel, tell your friend Ceri. You know it's good to share.'

'Promise not to tell?'

'On my word.'

'I've invited Roki over to the shack.'

'Oh, now that is progress.'

'He's taking the night off from his night shift at the paper. We're going to talk a bit of business, but you know how things work, we could get our shit together. Do you think you could delay your return?'

'How late? Midnight?'

'Cool,' Melita thanked me.

I was a bit surprised, but glad for her that she and Roki could become an item. I came to India to discover my gypsy roots, so Hari and I could have been a serious possibility. But here was I, hanging out with a Uke, who everyone thought was bad news. Funny how people get attracted to each other.

That evening in the church hall, there were long tables set out for up to a hundred people. Everyone had prepared a dish or dessert. There was a gift of beer and rum from the Beachboys on every table. Michael arrived late with Scorpion and came to sit next to me. The hall fell silent and I felt one of Michael's sermons coming on. Instead he clinked a glass and said, 'Hello everyone, nice to see this wonderful feast in front of us all. May I say grace?'

No one objected.

'Bless us, O Lord, and these thy gifts, which we are about to receive. And may we accept all those within our midst tonight like you would have taught us, that he who is without sin should cast the first stone. Bless you all.'

I really liked this priest and thought there should be more like him. Scorpion eased up. My strongest memory of Scorpion was when he tried to drown me in a bucket. Things had changed a bit since then and now I bucked up the courage. 'How you doing, Scorp?'

'Ah, mostly bad, but getting better by the day. How's things on the beach?'

'Same old, same old. I've been helping out here with the kids. Much more fun.'

Ethel from the Bodega, the last person I expected to see here, came over to say hello. 'Well said, Father. You know I was so impressed by your stand the other day at my place, that when I heard about tonight, I had to come. You may see some of my special red velvet cakes.'

Ethel was dressed in a simple black lace dress with pearls, probably real ones, unlike the fakes that we sold. She pulled up a chair and joined us at the table. There were a few Beachboys I recognised and one of them handed me a plastic glass of neat rum saying, 'A gift from your old friends.'

I wasn't going to turn it away, so I smiled and accepted.

'Come and join us at the other end of the table, there's more rum up there.'

The fire in Scorpion's eyes, which previously put me on edge seemed to have gone. Somehow I couldn't quite believe that this dude, who had nearly killed me, was now sat calmly at my table, eating Ethel's velvety cakes. 'So, Salvador,' asked Ethel, 'I'm sorry I just can't get to calling you Scorpion. What do you think of my cakes?'

'Quite good, but the rum is kind of drowning out the real taste.'

'Now this is just an idea, but I'd really like someone to help me run the Bodega. I'm getting on you know and I'd like a few days off now and then. You've run a great racket in the past, so how do you fancy helping me run a legal one.'

Scorpion looked at Ethel as if he hadn't quite understood her. 'Wadya think then, eh?' she prompted.

'Oh, I don't know, Ethel, running a drinking joint and knocking shop for punters is one thing... but a cake shop, really?'

'It's legal man. You need something within the law for a while. Something safe and out of the eye of the police.'

'I tell you what, I couldn't do front of house. Too many people know me. Behind the scenes, in the bakery could be better for me.'

'Well come around tomorrow. I could certainly do with a hand in the bakery.'

I never could see Scorpion kneading dough or decorating Ethel's velvety cakes with pink icing and wondered how his attempts to turn over a new leaf might work out. Scorpion made sure my plastic cup of rum was full and I don't know how I got home or with whom that night, but it was definitely well after midnight. Funny how this shack now felt like home, despite the dangers of two gangs after my blood. This was where I belonged, on the beach. Melita was fast asleep on her own, when I awoke the next morning with the mother of all hangovers.

I'd no idea what I'd been given to drink, but whatever it was, my head throbbed no matter what I did to get rid of the pain. My only consolation was my memory of the kindness that Michael and Ethel had shown towards Scorpion. It had given me back some faith in this tight-arsed, Catholic Goan community.

Chapter 24

A night with the gypsies

It looked like Melita had been stood up by Roki, which didn't surprise me. He didn't seem the sort that would be comfortable about cosying up to a girl like Melita, not with his strict traditions in dealings with us girls.

'He sent me a message at nine thirty last night, to say his mother was ill. What could I say?' The disappointment in Melita's voice was clear.

'Well… don't fret, just wish me Happy Birthday.'

'Birthday?'

'Yeh, sixteen.'

'Awesome, let's get you a cake at least.'

'I'd love one, with lemon icing. Where would you get one of those?'

'Hey, the Bodega of course.'

We were soon riding in a fut-fut up to the Bodega, where I asked Ethel if we could go into the bakery at the rear. There we were greeted by the new assistant baker, Scorpion. I blinked and Melita froze until he broke the ice. 'How do you like the white apron then? New leaf now, thanks to Ethel,' he joked.

'I'd like a cake with lemon icing, please, for our Ceri here. It's her sixteenth birthday.'

'No shit, now you two girls get a seat there by the window and I'll see what we can do.'

Scorpion emerged half an hour later with a cake, a candle too and a pot of glorious Nilgri, which beat Tetley hands down.

'Any wishes, Ceri?' inquired Melita.

'I'd wish I could be nicer to my mam.'

'What else?'

'World peace?'

'Come on now, be serious, tell.'

'I'd like to be with Igor tonight.'

'Wooah. Now don't wish for trouble. You know that's full of danger. The Beachboys are out to get your gigolo in revenge for what he did to Jaz. You've got to watch you don't get hurt in the crossfire.'

'I haven't seen him since the Carnaval, although I did get a couple of text messages.'

We jabbered away like ten-year-olds, until the Bodega filled up for the late afternoon session of teas and cakes and Ethel was having trouble finding everyone a table.

It was time to get back to our shack and watch the sunset on my very significant birthday.

We got back just before sunset. I dressed for the evening in my favourite red bikini bra top and a pair of white shorts, the ones I wore for Carnaval. Melita stayed with me like a good old friend, knowing that it would be rotten to be on my own on my birthday in a foreign land. She was being extra nice to me, which now on reflection must have been because she thought my lover was being targeted by the gang. Did she know something I didn't?

We sat at the steps of the shack, linked hands, and watched the sky darken to blood red. It amazed me how often we could watch that happen and never feel bored by a sunset, the passing of a day, and the anticipation of the night ahead. I felt rejected. Igor was never going to come for me on my birthday.

And then I heard the unmistakable throb of an Enfield motorbike parking up in the area behind our shack. I looked at Melita and she saw the joy in my face. I kissed her, saying, 'Thanks, *bach*.'

'Happy birthday, *Mnohaya lita*,' shouted Igor, as he came walking down the slope towards me, his arms flung open wide. We hugged. Really hard, as though fate was about to tear us apart forever. 'You look fantastic. Let's go.'

'Where are we going?' I asked.

'Somewhere special, to help you celebrate your birthday in a way that you will always remember.'

'I can't wait! Hey, what's up with that eye?'

'An argument with a door.'

He kick-started his chrome steed and I hopped on the back of this black beast that was going to take us to some place, I didn't know where. It could have been the edge of time for all I could care.

The evening's smoky haze, brought on by small fires lit to boil rice or cook a quick evening meal, filled the air as we passed through the tightly packed slum homes, where thousands of people lived cheek by jowl. Then the air cleared, and we were in open countryside. I held on to Igor with the side of my face resting on his back, my hair in full flight.

Now, nothing else seemed to matter. I had given up total

control of my life to this man, who most people said was best avoided. This was the guy accused of killing Jaz. Did he really have a hand in releasing Karina? Was he now under the command of his father and were we heading off somewhere for me to be sold into white slavery at the age of sixteen?

Right now, as we rode in total darkness along a rutted road, with the reassuring throb of the engine beating all through me, I felt an excitement like the day Harpo kidnapped me. The feel of the delicious warm air passing over my skin, my hair flying over my face like drunken moths, and my mind lost to this man leading me somewhere into the distance, all seemed like a dream. A lush dream. All that mattered was that Igor was with me. He had turned up to carry me away somewhere special on my birthday.

I saw the glow of campfires in the distance and the faint noise of people chanting, then children playing, all above the throb of the Enfield's engine. As we got closer, I noticed the tents and men in red turbans, women with their hands up in the air, dancing a traditional folk dance.

We drove into the gathering and a dozen stray dogs came up to us, barking to challenge our rude entry onto their territory. Igor switched off his engine and the dogs continued to bark, until a voice called out for them to stop. It was Hari who came to our rescue. He kicked one away, silencing them as they slunk off to lie by the campfire.

'Welcome to my family tribe,' he greeted us, and held his hands together in a *namasté* greeting. Then he garlanded us both with sweet-smelling, white jasmine, the most magical scent in the world. 'Tonight, we're celebrating the death of my grandfather.

'I'm sorry to hear that.'

'Oh no, we celebrate death, as it releases the soul. Tonight, we'll be singing songs, dancing and playing music to remember him.'

Hari wasn't wearing one of his T-shirts tonight. He wore a long black *kurta*, with trousers to match and red slippers. His traditional garb made him look quite tidy, as it did everybody else around me. It looked like a film set.

'That is fantastic luck for us,' Igor thanked Hari. 'It's Ceri's birthday and we're celebrating it by coming here. Sixteen, she is.'

'Oh! That's special?'

'Not in your tribe, I know,' laughed Igor. 'All married up and kids by then, eh?

'Oh yah, my wife is fifteen, that's her dancing over there.'

'Your wife?'

'Yah, I had to kidnap her from a tribe in the south and bring her here. She cried for months, but now it's okay. She likes me.'

'That's barbaric, Hari! I didn't know you were married,' I said, and there I was once thinking that we might get our stuff together.

'It's our culture, we've been doing it for many hundred years, and nothing's changed it. See how we live outside, under the stars. But come on now, we must take some drink and celebrate your birthday.'

'Have you any vodka?' asked Igor.

'No, tonight we have rum. I have some special foreign bottles that were smuggled over by the fishermen at Calangute.'

We sat down by the campfire, while someone continued playing the *poongi* and two girls danced in time with the music, which was played very fast, at a tempo I wouldn't even begin to describe. The elders talked, some seemingly arguing, while others laughing out loud. Hari poured out two polystyrene cups full of rum and handed them to us. It was good, smooth, and packed a punch, as I took the first few sips.

'This is the music that has been the basis of so much other music… Flamenco, Klezmer, Gypsy Jazz. It's been stolen by many great composers. These were the songs of the Romany people, who are directly related to these *Banjara*,' Igor explained, while listening and swaying to the music and the dancing. 'Don't you love it?'

I was lost in awe of everything going on around me, as if I'd suddenly discovered the origins of the human race and was trying to piece it all together and to make sense of everything I saw.

'Did your wife's parents come looking for her?' I suddenly asked Hari.

'Yes, they were very angry, because girls are worth more than boys. Girls are working hard on roads and buildings and cleaning beaches, picking up plastic. Boys just playing around with horses, mobile phones, or having fun. Some getting drunk every night.'

'So how did you manage to keep her?'

'Her parents asked her "You want to come back?" but she said no.'

'Why?'

'I think she became to like me.'

'How come? What did you do to make her like you?'

I played her *poongi* every day and made jokes. She began to laugh and stop crying. I think she liked me after that.'

'Do you love your wife Hari?' I asked.

'Love? What, like want to fuck her all the time?'

'Well not exactly, I mean, like, miss her when you're away working, or get worried if she is sick, that sort of thing.'

'Yes, yes, that sort of thing. Correct, I love her. I want her to have my children, too.'

'Hari,' said Igor, 'it's the same everywhere. I love Ceri in the same way.'

'So good then, why don't you kidnap her and take her away to your family?'

'It's not that easy man.'

'Why? Nice girl, Ceri, your father will be very happy.'

'Hari, we have a much more complicated system in our world, it'll take a lot to explain.'

'Okay, but think about the kidnapping idea, hah? It's good. You can get to know if you really love each other.'

'But we're already in love, at least I think so,' I said.

'And you think so too?' Hari asked Igor.

'Sure, I miss her very much and very much like to fuck her also. All those things.'

'So, let's have some more rum and drink to love!' cried Hari, calling out to his wife, who approached us shyly with the headdress of her sari covering her face. He said something to her and she removed it, but didn't make eye contact.

'See, this is the girl I love.' He appeared to translate it for her, and she laughed shyly.

'Hari has been telling us all about you and how he

247

kidnapped you,' I said, speaking to her while Hari translated. She laughed.

It was weird the way the four of us managed to talk the rest of the night, despite being worlds apart from where we came from. These were the people that Harpo had told me about. My dad was almost certainly eighty percent *Banjara,* like the gypsies in Europe and I would have half his genes. I felt that I had come home, and I don't think it was the rum in me making me feel that way. Like we Welsh think of *hiraeth* as a sense of longing for our home in Wales, I too had my *hiraeth* for the *Banjara* right here, in the middle of this night. It was pulling me stronger and stronger into their arms.

Hari's wife leaned over and stroked my cheek softly and then my bare arms. She hadn't met anyone white before, so I assume I was a novelty and she wanted to feel my skin. Was it plastic, stone, or even ivory? Her face showed surprise as it felt the same as hers, warm and smooth. We were the same, weren't we, just in a different skin?

'Like a bit of *bhang*?' invited Hari.

'What's that?'

'It's a sacred drink that we make. Better than rum or all these things you have which are poison. *Bhang* is drunk at special times when we worship our gods or now, tonight, when we celebrate the death of my grandfather. Try it, no headache, but very good feeling.'

'Sure man, I've done *bhang*, it's cool,' answered Igor, 'Let's do some *bhang*.'

Hari left us and brought back three terracotta cups of liquid. 'Your wife doesn't drink?' I asked.

'No, she won't.'

I didn't ask why. We took the cups and drank the sweet liquid slowly. It tasted a bit like a milk shake, nothing I'd rave about.

'Just wait,' said Igor. 'This is going to work its magic in a few minutes. You better be ready for the experience.'

Hari gave Igor a *poongi* and the two of them began to play. The other relatives applauded and began to clap. Hari's wife got up and began to dance and beckoned to me to do the same. Whatever was in the sweet milky drink was starting to take effect. I felt so good about where I was and the people around me. Dancing was the only way I knew I could express my elation. I followed her gyrating movements, noticing her belly button that had something shiny stuck in it.

But when the other women began singing, I imagined I knew their song and started singing along because it sounded like the song my mam used to sing, 'I will survive.' They thought I knew the song and clapped and came to hold my hand to join them. I continued to sing at the top of my voice and was probably horribly out of tune. Igor looked at me and rolled his eyes. I could have sworn I was Gloria Gaynor.

I danced, finding energy in my body I didn't know I even had, until I fell over with exhaustion and Igor came over to me. 'Drink some water now and then we must go.'

'Go where?' I asked. 'Aren't you going to kidnap me and take me away forever, Igor? Please, please, just you and me.'

'Hey, you guys,' shouted Hari, 'how do you say, *get a room*, hah? There is one right there under the stars, just follow that path.' He pointed out to the perimeter of the camp.

Igor took my hand and led me away towards the footpath, and the women began a shrill mouth wailing, warbling sound. Igor chuckled. 'That's the sound the women make at weddings, when the bride and her husband are going away for their first-night of sex.'

We followed the path lit by the dying glow of the campfire and came into a clearing of straw or hay that had been spread, probably for the horses or goats to sleep on. Igor dragged me down onto the ground. 'Let me kidnap you, yes?'

'Oh, alright then, where to?'

'It's a secret. You can't kidnap someone to somewhere she knows, otherwise she'll run away.'

'Okay, provided you're always as much fun as you are now and as good a lover. Let's take our clothes off and you can prove it again.'

Slowly we took each other's clothes off and spread them on the soft straw. He left on my jasmine necklace, and we were entwined as one. The sweet smell of the jasmine, mixed with Igor's own sweat and the earthy aroma of our straw bed, combined with the now peaking effects of the *bhang*. It provided a heady combination to our lovemaking. The music and the laughter in the distance added an extra accompaniment and I couldn't think of a better way to have celebrated my birthday.

Then over the sound of the music I became aware of the frightened screaming of an animal, which got louder and louder and more agitated. 'What's that?' I asked Igor.

'You don't want to know about that.'

'Tell me, I need to know.'

'It's a horse.'

'A horse? Making that sound? What are they doing to it?'

'Tying it down to the ground, I think,' said Igor sitting up and holding me to him.

'Igor, tell me the truth.'

'They are about to kill it. It's their custom when someone dies. Part of his soul stays with his possessions and they have to be burned with him.'

'Oh my God no, they can't do that. I must stop them. That poor horse did no one any harm!' I shouted, putting on my red bra top and slipping on my shorts, I ran down the path back towards the campsite.

'Hari, Hari, you can't do that to the horse, no, no, please!' I continued to yell, but my shouts were now being drowned out by the screams of the horse in the last throes of life, as it stuttered into a stillness. I went to hold it, but there was blood everywhere and Hari held me back.

'Please, this is our sacred custom, you can't make problems. Just think of my family.' He continued to hold me in a tight grip until Igor arrived. He released me for him to hang onto me. The heady effects of the *Bhang* had begun to diminish, and I began to feel tired and drained.

This was not a place I wanted to be anymore.

'Do you have to kill this poor animal?' asked Igor.

'It is no matter to you. Please leave now. She is making trouble here for me.'

'You're no better than those Ukes,' I shouted. It was the *Bhang* talking.

'Go, go!' Hari shouted angrily, in a way that really surprised me. Had I mocked a very delicate part of his culture.

'Take me home, Igor,' I demanded. He knew by my tone that if he refused, I would have just walked out into the night, in the direction of the brightest star in the sky that I believed would have eventually taken me back to Anjuna.

Igor tried to apologise to Hari, but Hari just turned his back. I just sulked away into the night.

'Hari, let's not fall out over this,' pleaded Igor. I heard Igor fire up his bike and come looking for me down the rutted track from the camp. He finally caught up. 'That was rude, Ceri. You cannot take some parts of a culture you like and piss on the things you don't. How do you suddenly become a judge?'

'They need to know that what they did was barbaric.'

'They kill hundreds of horses every day for meat, as well as cows and camels and many other animals. Is that okay?'

'That's 'cos they are being bred to be eaten, not that poor horse. All it did was serve its master. Anyway, let's go now, please.' I was speaking with a slur due to my tiredness and all I wanted was to go to bed and sleep for hours and hours. That *bhang* had been fun for a few hours, but now it didn't seem a great idea after all.

Igor shook his head. We argued for a while. Igor thought I was being insensitive. I said you couldn't compromise on certain things. Eventually my tiredness got the better of me and I got on behind him. We were soon speeding away from the camp. I think he was angry with me as he revved his engine harder, so we accelerated to quite a speed. The coconut trees whizzed past in a blur and I was sure Igor was trying to teach me a lesson for my outburst, which had probably ended his friendship with Hari. Perhaps he thought I'd ask him to slow down, but I wouldn't. I was not one to be scared by anyone.

We were soon passing more houses and little settlements by the roadside. Igor continued his full throttle assault on his old Enfield that struggled to respond uphill, but gave him the speed he desired on the downward descents. He kept swerving to avoid the potholes in the road and I had to hang on to him in case I lost my balance and came off the bike. This was the first time I'd seen his aggressive side, trying to exert his control on me. I'd seen boys play those sorts of tricks before.

We were coming down a steep dip in the road at quite a lick. I'd heard the sound of a barking dog from afar interrupting the sound of the Enfield's throbbing engine. The animals were a threat to cyclists and bikers along the main 66 road and I'd seen people coming off their two wheeled transport, caught out by the suddenness of these attacks. There was something that set the dogs off into a rage and I heard Igor ease off the throttle.

Then suddenly something hit us.

We were both flying into the air as the bike continued on its journey without us. We both flew in different directions. One of the last things I remember was seeing my favourite Evening Star pass by in slow motion up ahead, as I travelled in the air from the back of the bike. I hit something hard by the roadside and then was rolling over a few times, coming to rest in the verge.

The impact knocked me out cold.

Somewhere inside my mind I could see my brief life flashing by. I kept telling myself that I didn't want to die young. Thanks to Igor's recklessness and the antics of a pariah dog, I had been robbed of a great celebration on my sixteenth birthday.

Part Five

Chapter 25

The clean up

Igor lay on the ground unable to move his legs. He was in the middle of the road, the dog continued to bark and then scurried off somewhere into the darkness, content that it had managed to defeat its imaginary attacker. The Enfield lay on its side a few meters away with its rear red light still on. The smell of petrol from its tank spilled over onto the road and filled the air. Igor and Ceri both lay still for a while. Then Igor began to open his eyes and become aware of his surroundings. He thought he could hear voices disappearing into a car, the doors slam, and the car being driven off. Had someone stopped to check on them and then driven off to leave them to die?

Through the darkness he saw Ceri lying on her front on the verge, her arms splayed out. He had a searing pain in his right hip and a numbness in his lower body. 'Darlingska,' he moaned. There was no reply. He pulled out his phone from his shirt pocket to switch on the torchlight. He could see there was blood streaming out of her head on to her face, her mouth was bruised on the right side, and her arms and face looked scarred, from the effects of been thrown off the bike onto the road.

'Ceri, Darlingska, you okay?' But her limp body was

unresponsive. He felt like crying.

'Shit, oh fucking shit!' he swore, as he banged one fist on the ground. Then panic set in. Igor's life had been carefully controlled by his father Vlad, every step of the way since his mother's death. He was ill-prepared for dealing with emergencies on his own.

Igor was marooned, in pain, his mind was spinning out of control, and he was paralysed from the waist downwards. He could only think of one option now and that was to call his father, the one person that could save Ceri's life. He hated the idea of being rescued by his father, but knew of no one else to call.

He held his breath, then pushed the numbers on his phone.

It rang a number of times, it was two in the morning, then there was an answer,

'*Da*?'

'Father, it's Igor.'

'Igor? Do you know what time it is? Where are you?'

'I've had an accident. I've hurt myself. My bike is twisted.'

'No fuckin' way. Where?'

'About ten kilometres away on the 66 near Nuvem Church.'

'Can you walk?'

'I don't think so, but…'

'But what?'

'I think I may have killed someone, Father.'

'Holy shit! Who?'

'That girl from the Beachboys.'

'That fucking whore! You're such an idiot, son. Well, she's

258

better off dead. Wait where you are, and I'll get to you in ten minutes.'

Vlad rang off. Igor was already regretting making the call. Things had suddenly begun to go off in a bad direction for him. It wasn't just that he'd probably killed his girlfriend or even possibly his wife-to-be, he had capitulated full control of his predicament to his father, a decision he might forever regret.

The ten minutes seemed to last forever. Pinned down by his bike, unable to move, the rest of his life sped past him frame by frame. Flashes of Ceri's face drifted in and out of view, and he imagined her reaching out to grab him with her hands. Instead she lay lifeless on the road. Was it his recklessness that had killed her? He could remember reducing power and then there was this jolt that hit him in the chest and sent them both flying. And the sound of voices when he came to. Had he imagined them? He thought of the one person he had truly loved. He thought he heard his mother call out to him, but realised it was just his imagination.

All the while Igor lay by the roadside waiting, he kept the light of his mobile phone on so that drivers might see him, but none of the few passing vehicles stopped. There had been hijackings of trucks along this stretch of road at night. Most drivers would not stop for any stranger on the 66. Igor watched for oncoming vehicles then finally noticed the distinctive headlight profile of Vlad's Hyundai pickup truck. He waved his phone light and the vehicle skidded to a halt near him.

Vlad, bare chested in a pair of cotton shorts that he must have been sleeping in, jumped out of the cab. There was someone else in the cab with him. His father had a torch, which he flashed around to survey the accident scene and kept shaking his head. 'How could you do this, you dimwit of a son? *Ah ya, ya!*' Igor kept silent, like he had got used to doing for the last ten years since his mother's death.

Vlad felt Ceri's pulse. A lorry passed but didn't stop.

'Right, we've got to remove her before the police get here and start asking questions. The whore goes with you,' he ordered the guy in the truck. 'I'm going to wait for an ambulance. I think he's damaged his spine. Moving him will need special stretchers and medics.'

Aleks, the Uke with him, lifted Ceri and dumped her in the back of the truck as though she was a sack of rice or pulses. Then suddenly Igor thought he heard her cry out.

'Ceri, Ceri,' he groaned, but there was no reply. 'Ceri, Ceri!' he shouted again.

'Shut up,' said Vlad, 'the slut is dead.'

'No, I heard her crying out.'

'You're going crazy. Now lie still,' insisted his father.

In the headlights of the pickup truck, Vlad saw a thick cable across the road.

He flashed his torchlight at it and noticed it was tethered to a tree by the side of the road with a piece of card tied to the tree and the words *For Jaz* written in black marker pen. 'Fuck! You bastards will pay for this,' he shouted into the night for someone to hear. Vlad figured out instantly that Igor had fallen into a trip-wire set up by his enemies.

Someone must have tipped off his attackers that he would be travelling back down the 66.

'Right now, leave that whore somewhere where her friends

will pick her up,' Vlad ordered Aleks. 'Let those vermin get a taste of their own medicine.'

'Where is that boss? The Sunset Lounge?'

'Oh, just get rid of her whatever way you want. I don't know. Use your head, man.' And then Vlad lowered his voice and spoke in Aleks's ear, 'Just make sure you do a proper job, understand?' Aleks nodded.

'No, father, I want to be with her,' moaned Igor. 'She's still alive.'

'Shut up, you idiot, you need special help, or you may never walk again.'

'No, no, no,' Igor groaned, but his protests were drowned out as the truck started up and drove away into the night. Vlad next called a private doctor, explaining that his son had been in an accident and needed urgent help. He then began to take a closer look at his son with his flashlight.

'I'm going to remove your shoes,' he told him, undoing the laces on Igor's boots. 'Can you move your toes?'

'No, I can't feel anything down there at the moment.'

'Shit, of all the places for this to happen.'

They sat in silence for a while.

'Father, do you think this is punishment for all the bad things we've been doing?' asked Igor, breaking the silence.

'Punishment, by whom and for what? I'm only a businessman trying to make a living.'

'My God!'

'What are you talking about? Who's been putting these silly ideas into your brain? Not only are you screwing around with a railway station whore, but you're also believing in these ridiculous myths about Gods and punishment.'

'And you have been making money through the suffering of others.'

'Don't talk rubbish.'

They saw the blue flashing light in the distance approaching and knew help was at hand. Vlad waved his phone around until the ambulance could see him and Igor by the roadside.

'Be very careful in moving my son. He has damaged his spine. I will hold you personally responsible for any mishandling.'

The paramedics set to work, sliding Igor carefully on to the stretcher and giving him a shot of something to kill the pain. Igor closed his eyes, but before he drifted off he heard his father say, 'Don't blame me for all this, I'm still your father and will always be.'

Vlad rode with his son in the ambulance to the hospital. A mixture of anger and remorse ran through his mind. Had he failed to be a good father? Was this really all his own fault? Igor could end up in a wheelchair for the rest of his life, and Vlad didn't like the idea of being responsible for that. It was he who had decided to take on the Beachboys and burn down the Sunset Lounge. He had run the terror campaign on Anjuna, taking over with local businesses that were protected by the Beachboys.

The sorry state of his son could all be traced back to his own actions.

Part Six

Chapter 26

The big scoop

In the seventies Anjuna was a thriving fishing village, where fleets of wooden boats would go out late at night into the Arabian Sea and cast their nets, pulling in vast hauls of pomfret, tuna and sardines. Their catches were quickly snapped up early in the morning, when they were landed, by restaurants, hotels, and servants sent by middle-class households. Goans had a rapacious appetite for fish of every size and description.

Two decades later, the sea had been robbed of its fish by large trawlers that came from all over Asia to suck local fishermen's livelihood out of the ocean. The small boats had to venture further out to sea to catch anything at all. The Anjuna fishing fleet had now shrunk to less than half a dozen boats that returned most mornings around six, tired and exhausted after their night at sea.

Two men on a fishing boat, returning early in the morning, spotted Ceri's body floating out at sea. They hoisted her half-naked body out of the water and brought her back to shore. All she was wearing was her red bra top. They covered her up with a gunny sack to await the police. Denzil Braganza arrived an hour later to investigate. Despite the early hour, there was a small crowd assembled, and someone had found a pair of white shorts not far away, which they handed to the inspector.

Braganza recognised Ceri immediately and instructed his men to take the body away to the Panjim mortuary. Someone called Roki Sequera at the *Enquirer*. The young journalist had established a cadre of informers, who kept him plied with gossip and news of significant events happening in and around Anjuna. It was Roki, who by-lined the story the next day, that broke into the news around the world.

British girl found drowned on Goa beach.

The headlines screamed in Goa, all over India, and in the British press. It showed a picture of Ceri dancing on the Carnaval float with Melita, describing her as a popular 'good time girl'. This was the kind of sensational story that Roki had been looking for.

He felt that it would be the beginning of his brilliant career.

Inspector Braganza of the CID was quoted as saying, '*We are treating this as a case of drowning through excessive drinking and use of a local drug, Bhang. The girl had taken off her shorts to go and have a late-night swim which is becoming quite a popular sport these days with tourists. They are warned against this nightly pastime when there is no lifeguard cover. The sea is dangerous at this time of year and all must be careful.*'

The journalist had a gut feeling that there was more to Ceri's death than a simple case of drowning, and he was prepared to dig in for more on this story. He knew Ceri to be a feisty young woman and didn't think she'd have been so foolish as to swim on her own in the sea, at night, under the influence of whatever drug she'd taken.

Melita had kept calling Ceri, when she hadn't returned home that night. By midday there had been still no sign of her. Her mobile kept ringing without an answer all morning. Melita called St Anthony's to see if Ceri might have gone there to help with mealtime.

It was Father Michael who spoke to her.

'Melita, I've got bad news about Ceri.' There was a brief silence.

'Bad news?'

'She's dead. Drowned, they think.'

'What is this, Michael, some sort of joke?'

'No, Melita, I'm really sorry. Ceri is dead. This morning. They found her in the sea.'

'Oh God, no, not Ceri.' she yelled into the phone. 'Those bloody Ukes. I don't believe this. What happened, Michael? Tell me.'

'I don't know the details. The police have her body. She was drinking a lot last night, her birthday and all. I'm going to the mortuary now.'

'I'm coming with you, okay?'

Melita hung up. She couldn't come to terms with what she'd just heard. The idea that Ceri might not be alive was the last thing that would have occurred to her the night before, when she was whisked away on a motorbike. Ceri was hard, resilient, and, as she kept reminding Melita, came from the toughest council estate in Fishguard. An early death was not a fate she deserved.

Melita met Michael outside the hospital which housed the

mortuary. The priest hugged her.

'Very sorry for your loss, Mel,' he said gently.

For a minute they were silent, then Melita spoke. 'They say she drowned after excessive drinking, but I think they're covering up something worse. She went out with her Uke boyfriend, he was with her, and I'm sure would have brought her home. I know both the Ukes and the Beachboys disapproved of the relationship, especially after Jaz's death. It just doesn't look right.'

'Oh?' whispered Michael. 'That would not surprise me.'

'Ceri was a good strong swimmer. I've seen her in the sea every day, cutting through waves several metres high. Just can't believe she'd drown, no matter how drunk she was.'

When they asked to see Ceri's body the desk clerk said that they would have to call back the next morning, as the mortuary staff had gone home for the day. The entrance was full of people, mostly relatives and friends of the dead, who sat or stood in quiet conversations, waiting for news of loved ones.

Melita began to shout at the clerk, who was resolute in his adherence to the rules that forbade them access. 'I want to see my friend now. I've come all the way from Anjuna to see her. Now please let me in.'

Father Michael looked the clerk in the eye. 'Please call the duty inspector, tell him it's me, Father Michael from St Anthony's church.' They waited.

That triggered a response and the clerk disappeared to another part of the room and called a number.

Minutes later Braganza arrived.

'Hello, Father, you're lucky to get me, I was just about to

leave. You can understand that it's been a busy day since six o'clock this morning.'

'Denzil, Melita here wants to see her friend and identify the body. She's sure there must have been some mistaken identity.' Melita nodded.

'I can assure you, that I'm one hundred percent certain that it's her.'

'Sure, but please allow a close friend a chance to say goodbye. It was all so sudden.'

'Okay, but it's to be a quick look and you can't touch the body in case you contaminate any evidence.'

'Thank you, God bless you,' Michael said.

The mortuary room, tiled in white, was cold compared to the twenty-five degrees of humid evening heat outside. The floor was wet and slippery. One of the neon lights had a stubborn flicker, which interrupted the bluish haze of the room. The clerk opened cabinet 23 and pulled back the zip of the bag that contained Ceri. Both her eyes and mouth were wide open. Melita gave out a sob and held her hands to her face.

'Are we satisfied now with the identification?'

'Yes, that's her. Oh Ceri! Her left eye, it's all bruised and swollen. And her face is scarred down one side. Can I touch her?'

'Thank you, Madam, for the identification. Unfortunately, I cannot allow you to touch the body, as it is still due for further post-mortem examination.'

'I thought you said she died from drowning?'

'The preliminary analysis is death by drowning, we believe, due to a lethal cocktail of alcohol and drugs.'

'She was such a good swimmer. She's been in the sea since she was two. I need to see more of her.'

Melita was quick. She unzipped the rest of the covering before the clerk could stop her, then yelled in horror, 'What a fucking mess!

'Madam, I'm very sorry for you,' the clerk said.

'Her whole body is covered in bruises. She's been beaten.'

'It has been noted that there is some injury to the body that may have occurred.'

'Look, her eyes and mouth are open. If that's not a sign of a violent death, I don't know what is?'

'Not necessarily, the same thing can happen by drowning, madam.'

'That is total crap. Can't we get a thorough, independent post-mortem.'

'Madam, it is not possible.'

'Inspector Denzil, this is highly suspicious,' Michael objected. 'How could anyone accept the verdict of drowning? You should ensure a full autopsy is carried out as soon as possible. Can I have your assurance?'

'Yes, Father, but I will need the approval of my commanding officer.'

'If I can help to persuade him, let me know,' offered Michael.

'I want to touch her, my sweet girl,' moaned Melita.

'I'm very sorry but that is not possible, we can't contaminate any evidence we may have on the body,' the Inspector refused.

'But she's my close friend, you can't keep me from her.'

'I'm sorry… Really.'

'Sod you, sod this country, sod the whole sodding lot of you.' Melita began to sob, a slow pent-up whimpering and then a full-flooded howl of despair.

In the neon-lit, pale, lifeless body of her sixteen-year-old friend, she saw the weeks they'd been together, their wheeling and dealing on the beach, how cleverly Ceri had dealt with Braganza's relentless pestering, and the countless times they'd staggered back from the Sunset Lounge, giggling and laughing like ten-year-olds.

Michael knew that Braganza would not allow any further interference with Ceri's corpse, so he held Melita's hand, and led her away out of the mortuary.

'Have you interviewed any of the Ukes yet?' she asked Braganza as she walked away. 'She was last with Igor, the young one. I saw them go off for the night on his bike.'

'No, no he is under sedation and probably won't walk again. I have made a few preliminary enquiries,' Braganza replied. 'He was nowhere near Anjuna last night. He left her with the *Banjaras* and went off in a huff. They had some sort of tiff. I have my list of suspects. Please leave this to the police now and we will get back to you when you're needed to give any evidence.'

They walked out into the cooler evening air and Michael hailed a motor rickshaw. 'Let me take you back to Anjuna. You can stay with us at St Anthony's if you'd prefer.'

'I'm fine. I'd rather be on my own. Funny isn't it, Michael, how we miss people when they've gone and take them for granted when they're here.'

Melita returned to her shack by the beach. It seemed darker than usual. This temporary abode, which only stayed up for six months from October to March every year, had been their home. That evening she spent time staring out to sea, trying to make sense of what had happened. She had no way of contacting Igor. He had been the last person who may have been with Ceri. She'd asked Karina to try to find Igor, but his father was keeping him at a secret location. Maybe he'd been moved to Bombay to a private clinic. No one other than Braganza appeared to know much about him.

She gazed at Ceri's favourite Evening Star, as though her friend was sitting beside her.

Ceri's stories flooded through her mind.

The story about her nutting the PE teacher because he tried it on, about Harpo and the Wolves, and how she had never failed to accept any dare posed by her classmates. Melita had an image of Ceri tanned, bursting with joy in the tropical sun, reading a trashy magazine or gazing at a heavenly carpet of stars. They'd play a game of trying to count the stars before they fell asleep. Tonight, Melita didn't make it to twenty before her eyelids closed, heavy with exhaustion.

The next morning she awoke with Michael knocking on her door excitedly, waving a copy of the *Enquirer*. 'Look, it says they're reopening the enquiry now. The report says that the post-mortem found several hundred milligrams of alcohol, significant levels of cocaine, plus evidence of sex and brutality.'

'Let me have a look at that.' Melita grabbed the paper. There was her friend, on the front page, in a picture taken a few days earlier, looking every bit the party girl at one of Jaz's all-night raves, dancing with Melita.

'She looks very happy.'

'Just look at her! That beautiful girl.'

The tabloids in Britain were full of outrage at the latest news from Goa. One shrieked:

Ceri might have been raped. It is becoming clear that Goa has become a lawless state, where murder, drugs and prostitution go unchecked, even as thousands flee Britain for the sun and cheap holidays.

The Indian Minister for Tourism commented on TV that women should stay at home after dark to avoid unsavoury elements attacking them. There was immediate condemnation of his remarks by women's groups, forcing him to retract his comments. He was accused of giving oxygen to the rapists and misogynists. The minster was censured and shortly after removed from office.

The Russian Ambassador protested in a letter to the Hindu newspaper, saying that he would now have to give an instruction to all Russian women to avoid the restaurants, bars, casinos and nightlife in the evenings. For a few days, Goa's reputation as a place of fun and relaxation was in meltdown. Rumours abounded about the gang culture and the fights over territory by Russian Mafia. The world's press descended on this former Portuguese colony to interview shopkeepers, fishermen, and Braganza. Roki's insights into Ceri's life on Anjuna and the legendary Sunset Lounge were featured all over the world. The *Enquirer* collected a healthy income from the syndication rights for his work.

'This story is going to rock and roll, Roki *bhai*,' his editor congratulated him. 'I want you to suck up all you can find on this case and give us regular updates. Find her friends, go to that church to talk to Father Michael, and find out more about the Ukrainian boyfriend. You're a smart guy, now go and really put us on the map. It might stop our owners from shutting us down.'

Chapter 27

Just get it done

Braganza's boss, the Chief Inspector, phoned later on the day after the *Enquirer* had broken the story about the new post-mortem. 'Hello, Denzil, we've got to clear this one up pretty damn quick, you know what I'm saying? You've heard the *tamasha* going on. No ifs, buts, just results hah?'

'Leave it with me, Sir. Consider it done. I already have the suspect in mind.' Braganza put the phone down and held a quick briefing with his four constables.

'Now look, men, we have a very serious situation. That *ferenghi* girl appears to have been raped and murdered, judging from the latest post-mortem. We need you to go out there and bring in some suspects. Not tomorrow, but today, tonight, *accha*? Find out what the *gundas* are saying. Squeeze, threaten, do what you can.' The men nodded. There were scores to settle. This was the time to reach out to informants and bring someone in. One of the men put his hand up to speak.

'Okay, Fatty, what is it? Better be good.'

'Sir, there is one fellow who was getting very pally pally with the victim and her friend. He is a *Banjara*, and I know you may be thinking that's impossible, but I think she was encouraging this smelly chap.'

'Nothing surprises me about these *ferenghi* kids. Apparently, she visited the *Banjara* camp on the night of the incident. These kids just don't seem to have any morals or common sense. Imagine them with a low-life gypsy. Bring him in, I'll have a word with the sister-fucker.'

Inspector Braganza was a product of the Jesuits at St Xavier's in Panjim, who had no patience for dull boys who didn't want to learn. They doled out the cane liberally for seemingly innocuous infractions, from not knowing one's multiplication tables to talking out of turn. Once a teacher threw a wooden blackboard cleaner at Denzil, which hit him just below the left eye and rendered him half blind. Despite the tough life, he lasted the course and left at sixteen, barely passing his School Leaving Certificate.

His stepfather was a drunk, who thought nothing about giving the boy a regular slapping. He told Denzil he had three months to find a job when he left school. The police seemed an obvious employer of choice as he had no academic abilities, but would look good as a law enforcer. The pay was regular and for the first time Denzil could throw his weight around and feel really good about himself.

Hari went to do his beach rubbish collecting round on his own, two nights after Ceri's body was discovered on Anjuna, hoping that he might see her *bhoot* at the place where her body was found. The *Banjara* believed that the spirits of the recently- deceased could appear to their loved ones, especially if they had not re-entered the physical body of another living being. As Ceri had not been cremated, he yearned for the possibility of seeing her come to him.

Although Ceri was from a different world, Hari had

formed a strong attachment to her energy and vitality, often talking of her as sister. Thanks to her and Melita, he had gained a new confidence in dealing with people from her world, who had untold wealth and power compared to his own tribe. So her untimely death had affected him greatly and he longed for the chance to meet her again and say his goodbyes.

The beach was deserted that night, with only the tiniest sliver of a moon to illuminate the shore. He had walked the length of Anjuna twice, his bag of litter was only half full but he had lost interest in picking up pieces of plastic. He was tired after a long day and sat down to rest, closing his eyes, facing out to sea with the gentle sound of the sea lapping up to the shore.

It may have been a few minutes or an hour, but at some stage he saw the figure of what he was sure was Ceri walking away from him along the shore, paddling her bare feet in the waves as she went.

He walked towards her, called out 'Sister, sister' but Ceri didn't look back. No matter how fast he walked or ran, he could not reduce the space between them.

Eventually she turned around and stopped.

Hari saw her smile at him. 'Sister,' he cried, 'you came back for me.'

She didn't make a sound.

'I'm very sorry for the horse, it was our culture, you see,' Hari apologized, and Ceri turned back around and walked away from him.

It all ended when he felt a kick in the ribs.

One of Braganza's policemen growled. 'Sister, hah? What

sister are your calling out for? It's going to take more than your fuckin' sister to save you now,' he jeered.

Hari was stuffed into a police van. They had found him exactly where Braganza thought he might be. He always kept clear of the cops, who knew he was of no use to them, being a poor useless gypsy. You couldn't extort money from a boy who had nothing, but now suddenly he'd become hugely valuable. In fact, so valuable that Inspector Denzil Braganza's job at the Foreigners' CID, his position as a pillar of Opus Dei, and the reputation of the Anjuna district as a safe place to enjoy, depended on Hari.

Hari was thrown into a police cell after having been walloped with a *lathi* a few times to exact revenge for past humiliation. Denzil arrived early that morning, after he'd been called and told that his men had the prime suspect in custody.

He drove to the *Thana,* imagining how he might extract a confession in minutes, not days. How good it would be to call the boss. No, he'd go and see him in person to tell him the news. What a good day it would be for him and the force. He went straight to the cell holding his suspect. There would be no need for an interrogation room. He wasn't the sort of guy who did things conventionally.

He lit a cigarette. '*Achha,* now I want to hear the truth. Where were you last Friday night?' Braganza began, then took a long drag and blew smoke in Hari's face waiting for an answer.

'I was at the cremation of my *Bapi.*'

'And is it true that there were other *ferenghis* with you, hah?'

'Yes.'

'Did you know them? Or did they just come from nowhere?'

'Yes, Sir, the *engraji* girl I work for and her male friend. They are calling him Igor.'

'And why did they come to your ceremony? Related, were they?'

'No Sir, the man Igor brought the girl to see our dances and other *tamashas*. The girl was disturbed to see the killing and cremation of our *bapaji's* horse, and she walked off into the night. I didn't see her after that.'

'Did she? Look, there are people who have seen you trying to put your arms around the girl and being refused. Right?' the inspector paused to hear the rebuttal.

'No, Sir.'

'You wanted to stick your cock up her pussy, didn't you, you dirty son of a pig. And that night, at your camp, you gave her *bhang* and some very expensive rum, and thought you'd give it a go, hah?'

'No, Sir,' murmured Hari.

Denzil landed one of his best-in-class punches designed for maximum impact in the middle of the stomach. Hari doubled up and passed out.

'Get some water for this bugger,' shouted Denzil. Someone came with a jug of water, which he threw in Hari's face. Hari opened his eyes.

'No use you telling lies, fucker. I'm going to get the truth out of you, even if I have to kill you.'

'How would you do that if you kill me?'

Another hammer blow and Hari slumped again.

Denzil had learned that in exacting a confession, you had to target beatings where the after-effects weren't visible. He'd committed to memory the *Handbook for Attack and Defence* and practised it many times, mainly on unarmed prisoners.

The neat thing about hitting the solar plexus is that it contains a lot of nerves there, including the diaphragm that helps you breathe. A punch makes the diaphragm spasm, the person can't breathe and is often in a lot of pain. Even muscular guys can get taken down with this easily, as even if they're bodybuilders, then they can't develop muscle over that area. In fact, if they're lean it's perfect as they won't have any fat there to protect them.

Hari had been on the receiving end of two blows and was now unconscious again. Denzil had to make his mind up about what he did next. He'd get one of his men to come in and try the 'Good Cop' approach.

When he came around again Hari found himself sitting in front of one of the constables, the plump one, who had a cup of sweetened tea for him.

'I'm sorry about my boss today. He's very upset by what has happened. Have this tea and think things over, it might improve your memory of the night. I have a copy of the signed confession and it's very simple. You see, we may be able to get you a short term in jail, due to the state of your mind.'

'There's nothing wrong with my mind.'

'*Aré*, listen, that's just the excuse we give. Now, you don't want to go through another beating, do you? You may never work again. The boss will make sure of that. Your parents will be harassed forever. Why make it difficult for them? You're a *Banjara*, life in jail might be better than outside it.'

'My parents?'

'Yes, yes, they suffer the most. You're a strong young man and can take all this beating and stuff. But parents are getting old, they must not suffer.'

'They haven't done anything.'

'And neither have you, so you say. Look I believe you, it's the boss, he's not for changing his mind once he has made up his mind. I know, trust me.'

'I'm innocent, I wouldn't kill that girl after all she did for me.'

The constable shrugged his shoulders, 'It's just your bad luck, *baba*, being a lowly *Banjara* and that. You can't push water up a hill. Either you sign up and do a bit of jail and everybody lives happy ever after, or you stay under arrest until we get a confession and your family gets the wrong end of the boss's *dunda*.'

The mention of his family getting dragged into the case tipped the balance between accepting torture and giving in. He could not take the blame for their suffering. He'd seen other families driven out of the area because someone in the clan had displeased a rich and powerful man.

Hari gave in.

'Let me sign then,'

'I'm glad you have seen sense. We will get the court to be as lenient as possible.'

Hari could not read, so he held out his left thumb and touched the inked pad and then the document.

'*Shabash*, well done,' congratulated the Chief Inspector in a call that evening to Denzil. Roki, the reporter from the *Enquirer*, also called to interview Braganza at the Thana. 'This must be a very proud day for you, Inspector?' asked the young journo. 'Yes, I'm very proud of my men and the excellent policing we provide in the community.'

'How did you conduct the enquiry?'

'Well, as I was saying earlier, the face of the killer came to me in church, when I visited hours after we discovered this horrific murder. I closed my eyes and said a small prayer to ask our St Xavier to give me the strength to apprehend this man. And I saw him. I was able to draw up a rough identity kit sketch and give it to my constables, one of whom instantly recognised the *gunda*.'

'So, you believe there was divine intervention?'

'I can't think of any other reason,' said Denzil. 'I think our patron Saint Xavier wanted to intervene to stop another tragedy like this, and I was his channel to make it happen.'

'Would you call yourself a religious man, Inspector?' the journalist quizzed Denzil.

'I'm a Catholic and it's for my fellow community to judge me, but I try to be observant where I can.'

'Sir, there is a widely-held belief that there is a lot of police corruption here in the force. Do you agree with that perception and if so, are you personally playing a part as a good Christian to eradicate it?' asked the journalist.

Denzil paused to think about the loaded question. 'No police force is whiter than white, I might say. There are one or two bad eggs who spoil it for us all, but be sure they will not last long. Things are changing fast. You will see.'

The *Enquirer* ran a front-page feature on the amazing insight into the arrest, by their Law and Order correspondent Roki Sequera, who was widely praised by the Goan community for his in-depth reporting of the Anjuna incident.

Inspector prayed to catch murderer of teenager. In an unusual insight to policing, Inspector Denzil has claimed that he had a vision from St Francis Xavier when he prayed at St Anthony's church last Sunday. 'I saw his face clearly when I closed my eyes,' he said. This has led to the dramatic arrest and confession of the perpetrator, apparently known to the victim.

Chapter 28

Miscarriage of justice

The discovery of Ceri's body and Hari's speedy imprisonment, was again a tabloid sensation. Tourism could now breathe again.

The bad egg was behind bars.

But in Bencula, the news was a thunderbolt to the little parish. Father Michael had read the story about Hari's arrest and seemed outwardly pleased that Denzil, one of his prominent parishioners, had been successful in bringing a fugitive to justice. The news was all over the parish and people could talk about nothing else. The relief that the perpetrator was behind bars had meant that young women were safe again to walk home at night.

But Michael actually felt uneasy, as he knew Braganza to be a corrupt policeman. He was troubled by Scorpion's earlier visit to the confessional, where he had linked Braganza to a plan to kill the Ukes' leader, Vlad. Michael had had many people through his confessional since he'd been ordained a priest, and every now and then, one came along who posed a challenge to his conscience and his vow of secrecy.

He was also fearful that one of his own Goan Beachboys might have been responsible for Ceri's murder as a revenge attack, to get back at the Ukes. He remembered their conversations about prayer, how intelligent she had seemed for such a young woman, and how she had helped in the kitchens for the orphan children of the parish. It was always sad when someone died so young and even harder when that person had so much to offer the world.

Michael decided to hold a mass to commemorate Ceri, He invited Melita to say a few words as her best friend. Melita was filled with anger at the corrupt system of local justice and how Hari had been scapegoated by the police and the authorities. Her anger ran deep, as she mulled over her options to free Hari. She knew he was incapable of anything as violent as raping and killing Ceri. She had to find Igor to establish what had gone on the night they drove off together to celebrate her birthday. Ceri had been delirious with joy at being carried away for her surprise celebration, which made the news of her appalling murder even more unbearable.

The church was packed on Friday evening. There were people there that Michael hadn't seen for a decade. Even the Beachboys had turned out in force with Karina, their new leader. Scorpion, too, sat at the back wearing a heavy pair of aviator shades, trying to avert attention from himself and failing miserably.

'Welcome, everybody. It's nice to see you all here today united in grief, to commemorate the short life of Ceri Davies, one of the most vibrant young people we have had the pleasure to welcome into our midst. Death, in what we believe are such tragic circumstances, is hard to accept when someone is so young and I offer my sympathies to her friends here today.' Michael spoke from the raised altar, decorated with white funeral lilies that emitted their strong familiar funereal aroma.

The congregation was confronted by a picture of Ceri that had been erected below the pulpit. The one Roki had taken on Carnaval day. It was a picture full of joy and exuberance, which fuelled the feelings of sadness at the loss of such youth. The question on everyone's lips was, who was responsible for Ceri's death? Everyone knew it wasn't Hari, he was just an easy target for Braganza, whom few people in the congregation trusted despite his elevation to Opus Dei. Or was it one of the Beachboys, who had partied with her over the nights that she had spent at the Sunset Lounge, sitting right there in the front row, probably gloating at his deeds.

'We owe our thanks to you all who welcomed this stranger into our hearts,' continued Michael, 'I hope we can use Ceri's death as a wake-up call to get us to see what's happening to our parish, when we abandon the fundamental values of Christ's teaching. When I was a boy you could leave your house open day and night. Young girls could walk home at night without fear. The family was sacred and hard work and honesty were rewarded with prosperous happy times.'

There were nods of approval from the elderly, with some even expressing their approval vocally. Karina and the Beachboys, who sat in the front row, remained stoical in their demeanour. She had enforced a uniform regime of navy jackets and white shorts to smarten up her gang, making them look like members of a local sports club rather than gangsters.

'I ask you to bow your head in a minute of contemplation to pray for the soul of our deceased sister.' There was a moment of intense silence only interrupted by the endless honking traffic outside. 'I now call upon Ceri's close friend Melita to give us the eulogy.'

Melita took to the pulpit. She wore a blue and white floral dress, the only one she possessed. She paused, looked around her and for a moment you could have been forgiven for thinking that she was frozen with fear or at a loss for words to express her grief.

'Hello everyone, and thank you Father Michael for the opportunity to say a few words about my friend Ceri, who I will miss, probably forever. She was an inspiration to me and in the weeks we were friends, I learned so much about how to enjoy life, become a businesswoman, and help others. I hope that Ceri's death was not in vain and that we can learn something from it. I came from Birmingham in England some weeks ago, about the same time that Ceri arrived here. We were both in Goa for the first time. I was here in search of my roots as my parents were originally from here, in fact from this parish.'

There were nods again from the grey-headed contingent, with a few murmurings from those who had known Melita's parents.

'My mum and dad spoke so lovingly of the land of their birth, that I dreamt this to be paradise and a place that I had to come back to. I'm sad to say that I haven't found that yet and Ceri's murder has just put another nail in the coffin of my dream. I see in the front row my own friends the Beachboys, looking so smart and well turned out, and yet they are living on the proceeds of crime. I'm sorry, boys, but that is the truth isn't it?'

Karina at this stage got up to walk out and take her gang

287

with her as a protest.

'I'm really sorry to say this, but for the sake of my dear friend you should stay and listen to me for another minute,' Melita insisted. Karina looked at one of the Beachboys, who said something, and she sat down again.

'But the real problems start at the top, starting with the Minister here in Goa and with the police, who have been lining their pockets, allowing us to sink into the state we find ourselves. Look amongst us. Inspector Braganza, who has been knighted by Opus Dei, is one of the biggest sex pests I have ever known. He could never keep his hands off Ceri.'

A loud rumble of tut-tutting broke out. Michael arose from the altar, waving his hands to signal to Melita to stop, but she went on. 'And now an innocent man lies in jail for the murder that he definitely didn't commit and a guilty party roams free, all thanks probably to a bribe paid to Denzil to suppress the truth and frame an innocent *Banjara* youth. What happened to Christ's words of *Blessed are the poor*, Denzil?'

Braganza got up to go.

The congregation began a slow handclapping, which continued well after Melita had come down from the pulpit, and only stopped after Braganza had left the church. Melita stayed at the pulpit to acknowledge the applause, then took deep breaths until she felt she could breathe easily again.

She had never addressed a public audience and had it not been for the passion she felt to expose the hypocrisy, she would not have been able to mount such an eloquent speech. She had lifted a curtain that held a myriad of truths and conceptions about Braganza that had not been voiced in public before. The constant sexual harassing, the corruption, and now the lies and cover up of Ceri's death had triggered a fierce desire to expose Braganza. She knew she would eventually face expulsion from Goa.

This was her only chance tell the truth in public.

Michael continued with the mass without referring to Melita's comments, which had given the ceremony a new sense of relevance and fuelled the flames of the priest's previous comments on the state of his beloved land. Now his worst fears about Braganza had just been confirmed.

Melita wanted to slip away before the Beachboys or Karina got to her, but then Roki stopped her. 'Hi, that was just great. Was it all true? You've got real balls, girl, doing that in front of all those deadbeats.'

'What do you think? Would I have risked saying all that in public if I wasn't sure?

She was my friend and I want her real attacker brought to justice.'

'Why do you think the *Banjara* fellow is innocent? It seems obvious if he was seen with her, hugging. You know these are simple people.'

'He worked for us. I probably know him better than anyone around here. He is a shy boy around women. Anyway, I last saw Ceri go with Igor, the Uke, on his motorbike. Who knows where he is now?'

'Has he been investigated by Braganza?' asked Roki.

'Not likely, it's common knowledge amongst the Beachboys that the Chief of Police has been paid by his father to allow them to conduct their illegal business.'

'You make a lot of unsubstantiated allegations.'

'They're all true. But your newspaper only prints stuff you're allowed to say. I bet your editor won't publish a truthful report of this mass and my eulogy. But I can assure you, you'll gain the respect of the community you serve if you do. Everyone knows Braganza is a corrupt policeman, and the sooner he is exposed, the better for Goa.'

'I help to publish news that can be substantiated, anything else is liable to our libel laws.'

'Suit yourself. If you want to keep things the way they are, that's your choice. But nothing changes,' Melita said bitterly as she walked away. Scorpion came up and gave her a huge hug.

'Sister, that was brave, really brave, but watch your back. I'm here to protect you if you need me,' he offered.

'Thanks, I'm going back to my shack now. Hope we can get Hari freed. By the way, how's the café business?'

'Oh hell no, sister, I'm outta there. I got expelled like Ceri.'

'What did you do, make a pass at one of the customers?'

'Now that would be something, ha? No worse, I emptied hot coffee over some straight-arsed moron, who told me he didn't want to catch Aids from me and could I go bake bread somewhere else.'

'Wow, awesome. He got what he deserved.'

'Yes, and I got let go, so now I'm going to take Michael's advice and get some proper learning, become a chef. I've always liked the idea of cooking great food,' said Scorpion licking his lips. 'Mind how you go.' He hugged her again.

There were several elders who shook Melita's hand. 'You look the image of Roseanna,' said one, referring to her mother. 'No, I see Daniel's forehead,' said another, noticing her father's features. It was as if suddenly Melita had a following, after weeks of not being noticed around the parish.

The person most troubled by Melita's eulogy was Michael. Braganza knew that he was bomb-proof from the top of the corrupt establishment he was part of, but Michael carried the weight of Scorpion's confession that implicated the policeman in someone's murder. He would never break his vows, but the weight of carrying someone else's crimes on his conscience troubled him deeply. Braganza was one of his most prominent parishioners and a defender of the Goan pride in their identity.

Yet he was a crook, rotten to the core.

'That was one of the most courageous eulogies I've heard. You spoke with such conviction. You knew this guy in jail well, Melita?' asked Father Michael.

'No way is this guy guilty. I'm really sure. He was such a gentle boy and we both loved him very much. He knew his place. I'm sure he's been stitched up.' Melita had no doubt of that. 'Look, we must get to see him in prison.'

'Have you tried?'

'No, no way. If I went anywhere near that *Thana*, they'd throw me in there, too.

Braganza will now be gunning for me.'

'Surely you know Inspector Denzil, he's always popping down to the Sunset Lounge.'

'Slimy, that fellow. You don't know how badly he treats us girls, like whores, touching and making terrible suggestions.'

Michael knew that he had to do something to balance his conscience. Not only had Braganza wrongly imprisoned Hari to score a few points with his superiors, but he was depraved and treated women badly.

Hari had so far had no legal representation. People like the *Banjara* generally went without any legal aid, and as a result got the raw end of justice. However, Community Law Centres were gradually cropping up in parts of India to protect minorities. These agencies were an excellent training ground for young lawyers looking to gain first- hand experience after law school. Michael had to find someone to represent Hari.

Roki handed him a gift on a plate, by publishing Melita's eulogy in full, under the headline *Murdered girl's friend claims accused is innocent.*

A day later, a lawyer from Panjim managed to contact Melita via Michael and arranged to see Hari in a private interview. The conditions were strict, mandating that no one else must accompany him.

Hari had aged in just a few days. The T-shirt he was so proud of was torn and covered in what must have been vomit, probably a reaction to the blows to his stomach. The lawyer was only allowed twenty minutes to question him.

'My name is Bhatia. I'm here to help you get out of jail if you're innocent. How long have you been here?' he asked.

'I think since Monday night, so three days. But I really can't be sure,' Hari replied.

'How did you get here?'

'I was picked up on Monday night on Anjuna, whilst I was picking up plastic.'

'Did they tell you why?'

'No, not until I arrived at the prison, the next morning.'

'Did you willingly sign the confession?'

'No, I was beaten.'

'You agreed to sign the confession but didn't actually commit the rape and murder?' asked the lawyer. Hari remained silent. Then the lawyer spoke again.

'Look, I'm here to represent you. It's your right. There's no reason for you to go to prison for a crime you did not commit.'

'Sir, you are an upper-caste person, who went to school and college. But think of me, a *Banjara* with nothing, no education. It's my family who will be hurt. The police won't let this go without punishing them forever.'

'So, they threatened to punish your family if you didn't sign?' Hari nodded. 'And you're innocent?' asked the lawyer.

'Ask the girl, Melita,' Hari said. 'Does she think I'd ever do a thing like that?'

'Hari, we can do a test that can scientifically prove your innocence. It's commonly available now. Let's do that.'

'I can't allow any harm to come to my family. That is why I signed the paper. Can't you see?'

'Okay, I understand that. But let's agree this. Can I be your lawyer to be your representative in court? What that means is, I will ensure that you get the fairest deal. It's the law of India that everybody is allowed a fair trial.'

Hari laughed for the first time, 'That is so funny, the law hah? And the people who are looking after the law are who? These guys here, the ones that are beating me up and will soon turn on my family if I don't do as they say.'

'It's not perfect by a long way, I admit, but we're your friends and want to do what's best for you. So, will you agree to that at least?'

'Yes okay, but I'm not taking anything back,' agreed Hari eventually.

'Okay, now have faith in me. I'm going to help you fight this.'

Hari had now been held in jail for three days, without an arraignment or preliminary hearing to consider the legitimacy of his arrest. Father Michael and the lawyer Bhatia made a number of calls to make sure his case was heard before a magistrate, but the justice system was creaking in India and here in Goa was no exception.

Father Michael was known for his persistence, and he managed to get a magistrate to come off sick leave to hear the case against Hari, for the murder and rape of Ceri Davies.

Magistrate V.P. Anand was a past pupil of St Xaviers in Panjim and Michael often reached out to him for help in advising local parishioners who fell foul of the law. Anand's natural suspicions, were to suspect police motives and not blindly follow their recommendation, but he would publicly always say, 'They are the experts, why go and second guess them.'

The courtroom was a small windowless place in which one would not wish to spend much time. V.P. Anand sat at the head of the room, on an elevated table in the glare of bright neon lights. A police lawyer and Inspector Denzil sat on the left with Hari, in handcuffs, and his lawyer Bhatia on the right. Melita and Father Michael were in Court, too.

Denzil exchanged nods with Father Michael. It was not going to be a normal sort of day, he thought, when your parish priest turns up to support the guy you're trying to put away. Did he know that one of his star parishioners had something to do with the torture of Hari Lal?

The room was like an echo chamber as the police lawyer read out the charges. 'Sir, we are respectfully asking you today to consider holding the prisoner Hari Lal in custody until a full hearing. He was arrested at 11.30 pm, on the night of the 23rd March and has been held in Bencula Thana since then. On the 24th March at 2.45 pm, under interrogation by Inspector Denzil Braganza, he confessed to the rape and murder of Ceri Davies, whose body was found on the morning of the 21st March on Anjuna. He has been charged with the murder of Ceri Davies and has signed a confession to that effect.'

'Please tell me a few things before we proceed to hear the case from Mr Lal's lawyer: why is it that this case has gone three days without a preliminary hearing in contravention of the Penal Code Act? And please explain to me the circumstances as to how the original conclusion of death by misadventure, was changed after twenty-four hours to "murder and rape."' Magistrate Anand was already in a combative mood.

Just then the door to the courtroom opened and in walked Roki Sequera, nodding apologetically for disturbing the court. He sat down and pulled out his notebook.

'If I may come forward, Sir, to address the court?' Denzil requested. 'It has been difficult to get a magistrate to conduct a hearing, as there are big scheduling difficulties here in the State and it was only due to your kind agreement to be here today that we have been able to hold this court. As to the changes to the original conclusions following the discovery of the victim's body, we had not had a chance to study in detail the results of the post- mortem. As soon as we discovered the full implications, we immediately changed our declarations and informed the public.'

'Okay, I accept your explanation, but must remark that your actions were at best lackadaisical and at worst downright unprofessional. These are not the standards we expect from our police force today,' rebuked Anand.

'I'm sorry, Sir, we have a very heavy workload during this busy tourist season. Your point is noted,' Denzil apologised. He could see that the Magistrate was not going to give his side an easy time today.

'Now let us hear from the defendant's lawyer, Mr Bhatia.'

'Sir, please be accepting our case against the further detention of our client on the basis of the following: firstly, our client was not given any reason for his detention, nor was a lawyer or representative present at his interrogation. Secondly, this illiterate *Banjara* man was not made aware of his rights at any time during his arrest, or during his detention. And, finally, and perhaps most seriously, Sir, this confession was extracted from our client under torture and duress and fear of intimidation to his family. I would like to ask your permission for the client's acquaintance, Miss Melita Gonzalez, to address the Court.'

'Permission granted,' said Anand.

The police lawyer sprung up. 'We object, Sir. Miss Gonzalez is a person of poor character, who is a habitual drug taker and beach itinerant. She has been under CID surveillance for some time.'

'Overruled. Let's hear from Miss Gonzalez.'

'Miss Gonzalez, Melita, please be telling this court of your relationship with the deceased,' the young defence lawyer requested.

'Yes sure, thank you, I have been a close friend of Ceri since she came to live with her mother at Anjuna, we had made a little business together selling cheap trinkets and jewellery.'

'Which is illegal and has not been registered,' interrupted the police lawyer.

'That may be true, but then you'd have to arrest fifty per cent of the entire beach at Anjuna. I would put it to you,' countered Magistrate Anand. 'Let the witness continue.'

'We befriended Hari about a month ago,' Melita went on, 'because we liked his smile and also felt sorry for him, you know, as he is a *harijan,* an untouchable boy. He would say good morning to us every day, as he went about his job of picking up plastic bottles and rubbish from the beach.'

'And did he at any time, make any provocative suggestions towards you or the deceased?' inquired Bhatia.

'No, not at all. He is a mild-mannered young man. You see, everybody felt sorry for him and wanted to give him a chance in life.'

'You were taking a risk with this man however, weren't you?'

'I don't think so. He was very smart. He picked up English and French words very quickly from us, so we thought we'd give him a chance to sell our trinkets and he did very well.'

'The police lawyer may now question the witness,' said Anand.

The Police lawyer rose.

'We have people who saw Mr Lal trying to make sexually provocative teasing type of gestures towards the deceased.' He turned to Melita. 'Would you not agree he was sexually frustrated at the prospect of being suddenly befriended by young foreign girls like you, who have some reputation?'

'If you're saying that we were leading him on, then you're totally wrong. Yes, we did give him a friendly hug sometimes, and invite him out a few times for a drink, but he always refused, saying that he'd rather have the money for his family. Also, to help his family out, he was now doing two jobs, ours and rubbish collection at night, as he wanted to earn the few extra rupees from the hotel.'

'I hope that gives the court some comfort, Sir, that my client was of good character, looking to make his way up in this great country of ours,' interrupted Bhatia.

'Continue.' Anand told Bhatia.

'Please Sir, notice the marks on the defendant's T-shirt.' Bhatia asked Hari to stand up. 'These are vomit stains, Sir, the result of some severe blows to the stomach, which he sustained in detention. This was simple torture to get him to confess something he didn't do. The police have been under pressure to solve this murder and Mr Lal was an easy scapegoat.'

Denzil looked at the police lawyer to get him to make an objection, which he did hesitantly. 'Objection, Sir, the stains could have resulted at any time due to aggravation of the stomach or irritation of the bowel. There is no case to be made.'

'Sir, please may I ask my client to speak for himself?' asked Hari's lawyer. The magistrate indicated that he could.

Bhatia addressed Hari in Hindi. 'Are you frightened for the safety of your family?' Hari nodded. 'You have to say yes or no.'

'Hah,' said Hari, responding in the affirmative.

'Was it fear that made you sign the confession?' asked Bhatia. Hari remained silent, then spoke hesitantly.

'I'm a poor *Banjara* man. I wake up every day thinking 'How will I eat today?'

You all are all very clever and high up. I'm just frightened standing here.'

'You should not be frightened, young man. We're here to make sure the law of our nation is carried out and that the innocent are protected. If you are innocent you should have no fear,' instructed Magistrate Anand. 'Were you forced to make this confession?'

'Hah Sir, hah.' He lifted his T-shirt to point to his stomach. 'That policeman,' he pointed at Denzil, 'punched me here, so hard I fainted Sir. Not once but many times.'

'Please Sir, objection,' the police lawyer cut in.

'Let the witness continue, please,' instructed the Magistrate.

'So, did you decide to sign the confession because of the pain?' asked Hari's lawyer.

'No, Sir, I can take pain. They said they would hurt my mother, my family. I had no choice.'

'So, there we have it, Your Honour,' Bhatia resumed in English. 'The boy was ready to take the pain himself, but not have his family harmed. Thankfully, there are people like my client that put their families first. No more questions from me, Sir.'

'Any from the CID side?' asked Anand.

'No Sir.'

'Inspector Braganza? Have you anything to add?'

'I would just like to add that we have no other suspects at the moment and that all of our evidence points to this man. He has at no time denied committing the crime,' affirmed Denzil. 'If Your Honour releases this man, then I would respectfully suggest that he will think nothing of continuing to be a threat to women, particularly foreign tourists, who are not acquainted with the dangers at night.'

'And can you assure me that at no time the defendant was tortured or intimidated in your jail?'

'Sir, definitely not. That is not our procedure,' lied Denzil with an impeccably sincere look on his face.

'You see, Inspector, as a man who likes logic, I can't quite see why this fellow would commit such a crime on his young employer, even if he was mad about her. And furthermore, I don't see why he would have confessed his guilt without some inducement or coercion. It just doesn't make sense to me,' observed V.P. Anand.

'Please be bearing in mind what Inspector Braganza said earlier, that if the defendant is released and absconds, then we are back to square one,' warned the police lawyer.

'What is it?' said the Magistrate, as Hari's lawyer raised an objection.

'Sir, Your Honour, there is one other prime suspect that the police have not interviewed. I would like to return Melita Gonzalez to the stand.'

'Very well, I hope this is necessary,' said Anand.

The police lawyer rose. 'Objection, Your Honour...' but the Magistrate didn't let him complete his objection.

'Please tell the court about whom you last saw the deceased with, on the evening of the murder.'

'My friend Ceri was celebrating her sixteenth birthday and a Ukrainian man, who we know by the name of Igor, came to take her out for a celebration. They rode off on an Enfield motorbike, and it was the last I saw of her alive.'

'Please tell the court of the deceased's relationship with this man Igor,' asked Hari's lawyer.

'She told me that she was in a relationship with him and his father disapproved.'

'His father being the leader of the Ukrainian gang known as the Ukes?'

'Yes. Ceri, my friend, was associated with the Beachboys, a local gang and they gave her protection. I have tried to contact Igor over the last few days, but no one knows where he is.'

'You see Your Honour, the police are failing in their responsibility by not bringing this man, with known criminal contacts, in for questioning. This is a traditional gang feud, with the victim being caught up in it. Unfortunately, we are seeing so much of this gang warfare in our sunshine state, all fuelled by drugs and prostitution,' the lawyer deplored.

'Is this true, Inspector?' Anand asked.

'No sir, that is not true.'

'Which part isn't true?'

'Sir, I did interview the man in question in hospital, where he is hospitalised.'

'Hospitalised?'

'Yes, Your Honour. He was injured in an accident on his motorbike and has been paralysed. He was under heavy sedation at the Mahindra Hospital and was not available for interview. He was picked up by an ambulance on Route 66 on the night of the murder. I eliminated him from my enquiries at that stage.'

'But we must have his statement before we convict this man,' objected Anand. 'It is very improper not to do so.'

'Sir, I have witness statements that the two quarrelled and that the deceased left on her own.'

'That may well be true, but we need to have these individuals questioned under caution for us to have a full view of the events,' instructed the Magistrate, 'And bearing that in mind, I'm prepared to offer bail if any one of the defendant's well-wishers here is happy to put up the sum of twenty thousand rupees.'

Melita's eyes lit up immediately. She had at least double that in dollars, from the time Igor had bought her entire stock. Ceri had given the money to her for safe keeping as the 'banker' in the partnership.

'Yes, yes!' she shouted.

Hari's lawyer turned to her. 'Please now, we can discuss this outside. Sir, it looks as though we are able to take up your kind offer. Thank you.'

'I'm also instructing you, Inspector, that I want a full medical examination of the defendant carried out immediately, with a view to determining if he has suffered any physical harm in the last forty-eight hours. I also think in view of the gravity of these allegations, another more detailed post-mortem should be carried out. In fact, I'm surprised this has not been instigated already, and I want a full interrogation of the suspect named as Igor when he recovers,' concluded Anand. 'The session is now closed.'

Melita couldn't control her excitement that the money she

and Ceri had earned could now free Hari. She threw her arms around him in court as Denzil sneered. An official undid the handcuffs and said that Hari was free to go.

As they walked out of the court, Father Michael addressed Denzil. 'I hope you found Anand gave this a fair hearing. Everything okay?'

'Yes, I'm fine, just been very busy with this case.'

'Do you think you have the right guy?' questioned the priest.

'Oh, definitely. These *Banjara* people have a drop of grog and they're sexually possessed. A little encouragement from one of these white foreign girls and it all goes to their head.'

'But he seems a very gentle chap,' said Michael. 'Of course, only from what I could see.'

'It's a big act. I know. I've had a few years of dealing with these vermin.'

'Denzil, now, now. We're all creatures of God. That's not very Christian of you.'

'I've seen these people on the front line, Father. I'm telling you.' He paused. 'Anyway, how have you become so interested in this case? He's not one of ours.'

'Just a child of God like any one of us.'

'I see,' said Denzil, but the Detective Inspector had been a policeman for far too long to be convinced by his parish priest's words. He could tell he knew far more than he was letting on. Roki caught up with Melita.

'Hello,' she said. 'I remember you at the Carnaval. You must remember Ceri.

'I certainly do, she was not someone you can forget.'

'What does that mean?' asked Melita.

303

'Oh, very certain about herself, but also quite a flirt.'

'She gave as good as she got, if that's what you mean.'

'Oh.'

'Braganza was always trying to paw her when he visited the Sunset. He thought she was one of Scorpion's whores in waiting. She fought back well, verbally that is. Now she's dead, I think he's getting his revenge.'

'And this guy Igor?'

'She was madly infatuated with him. Definitely not with Hari.'

'That would have made the *Banjara* jealous, no?'

'No way, I had my eye on him, but now I've discovered that he is already married to a girl in his tribe.'

The *Enquirer*'s headlines the next day ran, *Suspect to murder released on bail*. And Roki had a scoop again. He pointed to Magistrate Anand's comments on an incompetent police force, dereliction of duty, and the safety of Western women who went out after dark in Goa. Roki's article kept silent, however, about the alleged indiscretion of Chief Inspector Braganza. Roki had to be careful that he didn't alienate the police, who were a major source for his leads.

The Minister for Tourism in Goa was furious. He called Denzil. 'This is a result of your incompetence that the alleged killer is now free, roaming the beaches of Goa, presumably to commit his next crime. We are looking like nincompoops.'

'Sir, please bear with us, the case is more complex than we thought. We need to compile a little more evidence.'

'Evidence, man? What sort of evidence? You have a confession, dammit!'

'Yes, but there is another suspect, who was seen with the

girl on the night of her death. The Ukrainian boy Igor, son of the gang leader.'

'But he's in hospital in intensive case. What nonsense is all this? Do you want me to take you off the case?' The Minister was getting aggressive.

'I've been ordered to do so by the court.'

'Very well, let me know when you do so. I'm sure it will be a total waste of police time again. In the meantime, I want you to serve a notice to terminate that girl's visa, the one that's been stirring all this problem and making us a laughingstock.'

One of Denzil's constables delivered the notice to Melita the next day to leave in forty-eight hours. It mentioned her business activities being in contravention of the conditions of her tourist visa.

Chapter 29

Mam on the make

Roki took a call shortly after getting to his desk at the *Enquirer* on a Monday morning from a woman purporting to be Ceri's mother. She wanted to tell him her side of the story, if he was interested in the 'real' truth. The story had already begun to get his name circulating in some of India's most widely read newspapers. Editors seemed to have a rapacious appetite for more angles on the Anjuna murder mystery.

The country was polarised around two different views. Was it the wicked gang culture, which the girl had been caught up in, that killed her, or was it, in fact, the inevitable result of Europe's export of their disaffected youth, in search of sex, cheap drugs, and booze? The papers took one or the other position.

'Mrs Davies, will you be travelling here to Goa to see the body of your daughter Ceri? Perhaps we could meet and get your end of this sad story as her mother?' asked Roki.

'I would love to, but I have no money at the moment. I'm destitute. I gave it all to Ceri so she could look after herself. Besides, the *Bhagwan* says it's better for me to engage in meditation and prayer at the *ashram* at this difficult time. Coming to Goa now won't bring my Ceri back from the dead, will it? What's done is done as far as I can see.'

'Very well, I will catch the next train,' Roki assured her.

'By the way, just one more thing, my name is Devi Rama now.'

Now Roki could have first-hand evidence from the mother of the deceased Ceri, providing yet another view. In India, the words of a grieving mother would carry more weight than any politician or commentator. His editor gave him immediate permission to travel to Pune, even by first class, if it meant he would be assured of a seat.

He caught the next available train out to Pune, where he had been given an address at the *Ashram of Bhagwan Sri Gopal*, arriving early the next day. The *Ashram* was located just off the main Laxhmi Road in the city centre, a short motor rickshaw ride from the railway station.

A woman in a white sari greeted Roki and made him sign the visitor's book after he had described the purpose of his visit. 'Oh yes, Devi Rama is one of our recent devotees. It is with great sorrow and regret she heard of the brutal death of her young daughter,' declared the woman, as Roki went through quite a lengthy signing-in process.

'It says here that a donation may be required to arrange the meeting?'

'Oh yes please, purely voluntary of course. We rely on our visitors to support our efforts here. You realise we're all in the hands of God for our daily physical and spiritual sustenance, as we have given up everything for the poor and needy.'

'I'm a struggling journo you know, so I only have a few rupees to get me back to Panjim. Please forgive me.'

The woman's sari, partly wrapped around her head, slipped

and she didn't bother to readjust it. 'It is fine then, but remember money won't bring you happiness my good Brother.' She left to find Devi Rama.

The walls of the reception room were festooned with fading technicolour and black and white photographs of the *Bhaghwan* posing with both Indian and international celebrities and some recent pictures with Bollywood stars. Roki recognised quite a few of them, but he had his suspicions as he'd never heard of the *Bhagwan* before. Were they real devotees, or had the *Bhagwan* merely acquired the pictures?

And then in walked the lone figure of Devi Rama, a short, grey-haired woman with very pale, almost pasty skin and vacant blue eyes that stared into the distance way past Roki, to some point probably a mile away.

'Namasté, good morning to you,' she said, raising her hands in a sign of greeting.

'Oh, hello, I'm Roki, the guy you called yesterday at the paper.'

'Ah Roki, you can call me Devi or even Sister if you prefer.'

'Good, Devi is good with me,' he smiled.

'Please sit down,' she invited, seating herself at the end of the solid teak glass topped table that looked like it had been in situ for a hundred years. Roki sat down at right angles to her on the closest chair he could find.

'I'm so happy you called me, Devi.'

'Why happy? I've lost my dear daughter, taken by those evil men. Do you know, on reflection, I'd like you to call me Sister, if you don't mind? You being a journalist and all that, it's more respectful hah?'

'Yes okay, Sister. What is your real name?'

'Real name? Devi is my real name and about as real as yours.'

'Ah yes, no, I meant before you took your new name here.'

'It matters not. That's then and this is now.'

'Okay, tell me, Sister, how do you feel now about the death of your daughter? Angry, sad?'

'Well,' she said, and then paused. ' The *Bhagwan* has taught us that anger is unproductive and leads to a loss of control. I feel sad. She was my flesh and blood.'

'Have you been to see her body?'

'It's pointless, she's gone. I have her only in my memory and that is much better. If I saw her in the morgue, I'd be in danger of losing my mind. What is the point of that?'

'Were you close? Her friends say she'd help you out financially.'

'Oh, yes. You see I have nothing here of my own. I depend on the generosity of others. By the way, how much does your paper intend to pay us for this interview?'

'Oh, I was not aware of any payment. My only hope was that you would give us the real story of Ceri, rather than what I have picked up from others.'

'Well, now let me see, you're going to make a killing by publishing my story and we here at the *ashram* get zilch? Duh! What do you take me for?'

'I'm sorry, Sister, but I didn't come with any money, just a few rupees to get back to Panjim.'

'Oh, and I thought your pockets were bulging with notes for me. Well, brother, no money, no interview. Come back when you're flush with cash. Let me see, it's unlikely I'll be sitting down with you for less than ten thousand rupees in cash.'

'Oh Sister, I've come a long way to hear your story. I'm a struggling journo, trying to make my way and get the truth told about your daughter.'

'The truth costs these days. That's just a fact of life. Everybody can make up lies, but I have the truth, the real truth from the mouth of a mother. It doesn't come more real than that, hah?'

Roki tried a mixture of charm, sympathy, and even a hint at shaming to get Devi to change her mind, but it was no use. It was as if suddenly the prospect of not receiving any compensation for the interview had thrown a switch in her mind and she was not going to cooperate.

The woman in the white sari came into the room with a cup of tea, but Devi rose. 'He will not be staying now,' she announced.

The woman looked confused, still holding the cup of tea in her hands. 'Please give me the tea, Sister. I've grown very thirsty from my journey. Thank you,' said Roki.

She handed Roki the cup of piping hot, sweetened tea. He poured a little into the accompanying saucer, blowing into it as steam arose. 'Oh, I'm going to enjoy this act of generosity from the *Bhagwan*,' he declared, and slurped the liquid noisily. 'Ah so good! This place is so full of love, peace, and tranquillity, I'm so pleased I came.'

'It's all thanks to the *Bhagwan*, without him none of this would have been possible,' said Devi coldly, walking towards the door.

Roki had been inculcated in the sceptic's school of Indian

mystics. 'If only we produced as many engineers and scientists as we do *Bhagw*ans we would be the greatest country on earth,' his father had once reminded him. If Devi would not talk without a considerable financial inducement, perhaps he could try a little blackmail.

Roki tried one last desperate tactic. 'Sister Devi, I'm sure I could help enhance the reputation of yourself and the *Bhagwan* if the world saw you in a more positive light.'

'We hardly care what the world thinks here at the *Ashram*, we came to get away from the world.'

'I don't think it would please the Bhagwan, if he read that the world thought you're a callous mother and this *Ashram* a decadent money-grabbing machine.'

Devi paused at the door. The woman in the white sari adjusted her head-covering again.

'Let me tell you what I've got, before we decide to take this conversation any further,' said Devi returning to the table, clearly open to bargaining her position in the best Indian market trader's tradition.

'Okay, what've you got?' asked Roki.

'Her text messages. Doesn't get much better since I believe her phone is missing.'

'Let me call my editor,' Roki shot back, knowing when he was onto something invaluable.

Roki returned a few minutes later. He had the money secured, not from his editor, but from his wealthy father. 'My editor is prepared to offer five thousand and wire the money here in the next half hour if you want. That's a final offer,' he lied.

'Okay, it's a deal then. Get that money over and come back

here when you're done. You can get screen grabs of all the telephone messages. She didn't do email.'

And that was Roki's big scoop. Through a few dozen messages, the last few weeks of Ceri's life were documented in words of few syllables, expressing her roller- coaster emotions of joy, frustration, love and sadness. They corroborated her love for Igor and recorded the first time she met him, her hateful thoughts towards Braganza, her admiration of Hari, and plenty of comments about her friendship with Melita.

But there was one message that took Roki's eye and which he copied a few times, as he was sure it might provide strong clues to Ceri's murder. Hari was out on bail and hadn't been completely cleared of the crime. These messages would almost certainly clear him once and for all and nail the real killer.

'I hope you help get the villains that killed my baby, I hope they get all the bad karma that the divine can cast on them,' Devi told him as he left.

Chapter 30

Confession

The Mahindra private spinal injuries hospital in Panjim was a state of the art unit with a top consultant, a member of the Royal College of Surgeons. The consultant performed an eight- hour operation on Igor to try and repair his damaged spinal cord. He expressly forbade anyone to disturb his patient, until the effects of the sedation had worn off and Igor was able to conduct a conversation without being distressed.

Melita had less than two days to leave Goa and knew she had to work fast to find out the real truth behind Ceri's death. Armed with the knowledge that Igor was in the Mahindra Hospital, she decided to use whatever method she could to get to him.

She concluded that the best way was right through the front door, posing as his girlfriend. She had to try to speak to him! She walked past Reception, following the signs to the spinal unit on the second floor. The lift doors opened and there were more signs to a private ward.

There was a board above the administrator's desk which had the names of the patients written in marker pen, along with their room numbers. Melita wore a head scarf with sunglasses as she thought it might age her. She smiled at the attendant nurse, who told her, 'You are early for visiting times.'

'Mari?' Melita questioned.

'Excuse me? No, I'm Maddalena,' replied the nurse.

'You look just like my best friend's sister. Her name is Mari. I'm really sorry.'

'Oh, that's ok.'

'Please, I've come from England to see my boyfriend, who has been injured,' pleaded Melita, accentuating her Goan accent.

The nurse who was busy filling out forms gave her a nod, Melita waved and followed the corridor to Room Two. She peeped through the glass in the door. Igor was sitting up in his bed alone, with traction pulleys fitted to his legs. She entered. At first Igor didn't move his head. His unshaven face and bloodshot eyes had aged him by ten years.

'Igor, it's me, Melita, come to see you.' Igor moved his head to face her without any expression. 'How are you feeling?'

'Feeling? Well I'm not feeling much at the moment,' he responded wryly. 'I may never walk again, they say.' He tried to point at the contraption of pulleys and wires that were attached to him.

'Oh Igor, I am sorry. Can I hug you?' Melita leant over to stroke Igor's face. 'I had to come and see you, Igor, I hope you don't mind. I brought you Ceri's diary to show you what she last wrote while she waited for you on her birthday.'

Igor held it in his hands and kissed the page. Melita read the entry out softly.

As I write this, I am sooo sooo feverish with the excitement

*of being carried away by my one and only love. Oh, Igor
bach, my gentle genie, whisk me away on a magic carpet
or a handsome white horse with wings, to a place where
we could do unimaginable things that give great pleasure.*

There was a tear in Igor's eye.

'I thought she was dead, but then I saw her move when
they carried her away,' he murmured.

'You saw what, Igor?'

'We hit something on my bike and both of us came off.
Ceri was knocked out, but I'm sure she was alive when my
father's driver took her away.'

'Igor, do you know there is an innocent man now accused
of raping and killing Ceri?'

'No, that can't be true,' retorted Igor, looking at her in
disbelief.

'And that man is Hari, you know the *Banjara* fellow that
you have played gypsy music with. They have tortured him to
confess to a crime he didn't do.'

'No, not Hari…'

'It is Hari, Igor, and you've got to tell your story to the
police before he is jailed again, possibly for life. You can't live
with that. Look,' insisted Melita, holding a picture of Ceri's
bruised and battered face that she had taken on her phone in
the mortuary, when Braganza's attention had been diverted.
Igor stared up at the ceiling and shook his head confused.

There was the sound of a man shouting outside. The door
to the room was flung open and a tall heavy man, Igor's
minder Aleks, rushed in. He grabbed Melita by the hair and
flung her out into the corridor as she yelled in protest. A

315

hospital orderly came by to see if he could offer any assistance, but Melita knew she had to leave quickly.

His visitor had shaken Igor.

Due to his inaction and silence on the events of the night Ceri was murdered, Hari would languish in jail.

That night he lay awake mulling over the few options he had left. In all probability he might never walk again. If so, would he want to go on living? Igor thought he would most probably want to end his life if that were to happen. If so, was it worth making Hari's life a misery?

If it was true that Hari had suffered at the hands of Braganza and been threatened with his life when he was totally innocent, Igor realised he had to do something to put the injustice right. And Ceri, his darling Ceri, with her face bruised and battered in a way that could not have been from the motorbike accident. She had been beaten and almost certainly killed by someone. Igor had to do all in his power to free Hari, but at the same time get back at his father, who was no doubt responsible for her murder.

Braganza, now on Magistrate Anand's instruction, made another approach to the hospital with a court order for an interview with Igor. This was granted on the third request. Things were going well for the chief inspector, now he had the court's authority to interview one of the Ukes. He had been prevented from doing so previously, due to the substantial sweeteners from Vlad that had flowed to his boss, the Minister of Tourism.

Vlad had employed a lawyer to be present for the interview, who sat by Igor's bedside, ready to stop him giving away anything that would incriminate him.

'Good morning, Mr Kravets, Andrei Kravets, correct?'
Braganza greeted the lawyer, as he entered the room,
accompanied by a clerk to record the interview.

'I am here to represent the interests of my client,' warned
the lawyer. 'Please be aware that he is under no obligation to
answer your questions if he so wishes and his right to silence
must be maintained.'

'Yes, thank you. Now may I ask you to leave, as I need to
conduct this interview in privacy and your legal services will
not be necessary?' Braganza replied, applying the Indian
Penal Code, which does not support the right for a lawyer to
be present throughout an interrogation.

'But Inspector, it is my client's wish for me to be present
throughout this interview.' But Igor waved the lawyer away.
'Neither of us need you,' Braganza stated. 'Now please go
outside.' The lawyer disappeared out of the room without any
further challenge.

'Please start recording this interview at Mahindra Hospital,
Room Two of the Spinal Injuries Unit, at 10.30 am, on
second of March, two thousand and ten,' he instructed his
clerk.

'May I call you, Igor?' He received a nod of agreement.
'Very well, now, were you with the victim Ceri Davies on the
evening of her murder?'

'I was, and yes, it was me. I murdered the girl,' stated Igor
without any further interrogation.

Braganza sat back and looked at the clerk.

The clerk looked back, as if he corroborated what Braganza
had just heard. Igor had decided that the only way he could
get Hari free, was to lie that he had been responsible for Ceri's

rape and death.

'Er, could you repeat that, please, for the clerk?'

'I said, I raped Ceri. And I'm sorry.'

'Did you beat her and rape her before you murdered her?'

Igor hesitated for a moment then admitted, 'Yes, I forced her to have sex with me in the forest and then drove her to Anjuna.'

'Why? What was your motivation?'

'I was jealous of her affections for Hari, the *Banjara* man.'

'It seems a very violent thing to do,' observed Braganza.

'We had an argument the night I took her to the *Banjara* camp. I could see her looking at Hari with sexual eyes, you know, like girls do. I was furious and we had an argument, then she walked away into the night. I was so very jealous, and it drove me completely crazy, you know. I found her walking on the road in the dark and told her I'd take her home, as it was twenty kilometres or more to her home.'

'So, she agreed to go home with you on your bike because she had no option.'

'Yes, the 66 is a scary place at night for anyone on their own. I drove her to Anjuna on my motorbike, and forced her to admit to carrying on a relationship with Hari. When she refused to admit it, I raped her on the beach and beat her head against a rock, then drowned her.'

'Didn't you think her body would be discovered at some stage?'

'Yes, but your system is so corrupt. I knew that you'd go for Hari as the easy option, and then he'd rot in prison forever.'

'So why are you now confessing to this?'

'After I left the scene in a rage, I felt that I'd purged the devil from my body. I was high, like on drugs, and I raced to my home at maximum speed. That was when I hit something and came off my bike. The last few days, since the moment I discovered I may never walk again, my mind has cleared and I'm full of extreme sorrow.'

'You've forgiven your friend Hari, too?'

'I realise it was all imaginary. Probably the *bhang* we were taking had made me think Hari was fucking Ceri. I can't let him suffer because of me.'

'So, you're prepared to go to jail hah?' said Braganza.

'Maybe not. I'm sure my father can influence someone, even the jury perhaps, to get me off. This happens every day, doesn't it?'

Braganza had conducted a number of interviews with suspects, but this one had taken a very different turn from the way he had imagined. He called in Igor's lawyer from the waiting room, to verify everything he had just heard. The lawyer was speechless at first, and then said that his client was still under the influence of drugs and that his testimony could not be trusted. So Braganza called for a doctor to verify that Igor was of sound mind and capable of giving his testimony, which the doctor duly did.

'I will now be placing your client on a twenty-four-hour watch and I would ask that you hand in his passport immediately.' Braganza ordered, relishing the thought that he had the confession.

The chief inspector felt that he was slowly twisting the knife into his adversary's ribs in a way that previously he had been prevented from doing. But Braganza knew that Igor's testimony was full of flaws and was inconsistent with the nature of the young man he knew.

Who was he trying to protect? Hari, or his father?

Braganza was, however, going to enjoy the conversation with the Minister when he told him that he had a confession from his sponsor's son. Under Judge Anand's protection, Braganza could proceed directly to a prosecution without running the risk of having to quash the conviction later on.

Melita went around saying her goodbyes to the people she had worked with at St Anthony's. Michael said he couldn't believe that Braganza could have been so vindictive as to get rid of her, and that he would try and get him to change his mind. Everyone was talking about her damning criticism of the corruption and praising her for her bravery at doing so.

To celebrate her last night in Goa, Melita decided to have her final fling at the Sunset Lounge. Like a phoenix, the Sunset had been partly resurrected from the charred remains of the old tented lounge, with the still remaining wreckage screened off behind the bar. Jaz's old mahogany bar was the only furniture that had survived from the Sunset's previous incarnation. It was a Friday night, when the Bombay crowd flooded in for the weekend to indulge in the decadence on offer.

Karina had made a few changes since taking over from Scorpion. She was harder on the boys' appearance and demanded that they show impeccable manners to their guests. She had implemented a navy blazer, white shirt, and grey chinos policy, which clearly set them apart from the other male guests, and she policed their sense of grooming like an army sergeant.

'I'm wanting my boys to be gentlemen, lovers and studs, all

rolled into one,' she kept reminding them. She also toned down the sluttish dress code of her women. 'Girls, I want you to be more Chanel than *Baywatch*. Men are liking the posh-girl-next-door look, rather than the dumb blonde that everyone's fucked!' she kept reminding them. She recruited an excellent tailor from the Mapussa Road to replicate the French Chanel styling and the women loved their new clothes. Karina hoped that gradually the reputation of the Sunset might begin to climb back up and Friday nights would return to their previous glory.

'Hey, Melita, I've designed a special cocktail and named it in your honour,' the new barman greeted her with pride, pointing to a chalk board marked *Special House Cocktail - Melita's Ruin*.

'You're having me on. You want me to drink something like that?'

'Oh come on, it's only vermouth and coconut milk, with a dash of gin.'

'Over my dead body!' Melita replied, then realised that her refusal had made Karina look glum. 'I'm sorry, I didn't mean it that way, no disrespect to Ceri and all that.'

'Yeah, I keep seeing her next to you. The Fab Floozies, I loved you together. You know this place hasn't recovered from the shock. Have you heard the latest?'

'What latest?'

'Igor the Uke has 'fessed up to Braganza that he did it, all to let Hari off the hook. It's hush hush, but Braganza told me.'

'I don't believe it. Never. Igor?'

'I don't think Braganza believes him either,' said Karina

shaking her head. 'Oh my God, speak of the devil, here he is now.'

The police inspector walked up to the bar where Melita sat. She stiffened.

'No need to fear me, my girl. I'm not going to hurt you, despite all that you've been saying about me from the pulpit. If you're nice to me, I'll give you some good news.' Melita smelled the stench of sweaty body odour from his clothes, which he had probably been in all day. 'Relax, I won't bite.'

'Hah, hah, Denzil, you're very funny and happy today. Would you like to try some of the special cocktail that I have prepared for Melita's leaving party?'

'She's not going anywhere,' Braganza answered. 'Melita thought she'd misheard what he had just said.

'There, you see, Melita. Denzil is going to wave that magic wand and you can stay and party with us forever!' laughed Karina, trying to lighten up the mood.

'I mean it. I'm cancelling your notice to leave the country.'

'Oh!' is all Melita could say.

'See, Mel, Denzil's not such a bad fellow after all, hah? Let's drink to celebrate you being un-deported,' invited Karina.

'Oh, and I'm releasing Hari's bail conditions, so you can have your money back.'

Melita was still speechless. Karina heard the last bit of the conversation and let out a whoop of joy, which rose above the sounds of Dab Danny's grooves. 'Now do I get a hug or not?' boomed Braganza, showing off his golden filling in his upper left incisor and opening up his arms.

Melita stiffened at the thought of the ordeal of being encapsulated within his malodourous body, turning her head well away to one side, so that he could not at any stage reach her lips. Those couple of seconds seemed to last for hours. Karina clapped at the end of it.

'One thing, I wonder why Igor told us another story. He said that he thought he killed Ceri when she came off his bike,' Karina questioned.

'Ah, that's police work you're on about. I can't discuss that here.'

'Perhaps you'd like to discuss it with me in private hah? There in my office?'

'I wish all my witnesses were as cooperative as you.' And Karina and Braganza disappeared behind the new velvet curtain to test out Karina's new 'Head Office'.

Igor's hospital recuperation room was now a prison cell in which he was being held, with a police guard outside, accompanied by Aleks, his father's minder. Aleks was about twice as tall and strong as the Bihari policeman, who was armed with only a walkie-talkie and a *lathi* stick. Over the days that ensued, Igor's two overseers became reasonable friends, taking it in turns to bring each other sweet tea. By night the Bihari was replaced by a Nepali policeman, who was less communicative with Aleks and far more diligent in his duty, staying alert at all times and refusing to engage in small talk.

Vlad had been away in Nepal for a week, presumably fixing up more contacts for his human trafficking activities. While in Nepal, Vlad heard his son had confessed to the murder, but only became fully aware of the full admission of guilt when he returned to Goa. He went directly to the Mahindra hospital.

His first words when he saw Igor were, 'I can't believe you are my son. Just so stupid. What were you thinking of? Do you know what these prisons are like?'

Igor stayed silent at first to allow his father to vent all the venom he could. 'Just like your mother, no idea of the practical realities of everyday, with her head in the clouds like you.'

The mention of his mother triggered an angry response from Igor. 'She was a human being, with feelings, not a senseless gangster like you. Living off the sufferings of other people is what you do. That's all you ever have done, other than a bit of diving.'

'I'm not going to take that rudeness from the boy I have financed and looked after for the last ten years. If you weren't all wired up, I'd thrash you here and now till you'd be black and blue. You don't spit in the well you drink from.'

'My life is over anyway, I'll probably be bedridden, or at best in a wheelchair for the rest of my life. You might as well end it now. Your words don't scare me at all. Don't you see, you should be praising me for letting you off the hook for covering up the accident.'

'I was trying to protect you, like any real father would.'

'And Hari the gypsy? It didn't matter I suppose if he was hanged and his wife and family suffered? In your world, other people suffer at your expense.'

'The world is not a fair place. Some win, some lose. That's the way it's been for millions of years. Howl with the wolves, or bleat with the sheep.'

'Father, you are a sick man, even more sick that I am. Just let one of your guys take me to the sea and drown me, like they did Ceri.'

'Don't speak such rubbish, it's clear that this conversation is going nowhere. I'm going to leave you now to sort out your stuff. And let me tell you something before you go. Those bastards the Beachboys set up a trip wire along the 66 with the idea of killing you and your tart. They were trying to get their revenge on us. I saw the wire and the note attached to the tree where you came off. Look at the mark across your chest. And let me ask you, who would have tipped them off that you were on your way back at night?'

Vlad stormed out of the room, taking his minder Aleks with him. 'Let's go, this boy is not my son anymore.'

When Melita called the Hospital later that day, the physio was massaging Igor's legs to aid the circulation of blood to his lower body.

'Come in,' he signalled. 'We're nearly finished here.'

Igor looked pleased, to see her as she pulled up a chair to sit next to him. 'I bought you some *laddus* from the fellow down the road. I just couldn't resist the look of them.'

Igor thanked her. 'That will cheer me up.'

Melita opened the cardboard box of golden round balls, made mostly of sugar and flour, and held them up to Igor, who looked at the box with wide-eyed excitement. If a few sweets could brighten up his day then this was definitely worth it. He bit a chunk and began to munch away, nodding with pleasure.

'Igor, I just want to understand how such a horrible thing happened to Ceri. You said that she came off your bike and hit her head on something, but when I saw her body she was bruised and battered as if she'd been attacked. And the coroner said that there was evidence of a vicious rape, in which she struggled to escape.'

'Arrgh! I just want to die! Give me some arsenic or something to take me away!' yelled Igor at the top of his voice, as if suddenly in terrible pain. The guard outside came into the room.

'What is the matter?' he asked.

'It's okay, okay,' assured Melita. 'He's just remembering something painful.'

'They tried to kill us, Melita.'

'Who?'

'The Beachboys. They set up a trip wire across the 66 in the dark. Someone informed them that we were driving back.'

'Shit! Hari?'

'And Karina would have given the orders.'

'Igor, that's unbelievable. She's been all sweetness of late.'

'I knew, I knew Ceri was alive when she left me. I saw her move. She must have awoken after she was taken away,' moaned Igor.

'Who took her away, Igor?'

'My father's driver, that thug Aleks. Oh, if only I could walk. I heard my father tell him to take her away, so it was he who must have abused her.'

'Does your father know? You can't be sure, Igor.'

'I think he does. That's why he was so angry at my confession. When I confessed, I had no idea of this.'

'Igor, you can't go to jail for a crime you didn't commit,' Melita insisted.

'Only I can handle this now, I think.'

'For God's sake don't do anything rash. Can I stay with you?'

'No, Melita, I need to do this myself.'

Chapter 31

My life cut short

There is no way I wanted to die so young. When my head hit that rock on the 66 and knocked me out cold, I thought my life had ended. For a moment the dark of the night completely blacked out and then gradually I saw the glimmer of far-off lights and I thought I was looking down on the road, seeing Igor lying there with his Enfield on its side.

In the glow of the red light, I could see his face grimacing in pain as he shouted out to me. I wished I could yell back, but it was like a nightmare when you want to scream, but your voice is muffled into groans. I could still see myself hovering over my body when his father turned up, and I came back down to earth with a jolt. My eyes opened slightly, but I was still in a daze.

I wanted to get up and run away, but my body felt like it was screwed to the floor. Every ounce of energy I had had been siphoned off. I heard Russian voices and a minute later I was picked up and literally dumped in the back of a pick-up truck, where I hit my head again on the steel floor of the vehicle. Any awareness of my surroundings was briefly shut out and only returned when the truck was moving again down a bumpy old road. I felt every lump in the road as I lay on the floor of this transport amongst boxes, cans, and bits of tubular steel pipe that rattled around me.

I was so sure of myself that I believed the condition I was now in would soon pass and that someone would take care of me quite soon. Just like Harpo had come to my protection at school and Scorpion had rescued me from ending up on the scrap heap in Goa, I felt that someone was looking out on my behalf.

I had so much to live for. So much had changed. Before I boarded that jet to Goa, I couldn't have cared much about my life ahead. My life in Wales was at a dead end, surrounded by no-hopers with very little future. I could see zero life ahead, with no prospect of any qualifications, with what would certainly be a miserable school report. But just a short time in Goa had turned my head. I could see how amazingly someone like Hari, who had nothing, could make so much out of so little. How the Beachboys could turn up at the Sunset looking like professionals, when they lived in such slummy conditions. How the orphans on their meagre portions of rice and lentils could go to school all day and believe that if they worked hard, they could set up a business one day or even become a doctor or a lawyer. They all lived in hope that something good would happen to them if they worked at it.

I now suddenly shared their hopes that I could pull myself up from being a loser to a winner. I knew I could, if I really tried. Death was not an option.

So, when the truck came off the hard-tarmac road and was rolling on something softer, I forced myself to lift up my head as my strength returned. It looked like we were on sand. I could hear the sea somewhere out there in the dark. The truck stopped.

As I sat up, I saw the hulkish Uke flash his white teeth at me and hop into the back of the truck. It didn't look good. I knew what he was after. He pushed me back down on the floor of the truck. My head hit one of the steel pipes and I yelled. The slime ball then heaved his repulsive body over me, and I felt him pulling off my shorts. I yelled again and tried to wriggle free, but I had very little strength left in my body. He punched me in the face twice, really hard to stop me moving. Each blow stunned me with pain, but I recovered to take a bite at his arm. I must have made an impact as he let go and swore.

However, I was gradually losing the battle to fight him off.

I felt one of the steel pipes roll into my right hand like a gift from heaven. I grabbed it hard to take a swing at his skull. This had to be my chance. I swung the pipe, whacking my attacker over the head with a clout so hard, to try and break his skull. I heard the sound of steel on bone and he slumped off me, rolling over to the floor of the truck with a deafening yell. I thought he was gone.

Now I had to get out and get away.

I was still in a daze, as I slid off the truck onto the sand. I paused for a moment to catch my breath and get a sense of where I was. I knew that the burned-out wreck of the Sunset was a few hundred yards away along the beach. I had to try and get there. I knew I could hide amongst the charred debris that still remained. But then I realised I was half-naked and my shorts were still in the truck.

I didn't care. I just had to get as far away from the truck

before that monster recovered and came looking for me.

I knew I had to get help.

The Sunset Lounge seemed further away somehow tonight, as I struggled to make progress towards my hideout. The soft but still warm sand was like walking through sludge and I stumbled and fell, as I moved forward one step at a time.

I was so drained of energy that I found it easier to crawl on my hands and knees. I began to shuffle towards my only oasis of hope. There I would find somewhere to hide, perhaps under the temporary staging, yes that would be perfect. Or behind the counter of the mahogany bar that had survived the fire. I only needed to hang out there for a few hours until daylight and then find Melita. We could seek help from Karina. She was management now. She was the strongest woman I knew, and I needed a strong woman right now to understand what I'd got myself into, and who could protect me. Karina and the Beachboys would look after my protection, I was sure.

I shuffled in through what had been the original entrance. The Beachboys had been working on the wreckage behind the bar to clear away the worst of the debris, but the smell of charred wood, plastic and rubber still filled the night air. Here in the wreckage, I should easily find somewhere to hide. Every inch of movement on the ground reminded me of how bruised and battered I was, but the pain was the last thing on my mind. Now I was away from the open beach, with a dark camouflaged barrier between me and my attacker.

However, it occurred to me that, when Aleks recovered, this would be the first place that he might come looking. Fugitives usually run and hide in familiar places. He would know that. I had to dig myself deep into some corner of the Lounge. There were few options for places that would conceal me. The fire had done its work and reduced all the soft furnishings to nothing. However the mahogany bar had survived. I remembered how it had been Jaz's pride and joy, as he would polish the shiny top every evening before the curtain went up for his show to begin.

I crawled behind the curved exterior and noticed that the deep shelves which held glasses and mugs were still intact. Far in the back of one of these shelves would be perfect for me to crawl into and conceal myself temporarily. I cleared away a space big enough for me to squeeze myself in and finally, I was curled up in the dark. The searing pain returned once the distraction of escaping ended. I was lying still. I breathed slowly to lessen the pain and calmed myself to the point where I retreated into sleep despite the agony of the several wounds inflicted on my body. I dreamt of Harpo, with me at St Non's, as he played his *poongi* and I danced on the soft green grass overlooking the cliffs.

I was so happy in my dream.

At some stage into this dream I heard a crash, which woke me up. I could see someone inside the Lounge flashing the light of a mobile phone around. Judging by the heavy crunching of boots on the floor, it was definitely Aleks. It looked like he was doing a systematic job of looking for me, as the flashlight appeared to dash back and forth. In a few seconds he'd be flashing his light into the shelves.

I was sure my torso was well concealed behind the glasses, but to be sure I decided to wriggle further into a corner and that was when one of the glasses wobbled a little, which emitted the slightest tinkle.

This was enough to give away my hiding place.

In that moment, the game of cat and mouse had changed in favour of the horrid creature chasing me. He was behind the bar within a fraction of a second, swept away the glasses with his heavy arm and reached out into the shelving to pull me out feet first. I slid out, but not before grabbing hold of two glasses, one in each hand. He hadn't seen my improvised weapons in the dark, but I could see his face silhouetted in the glow of the torch. My hands were at the same level as his face and I plunged the jagged ends of the broken glasses into each side of his face, while yelling like a crazed animal, which increased the shocking impact of my attack. He yelled, too, mostly in pain, letting go of my feet to hold his face, presumably to remove the shards of glass, which I hoped had gouged his eyes out and blinded him temporarily.

I ran.

Suddenly I regained new reserves of energy after my brief rest, dashing out onto the open sand away from the broken glass on the floor inside the Lounge. I headed for the safety of the beach. I knew that once I was in the sea, I could outswim Aleks easily.

The glass attack appeared to have only momentarily stunned the hulk, as I could now hear his heavy padding footsteps, pounding behind me. I was running on flat hard sand and accelerated immediately, until I started to feel the water under my feet.

That was when I stumbled and fell.

Aleks tumbled onto the sand with me. He was up on his feet before me and began to drag my head further into the water. He was shouting something in Russian and this is the moment I realised I had lost all my strength and every one of my nine lives.

My mind had begun to blank out and water started to enter my lungs as he pushed my head down in the waves. I still wasn't going to give up on my life without a fight and whimper to this scumbag. They say all living creatures summon up hidden sources of energy when death looks them in the face, and I was no exception, but I'd lost every ounce of oomph by now and I was just carried along by this ogre of the night.

He was using both of his arms to hold me in a vice-like grip, but my feet were still free, so I tried to kick upwards to free myself. But that didn't work. I bit his hand as hard as I could, but he held on as tight as ever. All the time I was swallowing more and more water and was losing strength. I was losing all hope of being able to struggle free, as my lungs began to ache unbearably. I knew that I was being starved of air and was about to die.

Just up until this moment, life had been good.

I know I had a crap mam with a habit, and that I came from a shitty town in west Wales, but I had a life far superior to most of the other locals on Anjuna, where every day was a struggle. Just imagine Hari and his sisters getting up every morning to pick up rubbish to make just a few pennies in return. Yes, they had a life, but what sort of life?

The world was so unequal. It was totally unfair for me and others like me to lord over our superiority, just by some accident of where we were born.

So fuck the world, I thought.

It's lousy, let them keep it.
I'm better off out of it.

Epilogue

Chapter 32

Revenge

Summer arrives very quickly in Goa. Well before the end of April the weather becomes hot and humid, the stream of tourists cease their occupation of the beaches and bars, and even the long stayers from Europe's more temperate lands, take off to avoid the ravaging monsoons. The beaches are deserted and most of the shacks have been taken away to bunker down for the summer.

Igor had begun to regain some movement in his legs and his daily sessions of physiotherapy were beginning to pay dividends. He could sit up unaided in his wheelchair and he would take himself out onto the veranda every morning, just before the scorching sun began to make it uncomfortable outside of the cool air-conditioned interior of the hospital.

There on the veranda, Igor would play his *poongi* for an hour after breakfast, much to the enjoyment of the staff and orderlies. He'd acquired a recording device onto which he'd record a track of a tune and then play it back, accompanying himself with a second rhythm line and a harmony. This kept him occupied for hours and helped him avoid diving into a chasm of depression.

Aleks, his minder, would come to check on him occasionally to sip sweet *chai* with the nurses. Hatred for his father and his henchman built up layer by layer, as Igor read regular reports in the *Enquirer* about his impending day trial.

The *Enquirer* had been distinctly quiet about the Anjuna murder and Roki was growing impatient with his editor for stopping him from publishing a feature on Ceri's mother and her indifference to the loss of her daughter. The journalist now had screen shots of Ceri's text messages and believed that the messages would cast further doubt on the impending trial.

In her text messages she had spoken of her love of Igor and said how happy she was to be with him. She wanted her mother to meet the man who set her heart on fire.

Melita had left for Britain and had promised to write to him, but nothing got through Aleks's security curtain. Igor's sense of isolation grew day by day.

With a week to go to the trial, Michael called on Igor to check on his recovery and bring him news from the world outside the confines of the hospital. With the exception of Denzil Braganza, who called every few days to see if his fugitive continued to recover and be well enough to face trial, Michael was the only other person who was allowed access to Igor on humanitarian grounds. Igor signalled to Aleks to leave them alone.

'Just wanted to check on you to see if there was anything you'd like to tell me,' Michael began. 'I know you're not a Catholic, but many of my hardest parishioners find it quite helpful to talk about things. You know, difficult things.'

'Ah, yes, so you can go and tell that Christian friend of yours, Denzil Braganza?'

'No, on the contrary. What we say stays with me. I'm just

here for you to off load your anger and motivations for what you did to Ceri. I'm not here to judge.'

'Michael, Mike, Father, what do I call you? You couldn't start to think of the evil that has gone on in my life.'

'Well, assume that I've heard a lot in twenty years as a priest, and Mike is fine by the way.'

'I loved Ceri very much, I didn't want to kill her, and now I feel very angry about what happened.'

'People do all sorts of things when mad passion takes over. It's a crime in the eyes of the law, but history is littered with perfectly reasonable people, who have been overtaken by anger and done bad things.'

'Mike, the bad things are going to happen in the future. You don't understand.'

'No, I don't exactly,' said Michael, breaking into a frown.

'I'm going to take a life in exchange for what happened to Ceri.'

'You mean kill someone else?'

'Yes. In my world, in my father's world, retribution is the only way to get revenge.'

'But that's not taking responsibility for your own actions, Igor. Maybe other people led you to do what you did, but that's no excuse. Hating your father is quite normal behaviour. Sons have been hating their fathers forever, if you believe the psychologists.'

'I've been doing much thinking stuck here by myself. I have no life ahead of me in the state I'm in. I'll probably be stuck in this chair forever. I need to find a way to seek my revenge for what has happened. It's the only way I will rest.'

'Revenge is never sweet, Igor. No matter how bad you feel.'

'Mike, you'll never understand. I think you need to go now.' He shouted out for Aleks, who came in immediately.

'Please take this priest to the front gate. Make sure he is out of the grounds. I do not want to see him again.'

'Don't do it, Igor. Taking another life doesn't solve anything. It won't even make you feel good.'

Michael was led out of the room. Aleks's cup of sweet *chai* lay on the table. Igor had to be quick in executing his plan. He wheeled himself to his bedside, where he took the three capsules that they gave him at night, and broke them to release the white Temazepam powder, which he poured into the *chai*. He used his forefinger to stir the now lukewarm tea and went to sit by the only window of his room, where the air-conditioner blew deliciously cool air. He closed his eyes.

Aleks was back in two minutes, grumbling about Michael and the sweltering heat outside the hospital.

'I'm sorry,' said Igor, 'I must rest now. That priest has made me very tired.'

'*Da, da.*' grunted his guard, as he reached out for the *chai* and gulped it down in one uninterrupted action. His face grimaced at the aftertaste, but the overpowering sweetness and spices had disguised the bitterness of the drug. He went to sit on the single sofa in the room, deciding that the cool bedroom was by far the best place to be, and began to thumb through a tired looking copy of *Maxim*.

Igor lay motionless with his eyes closed. Despite the cool air blowing over his head, he broke out into an uncontrollable sweat, cracking open his eyelids every minute to check if the drugs had begun to take their effect. With just a single capsule, Igor would be asleep in no more than five minutes, but Aleks was a big man, so he might take a little longer.

It took about ten minutes for the Temazepam to reach its target. The magazine slid, falling to the floor with a thud, leaving Aleks slumped in his chair. This was Igor's chance to disarm his captor, who he knew always carried a small Makarov pistol tucked into one of his trouser pockets.

He wheeled over to Aleks's sofa and began to pat some of the half dozen pocket flaps. The weapon was in his upper left-leg pocket. Igor zipped it open and pulled out the Makarov. He had used one like this before at target practice, when his father had tried to stoke an interest in guns in him, back in Odessa. Igor had never taken to the weapon, and found the process of shooting at targets uninteresting and a total waste of time.

Aleks's right hand moved in his sleep, as he sensed someone was relieving him of his weapon. He made a noise that sounded like a protest and tried to straighten his posture. Igor was now holding the black steely weapon, pointing it straight at Aleks. The man half opened his eyes and saw Igor's face looking at him behind the Makarov.

Aleks had trained in the army as a shooter and later as an assassin, before Vlad had discovered him and offered him a job for which he got paid two or three times more. The sight of a Makarov pointing at him, cut through his clinically-induced stupor like a red hot poker. He sat up erect at the edge of the sofa.

'Put that down now! I order you in the name of your father!' commanded Aleks, half-slurring his words but keeping up his defensive demeanour.

'Keep your hand up and prepare to die, you son of a pig!' Igor menaced. 'You're being very silly.'

'I don't think so. Now, before I kill you, tell me why you raped and killed my Ceri.'

'What are you talking about?'

'I know everything, so don't act innocent. She was alive when she left the roadside and you took her away. I've read the Coroner's report.'

'It was for your own good. I was only following orders from your old man. We do everything Vlad says without question. His wish is our command.'

'He told you to kill her?'

'Well, not in so many words, but it was clear that he wanted her disposed of.'

'And abused, raped?'

'Well, she was a bit of a whore, hanging out with those low-life black gypos.'

Igor yelled out in rage, a yell so loud that it shook Aleks enough for him to lean back and shield his face with his elbows. He could see Igor's trembling hand pressing on the trigger of the Makarov, his rage taking over any doubt or guilt about killing someone in cold blood.

Normally Aleks would have used his training to overcome such a hesitant assassin, but the drugs had made his limbs feel like lead, so he decided to plead for his life. 'Please, please it was your father's wish. It's him you should be talking to. I'm just his servant trying my best to protect you.'

Igor started to breathe heavily. Doubts about taking the life of his lover's killer were just enough to stop him squeezing the trigger hard to fire a shot. He had plotted and planned this assassination for days and now was his big moment to seek final retribution. Yet doubt about the real culprit, his father, was clouding his judgment. Killing Aleks had been his plan all along, and then turning the pistol on himself would be the final chapter in his mission to protect the honour of Ceri and rid himself of the shame of dealing with her death for the rest of his life.

'It was your father,' Aleks pleaded. 'He would fly into a rage many times and yell, *I'm going to get rid of her one day, that whore*, so don't blame me, I was only the hired hand. When I came that night to help you in the truck, he said the same thing, *Get rid of her*. I was only following orders. You know what your father does to people who disobey him?'

Now the door was flying open and two nurses came running into the room, alerted by the shouts they had heard. They shrieked in horror at seeing Igor pointing a gun only a couple of feet away from Aleks. One of them ran back out of the room to get help.

'Mister, mister, holy Jesus, no!' begged the one that remained. She had also given him several hours of physiotherapy. 'Please, mister, please!' she pleaded, getting down on her knees and clasping her hands together. 'Mister, see, you are standing on your own feet. You will have your life back now. Spare us.'

Igor looked down and could see he had stood up from his wheelchair unaided.

Was it the empowering force of a gun in his hand, or was it the result of his overpowering fury? He'd planned to kneecap Aleks, so that he'd never walk again and then turn the gun on himself. But now that he was suddenly standing up unaided, things were beginning to look different.

Outside on the veranda there was uproar. People were shouting at each other and more and more people came out of their rooms once they heard that there was a gunman on the loose. They, in turn, began screaming and the panic began to escalate out of control. Someone pushed the fire alarm. The noise was deafening. Igor stood there calmly, his gun firmly pointed at Aleks with grim determination. He could see his target was still drowsy and in no condition to react.

And then the noise outside subsided, the alarm was silenced, and Igor knew there was someone there. His door was flung open and in walked his father Vlad, with Father Michael.

Father and son stared at each other and Vlad shook his head. 'You can't shoot anyone, you know that. Think of your mother. What would she say?'

'My mother? That's very fine coming from you after you destroyed her.'

'You know that's rubbish. She had cancer. Now give me that gun.' Vlad moved forward towards his son.

Igor fired.

Both Michael and Vlad fell to the floor. The shot missed them and ricocheted off the metal fire extinguisher.

'Igor, calm down,' begged Michael.

'If you want to kill me, do it now, damn you. Kill your father!' yelled Vlad, getting to his knees. 'I know how you hate me.'

The sound of gunfire initiated another round of shouts of panic. Then above it all, Braganza could be heard outside. 'This is the police, put your weapon down.' He entered the room, pistol first, pointing it at Igor. 'Put that weapon down now. I have an armed response unit outside. You don't want to die.'

Igor dropped his gun to the floor and the room soon filled up with hospital staff, security guards, and various people purporting to be in charge. Vlad went to hug his son, but Igor turned away.

'I only wanted what was best for him,' Vlad pleaded, looking at Michael.

'Now how did all this begin?' demanded Braganza, 'Who gave him that gun?'

Igor stated loud and clear. 'I want to change my admission to the killing of Ceri, the British girl.'

'I wondered how long that would take,' Denzil responded. 'I hope you have a good reason why.'

'It's my father Vlad you want to charge, ask that man,' declared Igor, pointing to Aleks.

'Do you know who betrayed you?' Vlad yelled. 'It was that stinking gypo, so-called friend of yours. He called the Beachboys to tell them you were travelling back south on the 66 on your bike, and they set a trip wire to kill you.'

'You're lying, just like you usually do.'

'I squeezed that out from one of the Beachboys. I knew it was their work. I was so angry that night, all I wanted was to rub out that sluttish girl in revenge. She pissed off the gypo bloke big time and he betrayed you.'

The news of the arrests of Vlad and Aleks spread quickly, giving Roki the chance to pull together the story he'd been waiting to write with the headline *Gang leader ordered murder*. He described how Vlad, in an act of revenge, had given the order for Aleks to kill and dispose of Ceri, whom he considered being under the protection of the Beachboys, and how his henchman took gory pleasure in carrying out Vlad's orders. The Beachboys had been looking for a perfect time to ambush Igor. Karina had given Hari an ultimatum to inform on his whereabouts. Hari had sent a text to tell the Beachboys that Igor would be travelling home down the 66 that night.

Aleks was charged the next day with the murder and rape of Ceri, and Vlad was charged for ordering it.

Chapter 33

Harpo's lament

May at St Non's on the western-most tip of Wales is probably one of the most beautiful places on earth. Flowers of pink thrift carpeted the landscape down to the sea, interrupted here and there by sea campions, which relieve the abundance of pink flowers. Wheatears flash their white tails up against the blue sky, flying in and out of the gannets looking for food in the sea below.

It's here that Harpo came to celebrate the passing of his once betrothed. Ceri's story had been covered in the local *Weekly Echo*. Her mother Devi had held a special funeral service for her daughter, when her body was returned to Wales, but this was Harpo's own one-man tribute, sitting on the cliff overlooking the sunset.

Harpo had been released from prison early, less than twelve weeks after the incident with the wolves. While in prison, he'd read of Ceri's fate and the attempts by the Goan authorities to apprehend the suspect.

His wooden *poongi* wailed out a gypsy tune, which wafted over the cliffs out to sea, and the gannets and wheatears seemed to dance in the skies to the rhythm of the tune. In keeping with the old gypsy custom to destroy an item belonging to the deceased in celebration of a life lived, Harpo had brought with him the towel that Ceri had left in his van, the evening he kidnapped her from the beach and took her to St Non's.

First, he lit a candle and watched the flame flicker in the gentle wind that blew from the southwest. Then he set fire to one end of the towel which smouldered, as he blew on it to fan the flames, which eventually began to consume the entire towel. He'd kept the towel folded neatly in the back of his van since his return from prison.

As the white smoke rose up to the skies and the cloth blackened to a fine ash, Harpo remembered the evening, just two seasons earlier, when they had sat together and drunk cider and promised themselves to each other, while he sang the gypsy love song that had echoed around the cliffs of St Non's.

The gypsy rover came over the hill
Down through the valley so shady.

He whistled and he sang 'til the green woods rang
For he'd won the heart of a lady.

Ah-dee-doo-ah-dee-doo-dah-day
Ah-dee-doo-ah-dee-day-dee

He whistled and he sang 'til the green woods rang
For he'd won the heart of a lady.

Acknowledgements

Writing a book is a long journey for writers who do so for pleasure. Without the help and encouragement of my editor Anne Garside I would not have persisted. I would also like to acknowledge encouragement from fellow author Brenda Squires, Laura Gerard and Caroline Ignatius. Thanks also to James Essinger of The Conrad Press for having the faith to publish this book.

Acknowledgements